Entwined Publishing books by Alex Winters

Modern Herstory
In Her Regency Era

I0565751

Modern Herstory

IN HER REGENCY ERA

ALEX WINTERS

ENTWINED PUBLISHING

In Her Regency Era
ISBN # 978-1-80250-293-0
©Copyright Alex Winters 2025
Cover Art by Erin Dameron-Hill ©Copyright October 2025
Interior text design by Entwined Publishing
Published by Entice, an Entwined Publishing imprint

Published in 2025 by Entwined Publishing, United Kingdom.

Entwined Publishing is a division of Totally Entwined Group Limited.

IN HER REGENCY ERA

Chapter One

Carol

"WANTED."

Carol Swinton stopped in her tracks to admire the gaily colored flyer tacked to the already overstuffed bulletin board in the employee breakroom. With a sprig of bright red and green holly in each corner and a border silhouetted with gold and silver musical notes, it certainly stood out from the run-of-the-mill black-and-white "babysitter needed" and "earn cash from home" junk bulletins that surrounded it.

She inched a little closer, clutching her cup of vending machine coffee in both hands as she glanced around to see if anyone was watching. *Fat chance,* she thought to herself as she glanced back at the holiday flyer with renewed interest. This time of night, most of the office drones had already headed home, leaving just Carol and a smattering of the overnight "Study Buddies" answering calls from forlorn college students who sought out their Homework Helpers hotline to assist with their term papers, projects and finals 24/7/365.

With the first week of December in full swing and finals starting to crop up all over the country, it was a busy time of year and, as the newest call center floor manager, Carol felt dutybound to oversee the fresh influx of new callers. So…bitter, lukewarm coffee from the breakroom vending machine and a quick stroll around the mostly empty office suite had seemed a good idea at the time.

But something about that flyer had piqued her interest so now Carol read it in full, if only for something to while away another long, late worknight high atop the Birchwood Business Center.

WANTED: *Energetic, outgoing, flexible female singer for popular, award-winning professional caroling troupe. Evenings and weekends required. Mezzo-soprano preferred, contralto optional, talent MANDATORY. Email reggie@victorianvoices.net to schedule an audition time and please come prepared with selections from up to three of your traditional holiday favorites from the Regency and/or Victorian time period(s). And, for both our sakes, please, please, PLEASE know the difference!*

"Mandatory," she muttered to herself, shaking her head even as she struggled to deny the sudden surge of adrenaline that coursed through her veins. Christmas carol singers? Regency-era songs? She was tempted to squee out loud but she suddenly thought better of herself.

Good thing, too.

"Beg pardon?" A sudden voice from behind found Carol turning on her sensible work heels, the sound grating in the otherwise silent breakroom. Rome

Patterson stood, fidgeting with the fringe on one half of his bright red and gold scarf.

"Rome," she gushed, taking two involuntary steps away from the bulletin board as if to distance herself from the squee-inducing flyer. "I...didn't see you standing there."

Rome smirked, his rich ebony skin radiant beneath the typically unflattering fluorescent glow from above. "I...just got here."

She took another step away from the board but her ever-observant boss was *way* too smart for that. "Eyeing the Victorian Voices flyer, I see?" he harumphed while tousling the bottom of the flyer with one plump finger.

Carol let out a fluttery little laugh, the kind she made whenever she was too nervous to form a complete sentence. "The what now?" she murmured innocently, as if she hadn't the faintest idea what he was talking about. And, since the exchange didn't already sound quite awkward enough, Carol blurted a quick "Whatever do you mean?" just to make sure. She even clutched a few non-existent pearls around her neck for good measure.

"Victorian Voices," he explained, drifting casually toward the soda machine while he dug his ID badge out of the front pocket of his stylish camel-colored slacks. "They're a professional caroling group. You know the kind..." He paused in his explanation to make a selection and swipe his magnetic key card across the touchscreen on the machine to pay.

Carol took the opportunity to slide onto a stool at one of the four bistro-height breakroom tables in the corner. She sipped her coffee impatiently as he gathered up his can of grape soda and turned to face her. "Old Victorian garb, top hats and bonnets, mufflers

9

and pince-nez, evergreen vests and fake timepieces..."
His voice had taken on a singsong quality as he took
three bounding steps and sank onto the bench seat
across from her.

She smirked and patted his hand. "Sounds like
you've given them a good study, Rome."

"You could say that," he hemmed.

She gave him a conspiratorial little wink. "I...just
did."

They'd only known each other a few weeks and
were still feeling out each other's ups and downs,
schedules, mood swings and compatibility. But they'd
connected   immediately,   with   humor   and
understanding, the way coworkers who were destined
to become much more so often did.

"So," she pushed, nudging his chocolate-colored
loafers beneath the table, "are you gonna spill or
what?"

Rome avoided her eyes at first, fiddling with the top
of his soda can before blurting, "I tried out for them one
year."

"You?" Carol sat up a little higher. Maybe she
shouldn't have been so embarrassed about reading that
flyer after all. "I didn't know you were a singer."

He shrugged. "I dabbled in high school, went to a
few choral competitions my senior year, that kind of
thing." Their eyes met across the stylish breakroom
table. Like everything else about the wildly successful
college hotline, it was modern, hip and expensive-
looking. Rome paused to take a long, almost rueful sip
of his soda.

"And then?" she prompted after he'd had time to
swallow.

He rolled his eyes. "I was home from college. Winter
break." Rome waved the can of Goober Grape at the

fancy flyer with a slight air of disdain, an uncharacteristic glimpse of negativity from a guy who was normally so chill and cheerful. "Saw one of those at the gym and thought why not, right?"

Carol sat back, anticipating some kind of confession. "Your tone implies it didn't go so well."

Rome snorted, nostrils flaring in advance. "That's an understatement. Reginald, the troupe leader? Pompous with a capital ass."

Carol chuckled. Rome was so lowkey that she'd rarely seen him sneer or scowl, let alone cuss. Suddenly he was doing all of the above? All at once? "There *were* a few red flags in the flyer," she conceded.

He nodded. "It's the same one they put up every year," Rome explained. "Talent MANDATORY, in all caps. Gets me every time, especially since Reggie's such a talentless hack himself."

"Oh my." She giggled almost nervously, a rash idea bubbling just beneath her skin despite the many warning signs flashing in her peripheral vision. "So the band leader's a douche, but…is the troupe itself any good?"

"Oh sure," Rome insisted, back to his old convivial self. "Top-notch harmonies, everything period-accurate, right down to the accents and top hats. They're *so* good they win the Jingle Jangle Competition every year."

"Jingle Jangle?" A caroling *competition*? Now Carol's curiosity was thoroughly piqued.

Rome smirked, one bushy eyebrow arching above his superior scowl. "You really are new to Birchwood, huh?"

Carol ignored the daily jab, whittling down to the heart of the matter as that initial kernel of a bad idea threatened to pop into something hot, fresh and potentially regrettable. "If they're that good, why do they hang up the same flyer every year? I mean, shouldn't folks be lining up around the block just to join them?"

"Because the whole troupe is insufferable," Rome explained. "Pompous, arrogant and conceited, so the only people who will stay in the group are folks just like them, and I guess they're harder to find than old Reggie thinks. Trust me...you'll see them for yourself soon enough."

"How's that?" Carol struggled not to sound startled. Had her new boss read her mind? She certainly hoped not, particularly after the way she'd chided him — mentally, of course — for wearing stripes *and* plaids the previous day!

Then he rolled his rich brown eyes and explained, "You can't avoid them this time of year. Strolling through all the hoity-toity neighborhoods in town, strutting through the ritzy shopping centers at peak Christmas shopping time, belting out old Victorian carols at four billion decibels..."

By the time Rome was through dishing, he was nearly panting with righteous indignation.

"So if they're so obnoxious," she teased, leaning over conspiratorially, "why did you audition for them in the first place?"

He chuckled self-deprecatingly, sliding from his stool to indicate that break time was over. "I guess to see whether or not I had the 'MANDATORY' talent they require. You might say I'm stubborn that way."

Carol joined him as they tossed their empty cups in the breakroom recycling bin. "You should give it another shot this year," she urged. "Sounds like they have more confidence than talent, anyway."

"That they do," he agreed, lingering just inside the breakroom as though neither of them was all that eager to get back to work. "Trouble is, they don't really *want* talent. They want…obedience."

Carol nodded in tacit agreement. "Not your strong suit?" she teased as they drifted from the breakroom into the maze of cubicles that lined the call center floor.

Rome gave a bittersweet little "tut" sound before huffing. "Obedience? Naw, not even a little."

She nudged his hip as they wound toward their respective offices. "That explains a lot, boss."

Chapter Two

Gabe

"What, no ice cream cake this year?"

Gabe Maxwell stood empty-handed at the entrance of the rented storage shed, on a work break and still sporting his faded blue and pink Soft Swerve work tee, blushing as he stammered out an excuse. "I mean, last year, there was no electricity yet and it just melted before we got to eat it anyway, so..."

"She's only teasing," Ray Ridgeway explained unnecessarily, testing the bright red and green seams of his ugly Christmas sweater as he patted the foldout chair next to him.

"He knows that, Ray," Jasmine "Jazz" Radiance practically growled as she stood in front of them, clad in an emerald-green tracksuit that clung to her frosty, gym-sculpted physique. "No need to explain a joke."

"Not if it's funny the first time," Ray whispered, leaning closer to Gabe as he took his seat.

"Now that we're all here," Jazz continued, coal-black eyes settling on Gabe as he shifted uncomfortably in his seat, "we can proceed with this year's orientation!"

Jazz's mock cheerleader voice and contagious enthusiasm made it clear she expected a suitably lengthy round of applause in reply. Gabe and Ray golf-clapped dutifully, as they did every year, Jazz already pacing as her second-in-command, Mason Crawford, eyed her coolly from where he stood next to a dry-erase board, ever at the ready to do Jazz's bidding.

When the sound of four hands clapping became uncomfortable, Ray and Gabe stopped, hands on their knees like a pair of pupils in some prairie schoolhouse back in the day. "Now," Jazz enthused after her round of faux applause was over, pacing across the rented storage space floor in her rhinestone sneakers. "Even though it's been a whole year, the sting of last year's defeat still hurts. Am I right, gang?"

Gabe winced while Ray nodded dutifully. Of course, Jasmine was one of those public speakers who asked the audience over-obvious questions she never required an answer to in the first place, yet stood there patiently waiting for one all the same as the cringe factor rose ever higher with each passing moment.

He wondered why he put himself through this every year. The deranged orientation, the forced enthusiasm, the slavish devotion to Jazz and her egocentric whims. And for what? The chance to dress up like some English fop and stroll around town in ill-fitting, Regency-era boots, belting out Christmas carols for minimum wage while doing double duty back at one of his three ice cream parlors to make up for the time off?

Still, he couldn't help but feel the holiday spirit bubbling up in him alongside his annual cold feet. Fact was, Gabe was a sucker for Christmas in general and Christmas *carols* in particular. He loved learning new ones, even if they were from hundreds of years ago. Loved harmonizing with his troupe, the highs and lows, following the rhythm and creating something magical out of, well, thin air.

But most of all, he loved the sight of happy children, beaming housewives and grumpy businessmen alike applauding as the Mistle Tones finished yet another old-timey tune and left them with a smile, full of the holiday spirit that coursed through Gabe with every note.

That was why he came back to Jazz's mind-numbing orientations year after year. Gabe inched back into his seat to settle in for a full hour of Jazz's nonstop ramblings about sense and sensibility. Because, for better or worse, the Mistle Tones were his only chance to indulge his holiday habit and sing carols as they were intended — out loud, in public, to an impromptu crowd that gathered, larger and larger, with each lavish holiday tune.

"...thirdly..." Jazz was busy preening, jolting Gabe out of his mid-pep rally reverie to find that her second in command, Mason, had already scribbled two whole bullet points on the annual Holiday Reminder checklist he was quickly amassing on the dry-erase board at the front of the room. "Cleanliness," Jazz continued, her tone and her gaze both zeroing in on Gabe's squirming neighbor. "Last year, I had far too many three-star reviews on Carol-Critics.com about the state of our costumes."

Beside him, Ray's chair squeaked under his considerable bulk. "I mean, Jazz," he huffed, never one to mince words despite tempting Jazz's considerable wrath with every dissenting syllable. "Perhaps if you didn't require us to get our costumes dry cleaned after every performance, we could—"

"We could what, Ray?" Jazz huffed, inching closer as her elegant nostrils flared and she tapped the frosted tips of her manicured nails impatiently atop her platinum wristwatch. "Eat chili dogs and spill them all over our breeches to our little heart's content?"

"I couldn't help it, Jazz," Ray protested, sitting up in righteous indignation. "We'd caroled at three shopping centers that day and your ambitious schedule left us *no* time to eat, so when I saw that hot dog cart, well…"

Gabe stifled a chuckle. It was such a ridiculous argument, yet they had it year after year. "Well, what?" Mason interceded, ever the lapdog to Jazz's bling heels. "You just had to forgo a napkin and get it all over your brocade vest?"

"I used *several* napkins," Ray huffed, holding up three sausage fingers as if to prove it. "How was I to know they used super heat-seeking chili on their footlongs?"

"Maybe skip a footlong in the first place." Mason huffed. "Do you know what's in those things?"

"Yeah," Ray clapped back, a rarity, though Gabe suspected if his old caroling buddy was going to get passionate about anything, it would be food. Particularly junk food so big it had to be measured in feet. "I know what's in those things—pure, unadulterated deliciousness. And six inches just isn't enough of that deliciousness for my taste, thanks so very much!"

"Or how about if you must indulge in pseudo-meat tubes, you eat at a table like a civilized human being?" Jazz piled on haughtily, making it clear the last time she'd indulged in a hot dog was probably during some childhood picnic ages ago, long before she'd ever heard the words "carbs" and "cardio." "We *do* have an image to protect, you know?"

"I'm well aware," Ray grumbled. "God forbid we don't do everything in our power to mimic Victorian Voices to a 'T,' right, Jazz?"

Jazz paused, bejeweled finger mid-wag, vicious green eyes widening as poor Mason let out a garbled squeak of righteous indignation at the whiteboard next to her. "Did…" For once, Jazz's words failed her. In the split-second pause that followed, Gabe and Ray shared a foreboding "oh shit" glance that bordered on the cartoon comical. Moments later, the tidal wave broke predictably, right at poor Ray's feet. "Did you just accuse me of…of…mimicking our closest competitor?"

"I mean," Ray hedged anxiously, folding chair nearly quaking with fearful anticipation beneath him. "Isn't that what all of the Regency garb is for? All those musty hymns full of words none of us can pronounce? Chasing their tail year after year?"

"Hardly," Jazz said with surprising restraint. "I'll have you know, period fashion is hardly *their* domain. It's traditional, after all. Just like the carols we sing and the cadence we walk and the imported holly we pin to our lapels. And for your information? That was my idea first."

"*Our* idea," Mason interjected, a rare occurrence indeed. "Remember, Jazz? When we first brainstormed our caroling troupe over coffee that Thanksgiving break all those years ago? We thought up the Victorian garb, the old Regency carols, even the imported holly, remember?"

"How could I forget?" Jazz huffed, turning her considerable ire on the only other founding member of the Mistle Tones caroling troupe. "When you remind me every year?"

"I mean..." Mason seemed unphased by the reversal of fortune. "It's only right, considering you're the self-designated front woman of our collective."

"With good reason," Jazz harumphed, shrinking into herself as she must have felt outnumbered during her shining hour. "After all—"

Behind them, on a table Gabe hadn't noticed earlier, a small timer dinged. Jazz deflated like a wavy inflatable arm balloon that had suddenly been unplugged, curling into herself as the timer's "ding" continued echoing through the rented storage space where they'd eventually rehearse daily until their first caroling gig sometime in mid-December.

"Already?" Ray asked, seemingly disappointed.

"What?" Gabe whispered as Jazz and Mason conferred about their own deflated sense of frustration at the front of the room. "You wanted to endure *more* of this?"

Ray shook his head, bald spot shimmering in the harsh lighting above. "Not necessarily," he mused, standing abruptly. "But I *do* look forward to this time of year."

"Me too," Gabe admitted with a crooked half-smile. "I only wish it wasn't so...tense."

They paused at the mouth of the long, narrow storage space. They rented a different one every December, Jazz too cheap to keep the same one all year. Gabe had to admit, despite the bleak aesthetic, the acoustics were great. Jazz was nothing if not detail-oriented and, despite her obvious outer flaws, her many professional assets kept them booked every night of the peak holiday season from mid-December all the way through Boxing Day. And that was no easy feat in a cutthroat, competitive caroling market like the one that existed in tony Birchwood, North Carolina.

"Okay, gang," Jazz rang out over their muttered goodbyes and bittersweet parting. "Our time for tonight's orientation might be up but I'd like to get back into the swing of things ASAP so...same time tomorrow?"

"What about our fittings?" Ray asked, reading Gabe's mind as they lingered side by side in the doorway. "We've got those at six, so..."

"Seven should be enough time for you both to get geared up, right?" Jazz pressed, already scooping up her expensive leather valise and taking a dismissive tone. She ran Radiance Realty in Birchwood, as successful at selling million-dollar homes as she was bullying Christmas-loving, foot-long-craving carol singers like Gabe and Ray into toeing the line for one solid month every year.

Still, Jazz wasn't holding a gun to their heads and, without her unique blend of swagger and sophistication, the two youngest members of the Mistle Tones would likely wander around singing *All I Want for Christmas is You* in ugly Christmas sweaters and matching reindeer sleep pants if left to their own devices.

Gabe and Ray nodded in unison, giving a backward little wave as they left the claustrophobic rental unit and stumbled out into the evergreen-scented air of their scenic little mountain town. "Tell me you're not still working tonight?" Ray whined as Gabe inched closer to his hard-to-miss pink and blue Soft Swerve minivan.

Gabe pretended to be disappointed as he nodded, heart racing all the while as he made his hasty goodbyes in order to be back to the shop in time for his last customer of the evening.

"Tomorrow then?" Gabe offered by way of consolation, sensing Ray wouldn't have minded a beer or two at Clover's Tavern the way they usually did every year after Jazz's annual holiday orientation.

Ray perked up slightly. Mission accomplished. "Yeah, sure. Meet you at the tailor's by six?"

"If I don't get there first," Gabe muttered impatiently, struggling not to peel out like some hot-rodding teenager for the short trip back to Soft Swerve.

And the sweet, non-dairy treat that hopefully awaited him there.

Chapter Three

Carol

"The usual?"

Carol glanced down from the chalkboard menu and struggled not to blush at the flirty counter boy and his wide, expectant grin. "Am I that predictable?" she asked. *So. Damn. Predictably.*

"I mean," he stammered, cool grayish-brown eyes alert and eager beneath the brim of his jaunty trucker cap. Like the logos on the windows and the white tiled walls and even the cute little minivan parked out front, the hat bore the telltale Soft Swerve mascot—a dancing ice cream cone in cute little black sunglasses, one hand waving a bright pink ice cream scoop. "Four nights in a row and you're here at the same time, lining up for the same order."

"I can't help it," she whined, watching him reach for a chocolate-drizzled waffle cone, hand-curled into the shape of a decadently sweet little bowl. "Your pistachio is just so good. And swirled with peanut butter?" She did an awkward little chef's kiss, made even more so by the work valise crooked in her elbow and the simmering case of nerves that had built up all day in anticipation of this very moment. "Divine!"

Good God, Carol thought miserably despite the cheery retro eighties ambience that pervaded every inch of the cozy, squeaky-clean ice cream parlor. *I am so bad at this!*

"Gabe," or so said the name tag clipped to his just-tight-enough work tee, paused to nod. "It is pretty lit."

"Lit?" Carol wasn't above a little harmless flirtation herself, batting her lashes and pretending to be unaware of the youthful slang.

He paused to stammer out a definition. "Sorry, it means 'good'. I mean, at least, that's what the kids who work here tell me. It could actually mean something totally scandalous, offensive even, but…" Gabe bit his lower lip, which might have actually released a tiny squeal inside of her, then admitted, "I'm too afraid to ask?"

Carol stifled a frown. After all, Gabe didn't look much older than a kid himself, with his eager eyes and hollow cheeks and thin, rangy body and those sweet, innocent eyes. "I hear my students say it all the time, too. I just…never bothered to ask either, I guess?"

Gabe perked up, still holding the empty waffle bowl in his gloved hand. "You're a teacher?" His voice was eager, his eyes probing, his tone intent, as if he might actually…care? Then again, who was she kidding? He was probably just asking to see if she qualified for some type of public-school discount or something.

"No, no," Carol rushed to explain. "I manage a call center not far from here. Homework Helpers? It's a hotline for college kids, staffed by college kids, so…lots of underage interaction and questionable vocabulary choices there."

"That explains it," Gabe marveled, turning to fill her waffle bowl with his lifegiving pistachio and peanut butter soft-serve swirl combo.

"Explains what?" Carol asked, admiring the breadth of his back and the way his buttery soft T-shirt clung so tenderly to it. It had been ages since she'd ogled anyone so shamelessly, but she couldn't help herself. Like the sweet treat swirling from the soft serve machine in front of him, Gabe was a nightly craving she couldn't resist, her willpower too weak to just say no and drive on by the Soft Swerve closest to home.

He turned at last, golden-brown waffle bowl about to topple over from his generous lack of portion control. "That explains why you consider ice cream a suitable dinner."

She snorted despite herself. "It's not dinner," she explained, not entirely helping her cause as an actual grown ass woman any. "That was instant ramen and vending machine coffee. Hours ago."

He frowned while handing over the bowl. Immediately, her lips formed an unconscious "O" to lap at the expertly curled tip. Suddenly, splendidly, soothingly, the creamy, savory combo jolted her back to life.

"So good!" Carol couldn't help but exclaim, body shivering with release.

"Maybe you should sit," Gabe urged, nodding to an open booth behind her. "So it doesn't spill over?"

"Good idea," she blurted, grateful for the invitation— a first after all her visits this week. Usually she just paid, pined and drifted out through the front door reluctantly, scolding herself for not making more small talk during the nightly exchange as she sat in the front seat of her car, scarfing soft-serve ice cream alone while she ogled fresh jailbait through the Soft Swerve windows until it was time to make the lonely, if short, drive home.

She set her heavy valise on one side of the booth and slid it over, sinking down gratefully onto the soft powder-blue leather beneath her. After pacing the maze of cubicles at work all afternoon, leaning down regularly to assist on a call or offer encouragement to a new employee, Carol was eager to spend the rest of the day in the seated position.

Her sore feet and quivering legs thanked her.

Gabe followed her out from behind the sales counter to the dining room floor. She struggled to ignore his casual, friendly gait, long legs poking out of breezy khaki cargo pants that made him look both collegiate and comfortable all at once. His black and white high-tops squeaked quietly on the similarly tiled floor, a throwback—like the rest of the parlor itself—to simpler, more youthful times. From unseen speakers nestled above them, instrumental eighties songs played in a steady stream of smooth jazzy covers that were at once recognizable but also...cool? Kind of?

An inspired choice, anyway.

There was a table for two midway between the sales counter and Carol's booth and, tentatively, as if he were the customer instead of her, Gabe sank into one of the two chairs.

"Will you eat when you get home?" he asked quietly, as if not to startle her. When a blank expression was all she could muster in reply, Gabe smiled encouragingly. "Something more substantial, I meant. A vegetable or two, perhaps? A little protein?"

"What?" she snorted around a mouthful of heavenly soft-serve swirl that always seemed to disappear far too fast. "After *this* monstrosity?"

Gabe's smile was sudden and sincere. "It's not *that* big," he insisted in a tone that implied they both knew better.

"The way you filled it tonight makes it bigger than ever."

Gabe gave her a boyishly cheeky wink. "Only the best for one of my regular customers."

Carol was taken aback. "So I'm a regular now?"

He seemed vaguely offended, the slightest hint of a frown pulling his soft, pink lips downward. "I mean, you've been here almost every night this week, so...I'd say that makes it official, don't you?"

Carol gazed around the cozy little ice cream parlor. It was deceptively large, considering its placement in the corner of an upscale little outdoor galleria on her way home from work. But surprisingly narrow, far longer than it was wide, making Gabe's seat, even while not technically at her table, surprisingly intimate.

Her gaze settled back on him, a prideful grin creeping across her own face. "Wow, I've...never been a regular anywhere before."

"No?" He seemed genuinely surprised, nodding as if to take in the small but stylish dining room. "We live and die by them."

"Really?" Despite her admittedly varied resume, Carol had never worked retail. Or was this service industry? Either way, as competent as she was in the academic world, she had no clue how a business such as Gabe's survived one way or the other.

"Sure," he insisted, sagging back in his chair all lanky and concave, a minefield of sharp edges and soft curves that found Carol forcing herself to avert her eyes from the especially tempting bits his posture had managed to put on display. "Soccer moms with a van full of kids after practice every day. Businesspeople from the research park around the corner stopping by after lunch for a little something sweet before heading back to work. The same high school couples coming in every weekend..."

Carol was impressed. She couldn't wait until she was as familiar with the call center as Gabe was with his job. "Your boss must appreciate you taking all this so seriously," she mused before her first nibble of the delightfully decadent chocolate covered waffle bowl.

Gabe snorted ironically. "He sure does."

"What's so funny?"

"Nothing, it's just..." Gabe's youthful, hollow cheeks blushed a softly quiet crimson as he finally announced, "It's me. I'm the owner. I'm...him."

Carol's jaw dropped. Literally. In all her years, that had never happened to her before. The jaw dropping, that is. "No chance," she snorted, sure the cocky little counter boy was just teasing her, taking advantage of her momentary sugar high to puff out his chest a little.

"Beg your pardon?" Gabe only pretended to be insulted.

"No, I mean, congrats if true, it's just...you seem so young."

"Youngish, maybe," Gabe insisted, wriggling higher in his seat as if to prove he wasn't just some junior high school part-timer after all. "But mostly because I skipped college and just started investing my money back into the business when I was actually young. When the old owner wanted to retire a few years ago, we worked something out and, well...voila."

"Wow, Gabe, that's...impressive. Seriously. I work with and talk to college-age kids for a living and ninety-nine-point-nine percent of them don't have a savings account, let alone a thriving business."

Gabe was still blinking his eyes, peering back at her. "How...did you know my name?"

Carol snorted. "It's on your nametag," she pointed out with a wave of her neon pink plastic spoon. "Remember?"

Gabe glanced down, as if surprised. "I try to lead by example," he stammered. "If the owner can wear one, then the part-timers can, too."

"Solid advice."

"But no fair," Gabe teased, seeming to ease back onto his seat, offering Carol a better view of his lean, rambling body and taut, sinewy limbs. "You know my name, and..."

"Carol," she blurted, wiping chocolate off her fingertips with a crisp Soft Swerve napkin, cute little ice cream cone mascot and all, before extending her hand. "It's...nice to meet you. Finally. Officially."

He took it gently, long fingers and big palm seeming to swallow her own up in soft, smooth flesh. She struggled not to shiver at the merest touch, but her sudden reaction was a testament to how long it had been since she'd been touched. At all. Period. By a man.

Any man.

"Same," Gabe said, finally relinquishing her hand. It tingled long after she returned it to the Formica tabletop, a savory sizzle just under her flesh that she knew would last all night long. As they sat, savoring a moment of awkward silence after their even more awkward "introduction," a door behind the sales counter swung open and a young employee paused, mid-stride, just shy of the cash register.

"Boss?" she huffed, and immediately Carol knew the spell had been broken. The look on Gabe's face — startled, then disappointed — made it clear he sensed the same.

Chapter Four

Gabe

"The pistachio machine's still full? I thought you cleaned that hours ago!"

Gabe jerked his head up, cringing at his young assistant manager's pronouncement. "Jalise!" he practically hissed, as if Carol wasn't right there watching the entire, admittedly dysfunctional exchange. "Please, we have" — his tone softened, as he waved at his newest, most supple and sensual late-night regular — "a customer."

The word rang flat on his tongue. After all, Carol seemed so much more than that. "At this hour?" Jalise was undeterred, shaking her head and not having her employer's late-night flirtations one tiny bit. At well over six feet and a few hundred pounds, his favorite coworker made an imposing presence.

"Wait," Carol stammered awkwardly before he could interject, "you're...closed?"

"Obviously not," Gabe insisted, running interference as he turned to Jalise with enough venom in his eyes to evaporate whatever measly amount of soft-serve mix was still swirling in the pistachio slot. "Right, *Jalise*?"

She ignored him energetically, rolling her eyes as she whipped off her work apron huffily. "I mean," she hedged cautiously, eyes widening as she finally took in the quasi-romantic scene unfolding in the ice cream parlor dining room. Jalise's gaze flittered around the room, as if seeing it for the first time. Then she and Gabe shared a quiet, almost conspiratorial look before her expression softened just in time to salvage the situation. "Maybe we forgot to post those new holiday hours again, huh, *boss*?"

Gabe sagged with relief, standing quietly so as not to startle Carol even more than his surly manager already had. "Yes, I meant to do that this afternoon, sorry..."

But Carol's eyes flashed with apprehension, and she stood abruptly as she crumpled the last of her uneaten waffle bowl in a wad of crumpled napkins. "I...I'm so sorry, Gabe, I didn't realize you were staying open late just for me."

"I'm not," he gushed, flashing Jalise a helpless gaze. "Honestly. Right, Jalise?"

"Sure, ma'am," Jalise insisted, even as she rushed to the door and held it open for Carol all the same, all but shooing her out. "We just haven't gotten used to our extended holiday hours yet, that's all."

Carol gave Jalise a silent appraisal. "And you probably have school still, yes?" she prodded, tossing her wadded napkin in the trash can by the door. "Not quite out for winter break yet?"

"No, ma'am, not until next week," Jalise announced, wearing a dramatically over-the-top hangdog expression. The same one she wore whenever she had a hot date and wanted to get out early. "So, yeah, that alarm's gonna be going off any minute now."

Carol nodded, sliding her sleek valise over an even sleeker shoulder. She gave Gabe a backward glance, auburn hair caressing her stylish silk blouse as his eyes traced every wispy strand.

"Sorry to overstay my welcome," she said, tone softening as their eyes met across the gaily colored dining room. For a moment at least, it felt the way it had before Jalise had burst onto the scene, literally — private, flirty, intimate. "I'll try to be a little earlier... tomorrow?"

Before Gabe could reply, she slipped through the door, sensible heels clattering on the formerly silent sidewalk outside. He watched her slink away, legs for days beneath her muted pine-colored pencil skirt. Her car was predictably sensible while achingly sleek, a luxury sedan that might as well have been yet another accessory as she sank into the driver's seat, gunned the purring engine and pulled away without a second glance.

The click of the front door locking behind her reminded Gabe where he was, and who he was with. "Young. Lady!" He turned on Jalise with a vengeance, only to find her leaning against the door, arms crossed over her voluminous chest and eyeing him curiously.

"Sorry," she said, the vague hint of her Puerto Rican accent more noticeable now that they were alone. "How was I to know you were out here macking?"

"Macking?"

"You know," she teased, nodding at the silent booth Carol had only recently vacated. The one he'd finally lured her into after four straight nights of relentless, if clueless, flirting.

"Yes, I *do* know." Gabe rolled his eyes, drifting back to the relative safety of the sales counter. "That's just... that's not...what was happening here."

Her sudden burst of laughter was gay and bright, sounding nothing like her imposing presence. "Okay, sure, boss."

"Honestly," he insisted, mostly to himself. "It's just nice to speak to someone my own age for a change, you know?"

Jalise frowned. "Your age?" she scoffed, setting about her side work duties of emptying the trash by the front door. "Bro, she's a straight-up MILF!"

"Ja-*lise!*"

She held up her hands, fingers tipped with her frosty winter nails, ice blue with miniature snowflakes dancing along their considerable length. How she didn't break three of them a shift was beyond him. "Sorry, but...them's the facts."

Gabe blushed. He'd been thinking the same thing, obviously. Night and day and day and night ever since the first time she'd walked in, after hours, looking as effortlessly radiant and confidently mature as the neon "Closed" sign over her head. The one, after all, she'd promptly ignored. "I prefer the term 'sexy librarian,' if you don't mind."

"Sexy *older* librarian," Jalise pointed out wryly.

Gabe's eyelids fluttered. "Right, that's what I just said."

"No," she corrected him, voice taking on that sing-song tone it had whenever she was teasing him. "You said 'sexy librarian'."

"Right? And..." Gabe didn't see the problem.

"Not all librarians are older," she pointed out.

"They seem older."

She rolled her pale-blue eyes. "Yeah, in your macho patriarchal fantasy, sure."

"Jalise."

"But you can be, like, twenty and have a librarian job. You don't have to be some drop-dead MILF to apply."

Gabe was tired. It was late. And, obviously, Jalise was splitting hairs. "You know what I meant." He sighed wearily.

Suddenly, Jalise seemed to have all the time in the world. To lecture him, that is. "Oh, yeah, I know your macho pigheaded fantasy, big glasses and hair up and silk blouse unbuttoned just so. I just needed to remind you that she's older than you, that's all."

"Not by much," Gabe hedged, even though everything about Carol screamed successful businesswoman, a feat usually achieved by someone in their mid-thirties, not twenties.

"Okay, sure," Jalise teased knowingly. "Besides, librarians don't drive Sierra Sports Flex, boss."

"Sierra what now?"

Jalise flashed him a healthy dose of "you're so lame" eyes. "Her badass car, bro."

Gabe nodded quietly, crossing the threshold from the dining room to the sales counter as he began shutting down and emptying the pistachio and peanut butter swirl machine. Jalise's boyfriend owned an auto body shop and was always picking her up and dropping her off in some newly souped-up hot rod. That was, when she wasn't tooling off on her motorcycle to this class or that. "And that's…a good thing?"

"Good? Boss, that car will set you back ninety grand, easy. And that's without all the bells and whistles, which a woman of *that* stature is surely accustomed to."

Gabe clucked absently, making short work of his nightly duties. "She *did* look successful," he mused, wondering what Carol's office looked like. Where she lived. What she slept in and, more importantly, who shared her bed. He scrubbed the thought away, smirking as Jalise prepared to clock out. "And what's this business about you having to set your alarm for school tomorrow, smartass?"

She blushed quietly, a complement to her smooth olive complexion and radiant, raven-black hair. "I mean, you were riffing, she was riffing, I just followed my gut, you know?"

"Yeah, well, if she'd known you were a sophomore at Birchwood State who didn't have her first class until noon, and only on Tuesdays and Thursdays, she might have stayed longer, dig?"

"Okay, okay, so I didn't think it all the way through." She held up her frosted nail tips in surrender. "I'm just…not used to seeing you so flirtatious, that's all."

"You haven't seen me flirtatious yet," he pretended to growl, the vain attempt at cocky machismo falling flat before it even left his lying tongue.

She rolled her eyes. "Yeah, well, if that was any indication? I still haven't."

He sagged against the counter behind him. "That bad?"

Jalise clucked a knowing tongue. "I mean, she seemed into it, but you were missing signals left and right, bro."

He nodded, glancing down at his black sneakers. "It's been...a while."

"I'm familiar." She pressed against the front door, glancing back from where it stood half-open. Never one to linger too small on small talk, Jalise typically bailed once she clocked out. He was impressed she was showing this much restraint. She even brightened with a most surprising offer indeed. "If it's any consolation, I'll work up a new store hours sign before my shift tomorrow. I'll make it look all official like, you know, snowmen and Christmas lights and whatnot. That way you won't be lying when you say we're open later in December."

"You will?"

"Sure," she promised, softening somewhat. "Least I can do after cock-blocking you tonight!"

Gabe was still laughing as Jalise gunned her bike and peeled out of the parking lot, leaving him behind with all of his side work...and half of hers!

Chapter Five

Carol

"And...your name. dear?"

Carol gritted her teeth behind a fixed smile. After all, she'd just spent the better part of twenty minutes filling out a thoroughly redundant application where her name was stated prominently right at the top, then sprinkled liberally throughout.

Plus, dear? *Dear*? Really?

"Carol Swinton," she chirped, ever the high school cheerleader before an imaginary pep rally crowd.

Carol had always tested well. If anything, she was usually over-prepared, far more than was necessary, and had the innate ability to swallow her pride to navigate the inevitable backhanded compliments, tiny jabs and sexist charade of a mostly male-dominated workplace.

Today, she'd hoped, would be no different. All the same, the resident douchebag in charge was surely putting her patience to the test!

Reginald Archibald the Third, or so he'd announced himself as she'd entered the rented office space midway down bustling State Street, peered down at her application with a self-satisfied smile.

"Ah, yes," he announced, lips thick and moist beneath an ostentatious mustache. "Here it is right at the top. And Carol?"

Reginald let the pause draw out so that she was forced to stand, literal hat in hand — or, in this case, her favorite cranberry-colored winter beret — as he fixed her with a disconcerting gaze. "What have you prepared for us today?"

She waved a sheaf of sheet paper unnecessarily, doing a ridiculous little curtsy to match the awkward vibe in the spacious office. It had once been a Quick Copy print shop, or so said the faded lettering on the storefront windows. Even now, giant printers and a faded "Fifteen-cent copies" sign were shoved against the far wall.

"Well, I dug deep to find a few chestnuts your fans might not have heard in a while," Carol offered.

Reginald turned to a large woman in an ornate scarf sitting beside him. His rolling eyes and pursed lips made it clear what a fool he thought Carol was. "Oh, I doubt that, eh, Bertha?" he said over-dramatically.

"Bertha" offered a similarly dismissive grin. "Good luck," she offered conspiratorially in a vaguely English accent, although her ruddy, windblown complexion and cheery "Elves Do It With Frosting" T-shirt made it likely that the closest she'd ever gotten to Britain was watching some detective series on BBC.

"Indeed," offered the man to Reginald's right. Rail thin and wearing a mustard-colored sweater to match his tweedy dress slacks and slipper-like loafers, the man peered down his long, slender nose with an inevitable scoff. "We've quite the library, Carla."

"Yes, well..." Carol ignored the trollish use of her non-name, an old and transparent ploy to put her off her guard. Mentally she pictured sweet Rome standing in her same position, wondering how he might have reacted to this very same trio's petty digs and deep-seated insults. "Be that as it may, I'll start with the *Birch Tree Blessing*, if I may?"

The glazed expressions and sudden seizing of the trio before her gave a good indication that they didn't, indeed, have quite as extensive a library as they thought.

"Interesting choice," Reginald muttered while casting an eye to the troupe members who sat on either side of him as if to say, "Ho hum."

"I thought so!" Carol brightened, sliding the unnecessary sheet music onto a stool beside where she stood. She set her new beret atop the pile, as if to signify just how prepared she'd come. "Penned by an altar boy in the tiny village of Blevin sometime around the mid-eighteenth century, the carol was sung exclusively in his home church until it gained some popularity after a visiting scholar heard it during Christmas Eve Mass in 1792, I believe?" Carol paused in her recitation to admire the slack jaws and blank stares of her executioners. Ehr, make that, *auditioners*. "After a brief run of popularity in London over the next decade or so, the carol faded back into obscurity once more, rarely sung anymore."

She gave a little hip wriggle and winked before proclaiming, "Until today, that is."

Reginald regained his previous composure, scoffing to his troupe mates while ignoring Carol as if she wasn't still in the room with them. With all of them. "A bit *too* obscure, perhaps?" he offered to the woman known as Bertha before returning his glazed expression back to Carol. "We find that the more overarching an explanation for a carol, the worse it usually sounds."

Carol ignored him, standing to her full height in the slinky cream sweater dress she'd chosen for the occasion. It was clingy, but not too tight. Form fitting, but not garishly so, with just the right hint of glitter in the creamy, off-white weave to signify the start of the holiday season. "Let's give it a listen and see first, shall we, gang?" she chirped, her tone, expression and posture making it clear that the question was all too redundant. Carol hadn't come this far, done this much homework and lost this much sleep to go home empty-handed now.

Then, before any of them could say otherwise, her lips carefully parted to control the measure of her breathing, Carol launched into the carol she'd been practicing for the last forty-eight hours straight. Acapella, unaccompanied and unbothered. She wasn't a true mezzo-soprano, as the blustery Victorian Voices flyer had requested. Indeed, her default setting bordered more on the alto range, rich and deep, but she was nothing if not an expert mimic.

Even now, eyes closed as she envisioned the faraway rectory where that creative little altar boy had penned his bittersweet song, feather pen scrawling against thick, off-color paper, the words trilled out, soft and high and sweet. "Birches stand, alone and white, a silent army on this night…"

The room fell to a quiet hush, Carol quickly watching the doubt disappear on each of the trio's faces as she leaned into the next stanza. "A crisp and quiet moon above, bare branches still below, the birches sing their carol sweet, snow drifting to and fro..."

The words slipped out, smooth and slow, the deserted office space a wise choice as her voice echoed along the silent walls, buffered by the cinder blocks and ceiling tiles until it funneled straight to her audience of three. She lost herself in the chorus, a bittersweet ode to days gone by. "Birches dancing, roots like feet, rise and join the carol sweet, dancing midst the forest glen, abandoned by the sons of men..."

Her tone was measured, passionate when the song dictated but reading the room all the same, softening the swell of the song's climax to accommodate for the size, or lack thereof, of her audience. She felt the lyrics deep in her gut, sending them crooning through her lips as if she were still alone in her laundry room, where the acoustics were almost as good as the deserted print shop's.

When it was over, Carol opened her eyes, but not before the sound of four hands clapping startled her out of her mid-Regency revelry. Bertha and her mustard-sweater-wearing companion were golf-clapping almost silently, their enthusiasm almost overwhelming their obvious regard for Reginald's feelings.

"I never thought it possible," Bertha exclaimed, all traces of her mock-English accent suddenly cast to the wind and sounding, to Carol's ear anyway, downright *Southern*. "A Regency carol I *hadn't* heard before!"

Carol blushed steadily under such high praise.

"Right, Felix?" Bertha elbowed the man beside her and, to his credit, Old Mustard Sweater Guy—of *course* his name was Felix—nodded appreciatively, still applauding. "I was skeptical at first," he said with a new warmth to his tone, soft blue eyes beaming under a healthy spray of salt and pepper curls. "But, by golly, that was…refreshing."

There was a vague pause, Bertha and Felix glancing at each other enthusiastically before giving a cautious gaze Reginald's way. He sat, rigid as ever, thick legs crossed one over the other, arms resting across a stiff belly. He wore a crisp suit, blue-and-white-striped dress shirt underneath, boasting a bright red snowman tie.

"I admit that song is new, even to me," he hemmed, the tinge of doubt creeping into his fatherly tone as he wriggled in an old desk chair. "Maybe we could hear what else you've prepared and see if it's equally…obscure?"

Carol brightened. It was far from a "yes," but it was just as far from a "no." She wriggled even taller in her clingy sweater dress, nodding as she licked her lips to prepare for her second selection. "I had to really dig deep to find this one," she offered, laying it on thick as if Reginald was the only one in the room. "For my second selection, I'll be singing *The Orchard Carol* and —"

"Another song about trees?" Reginald interrupted haughtily, Carol quickly noting the way Bertha and Felix shot him a warning look as he all but stifled a mock yawn.

Carol brushed it off with a fake laugh so convincing that even Reginald looked surprised by her generosity. "Maybe that's why they're so obscure?" she offered. "In fact, this is a solstice carol, popular for a few years in the *very* early 1800s. Designed as a round, you'll have to imagine the other three voices joining in. That is, unless…" She paused for a well-timed wink, glancing around the room and sure to make eye contact with each of them in turn. "You'd care to join me?"

There was a twitter of nervous laughter followed by Reginald clearing his throat. "Perhaps next time, Carol." His voice was stern and impatient, two layers thicker than his default tone of feigned indifference. "Now, if you don't mind, we have a dozen or more applicants we'd like to consider before making our final choice."

Fat chance. Carol admired the way Bertha and Felix were practically on the edge of their respective seats to hear what she had in store for them next. As if to delay the proceedings any further, Carol made an obvious glance toward the front of the deserted print shop, the storefront empty, to say nothing of the quiet side street in front of it.

Turning back around pointedly, she made a mock frown to let the fact be known that Reginald Archibald the Third was officially and unequivocally full of shit. "Oh, I'm sorry. I mean, I can stop now if you're *that* busy?"

She had no intention of stopping now, but Carol didn't need to let Reginald know that! "Oh, no," he blathered after Bertha shot him a searing glance from beside him. "I just meant maybe we don't need a history lesson before each song?"

"I quite enjoy them," Felix insisted, ignoring Reggie's laser-beam look of shock as he nodded encouragement all the same. "Please, Carol... proceed?"

She did that little curtsy again, cursing herself afterward. "If you insist," she said, mock-teasing, as she did just that. "As I was saying, the songwriter in question was a nun this time. Sister Helena Wittemyer ran an orphanage in the slums of London where, every Christmas, she put on a talent show as a fundraiser.

Tiring of the same old carols, the good sister wrote *The Orchard Carol* as a way to involve all of the children in her care by joining in praise through her quiet, understated hymn..."

Carol halted before she licked her lips and began the song in question. "Orchards bare this time of year, and only children linger here..."

Her voice was high, to match the key in which the song was written, but dropped lower as she continued with the next verse, "Frost upon the midnight ground, angels' feet don't make a sound..."

With her eyes closed, voice crooning quietly, a chair's squeak interrupted her before she could even begin the chorus. "Yes, yes," Reginald was saying, fumbling with the clipboard that held her application as he avoided her wide, vulnerable eyes. "Very nice, thank you, Carol. We...we'll be in touch."

Carol stood, stunned into silence as she nodded almost subconsciously, reaching for her stack of sheet music and peering back at the three faces across from her. "Of... of course," she stammered, slapping her long-forgotten beret atop her carefully coiffed head and backing toward the door, narrowly avoiding the desk chairs in her path. "I...I appreciate your time."

Outside the abandoned Quick Copy print shop, the chill December air matched her mood as Carol nearly stumbled along State Street to her car. Embarrassment rattled her nerves and self-doubt racked her brain as she slid into the driver's seat, shutting the door against the midday chill. She'd prepared so methodically, envisioned the audition down to the smallest detail and...things had been going according to plan. Had she erred in some way? Come off as *too* confident? Chosen songs that were simply too obscure? Gone too high or started too low?

She started the engine, Christmas carols blasting immediately from the car stereo. She shut them off, adjusting the heat to combat the seasonal chill. The day stretched out before her, long and gray, and for the life of her, Carol only wanted to go to one place for comfort, and not just the soft-serve variety.

Chapter Six

Gabe

"Why are they so tight?"

Ray Ridgeway struggled to button the front of his old-fashioned breeches, whining like a three-year-old struggling to get his hand into the cookie jar. It was an admittedly complex process for pants that *did* fit, but, even from a few feet away, Gabe could tell it was going to be a losing battle. Tailor extraordinaire Hammond Armond exchanged knowing looks with his assistant, Remy, as he inched toward the fitting rooms with a firm but fair expression on his face. "It's because you've gained weight, Ray."

"Not a chance," Ray insisted, sucking in his gut to no avail. Two of the six era-accurate brass buttons on either side of the fold-down front panel of his breeches were precariously secured but the top four? No shot. Not a chance.

"It happens, Ray," Gabe assured him, even as he wriggled into his own poly-wool blend trousers, a deep forest green and blood-red plaid befitting the season, thin at the ankles and flaring at the hips. Gabe always felt so prissy when pulling them on, and even more so when wearing them out in public.

"Indeed," Hammond noted, regarding his leather-bound notebook of regular clients' measurements. "It happened last year, too, remember, Ray?"

"That was different," Ray insisted, color rising to his full cheeks. "I'd sprained my ankle around Halloween and stopped going to the gym for the rest of the year."

Hammond and Remy exchanged another doubtful look while the tailor himself whisked in with a fresh swipe of his ever-present measuring tape. "Be that as it may," he murmured, sliding the tape around Ray's voluminous belly with an exasperated sigh. "The buttons don't lie."

Ray seized on this idea, grumbling as Gabe slid the puffy arms of his Regency dress shirt through a holly-covered vest of rich brocade. "They must have shrunk," Ray insisted, wriggling and holding his breath to try and seal the front flap of the Regency-era accurate pants once and for all. "That's the only possible explanation."

"Raymond," Hammond insisted, voice growing an edge more sinister with each passing moment. He was far from an imposing man, small and slight and as stuffy as he was fussy, but Birchwood's finest tailor certainly knew his business and was never less than professional. "We steam clean all our storage items. Not a washer or dryer in sight. The chance of shrinking is minimal at best—"

"But never zero!" Ray interjected, wagging a pale, plump finger, nails bitten to the quick. "Never, ever *zero*. Right?"

Hammond nodded begrudgingly. "Infinitesimal," he conceded. "But yes, never zero. So?" He clapped his hands and nodded toward Remy, enlisting the larger but no less fussy man's help as he held Ray in place while Hammond measured him once more. "Fine, yes, so we will let these out to forty-two and you will be more than comfortable for the holidays, yes?"

"Forty-two?" Ray nearly collapsed into the trifold mirrors where he'd been admiring the unfolding debacle as if a mere spectator. "As in...inches?"

Hammond looked confused. "What else, Raymond?"

Poor Ray looked like he'd just seen a ghost. "Y-y-you're saying I have a forty-two-inch waist?"

Remy and Hammond both nodded this time. "Is fine," Remy insisted through a thick accent. "Many Americans have this measurement, sir."

"Not *this* American!" Ray sank onto a long, padded bench just out of the mirror's range, as if to further distance himself from the maddening truth. "Gabe, help me out here."

"It's just a rut," Gabe insisted, slithering into his tailored evergreen riding jacket. It featured bolstered sleeves, two rows of shiny brass buttons on either side of the satiny black lapel and a fashionably high waist. "You'll be back down to your normal size by next year, bet on it."

Gabe preened in front of the mirrors as he tugged his jacket tight and made sure he had room to lift his arms, mimicking holding the thick songbook the Mistle Tones sang from each year. Thus satisfied, he reached for the top hat hanging from a rack just outside the mirror's range.

"Easy for you to say." Ray harumphed as Hammond and Remy conferred about his most recent measurements, alternately scribbling and haggling over Ray's listing in the notebook. "You're probably the same size as you were in high school."

"I mean," Gabe reminded him, "we're ten years apart in age, Ray. Plus we're different body types. That's what makes us look so distinct while we're caroling. Mutt and Jeff, you know?"

"So I'm Mutt?"

Gabe chuckled. "I'm not sure which is which, but what I do know? With your thick round glasses and mutton-chop sideburns, that unruly mustache and, yes, your specific waist size, you're the crowd favorite when we're out doing our thing. You want to throw all that away just to fit in a smaller pair of breeches?"

Ray frowned. "You're just saying that so I don't sink all the way into depression."

"I'm telling the truth," Gabe insisted, popping the high collar of his even higher-waisted riding jacket and admiring the way it nearly reached all the way to his ears. "It's why we dress this way, Ray. And sing the songs we do. She might be a petty taskmaster with definite narcissistic tendencies, but at least Jazz has that part right, anyway. People expect a certain vibe when they hear old Regency carols and, my man? You're definitely a vibe!"

Ray offered a begrudging smile. "Thanks for trying to cheer me up." He sighed. "And I know what you're saying." Ray twirled the corners of his thick mustache, the one that matched so well with his round, Benjamin Franklin spectacles. "I start growing this in July and everyone around the stereo shop knows why. By December it's thick and lustrous and folks start to get ready for our performances..."

Ray's tone was wistful and, Gabe reasoned, it had more to do with just his waist size. "But?" Gabe prodded, sinking onto the bench beside him. In his ridiculous Victorian garb, it was like trying to sit in a full-body cast. "Why do I hear a 'but' in there somewhere, old pal?"

"But," Ray teased, a smile inching across his ruddy face at last. "Wouldn't it be nice to...*not* do this every year?" He tugged on his britches, nodding as Hammond and Remy conferred over a tablet on the sales floor of their suit store. "Wouldn't it be nice to just...slip on our comfy jeans and an ugly Christmas sweater and sing something that wasn't four thousand years old?"

Gabe snorted, rolling his eyes for good measure. "Not this again?"

"Yes, this again," Ray insisted, glancing around the empty storefront as if somehow Jazz and Mason might be listening from behind one of Hammond's impeccably clad mannequins. "Range of movement, you know?" Ray insisted, wriggling his arms outside of his own brocade vest full of big brass buttons. "Putting our own unique spin on *modern* carols for a change."

"We go through this every year, Ray."

"I know we do, Gabe," Ray insisted. "Because it's a good idea, right?"

"Of course it is," Gabe reassured his old friend. "But remember the one time we had the balls to bring it up to Jazz?"

"Do I ever?" They both cringed at the shared memory. "I still have mild hearing loss from her outburst in the rehearsal space that day."

"So why bother?" Gabe nudged Ray's knee with his own. "Until we grow the balls to bring it up to Jazz again, it's a moot point, right?"

"I suppose." Ray sighed, slumping with the depressing developments of their annual costume fitting. "But a man can dream, right?"

Gabe reached over and patted Ray's knee. "One day, pal." He glanced around the tailor's shop as he pictured a time when it wouldn't be a yearly tradition. He'd miss the fancy breeches and elaborate buttoning process, but to be able to sit without assistance? Not get a vocabulary lesson from Jazz each year in order to merely understand the long-forgotten carols they were singing?

Why, 'twould be a fine day indeed, guvnor...

Chapter Seven

Carol

"I was just about to leave…"

Carol stood by her car self-consciously, admiring the gleaming pink and turquoise van as it parked beside her.

Gabe bounded from the driver's seat as if it was the beginning of their day and not the end, jingling the keys from his belt demonstrably. "We can't have that," he insisted, beaming as he nodded for her to follow him toward the front of Soft Swerve. She did so, feeling like she'd somehow asked him out on a date.

"I'm beginning to feel like these extended holiday hours of yours are total BS," she mused idly, even a tad playfully, as he struggled to find the right key.

He paused, keys in mid-jingle to peer back at her with that sweet, innocent face of his. "Why do you say that?" His voice, as ever, was earnest and curious.

"I mean, look around." Carol nodded toward the mostly silent outdoor mall that surrounded them, endless rows of high-end boutiques and quaint, charming eateries all shuttered for the evening. "None of your neighbors are open."

"That's because they're short-sighted business-people," he rallied, giving her a slow, charming little wink. "Can't see the bigger picture, that's all."

"The bigger picture..." She smiled back at him tentatively. They were standing closer than usual, huddled as it were in front of the door to his ice cream parlor. He smelled of some spicy man's cologne, youthful and brief as she continued to tease him as she might one of her young, enthusiastic employees. "Of staying open late for...one customer?"

"You're not *just* a customer," he insisted in that earnest way of his, warming her heart in ways it hadn't felt thawed in years. "After all, you could tell a friend that we're open late, and they might tell a friend, and soon enough...bam, this place is mobbed at nine PM every night."

Carol rolled her eyes playfully, feeling that nightly sense of giddiness that always overcame her in Gabe's humming, vibrant presence. "All the same, I call BS."

"Heck no!" Gabe turned, mid key-finding, tapping the newly posted hours sign with his free hand. "See, a sign and everything!" He squinted at it like he'd never seen it before.

Chances are, he probably hasn't. At least not since that saucy little assistant manager of his hung it up while he was out, that is.

"Hmmm," he muttered, very boss-like, as if he'd forgotten she was standing right there. "Those were supposed to be holly leaves, but I guess hearts will do?"

Carol chuckled. She'd noted the same thing earlier when she'd left her car to test the door, finding it locked, her hopes for another pleasant evening spent in Gabe's flattering, youthful company dashed. That was, until his van squealed into the parking lot just as she threatened to slip back into her car and make a hasty, unnoticed getaway.

"Maybe you're keeping them up through Valentine's!" she noted.

He eyed the jumbled-up December calendar with a shopkeeper's scrutiny. "Well, then we'd have to change the Christmas trees out here," he muttered, pointing to a cluster of clip-art evergreens in the top corner. "But I guess the little snowmen over here could stay, at least through February..."

She chuckled at his inner monologue, the meek sound lost in the turning of the right key at last. The lock opened with a satisfying *click*. "Yes!" Gabe cheered to himself, swinging the door open and the familiar scent of fresh-baked waffle cones and mint chocolate rushing straight to her overjoyed nostrils.

"So, the usual?" Gabe was all abustle, holding the door open just long enough for her to enter before bounding toward the cluttered pink and blue sales counter.

She heard the door shut behind them, following Gabe's long, jaunty steps to the by-now-familiar cash register. She noted how the row of soft-serve machines were silent, save for her favorite two.

"Actually," she teased, watching Gabe freeze in place as he swung through the little half-door beside the register. "I was hoping to try one of your seasonal flavors?" She made a big play of admiring the chalkboard menu above his head, tapping her chin with a silent finger as if thoroughly considering the creative menu offerings and not just trolling him. Big time. "Maybe the hot cocoa and peppermint swirl, perhaps?"

Her gaze swept down to find Gabe crestfallen, bordering on panic-stricken, eyes wide and jaw slack, a look she could hardly endure for another moment longer before she broke out laughing. "Just teasing, yes…the usual, please!"

His whole body sagged with relief, and he set about filling a chocolate waffle bowl with her favorite, pistachio and peanut butter swirl. Then, as if on a whim, he made one for himself. "Expecting company?" she teased as he came around the counter with one in each hand, guiding her back toward the booth where she'd sat the night before.

"I just realized I haven't eaten all day."

She sank into her booth bench, Gabe pulling out a seat at the same table where he'd sat the night before. "That explains it," she sighed, swirling a pink spoon to dab at her first bite of soft serve.

"Explains what?"

"Your girlish figure," she teased, ogling the way Gabe's thin Soft Swerve T-shirt clung to his boyish frame. Typically she dated older, more mature, more sophisticated, more masculine men. Not gym rats, per se, but definitely of the vaguely alpha, take charge but not *too* much charge variety. Not that they ever worked out, naturally, but she definitely had a type.

Gabe was so opposite from that type as to be completely foreign to her. *Is that the attraction?* she wondered, savoring the heady blend of sweet and savory soft serve. Was that why she was practically throwing herself at this poor, innocent young shopkeeper in the first place?

"Me?" Carol mused aloud, rejoining the live conversation after dousing the one in her head like a smoldering campfire. "I can't remember the last time I forgot to eat."

"Bad habit from high school, I suppose," Gabe mumbled, tucking into his own soft serve with gusto, the little pink spoon lost in his big, veiny hand.

"Sounds like a *great* habit to me," she exclaimed, self-conscious about more than just their age difference for once. At thirty-four, Carol had settled into a career that favored casual, but thorough business attire. Dresses and jackets helped camouflage the increasingly softer curves that resulted from more hours spent on the call center floor and less at the gym. She was far from, say, Rubenesque, but also a far cry from the spitfire, rail-thin tomboy who'd gone to NC State on a volleyball scholarship.

Gabe paused, leaving the pink plastic spoon wedged midway down his towering waffle bowl. "Why do you say that?" he asked, their eyes meeting across the small space between them. "You're perfect just the way you are, Carol. Skipping a meal would be unnecessary, and it's not much fun, trust me."

She cocked her head. It wasn't exactly Shakespeare, yet it was possibly the most romantic thing a man had ever said to her. "Okay," she gushed, uncertain how to respond when, after all, all Gabe ever saw her do was shove soft serve in her mouth night after night. "Well, thanks for that."

He beamed, tucking back into his cone as if he hadn't just soothed her soul with his balm-like praise. "You're welcome."

They ate in rare silence for a moment. Comfortable silence, that was. The same instrumental eighties music played in the background, fusing perfectly with the neon accents and "monthly special" posters that lined the dining room. On the wall facing them, high up and almost to the ceiling, a glowing monitor played old eighties and nineties cartoons on mute, as if to appease Gabe's youngest diners while their parents chattered away.

Eventually Carol nodded toward the empty sales counter. "Where's your partner in crime tonight?"

"Jalise?" Gabe hunched broad shoulders. "She was still scheduled for regular hours and one of the swirl makers started acting up at one of my other units so I had to pop over there for a quick fix and…what? Why the face?"

"Other units?"

Gabe smiled amidst a sudden blush. The vivid color lighting his pale, hollow cheeks complemented the soft, light-brown stubble that covered his head, reminding Carol that he'd gone hatless tonight. *In my honor?* she wondered wickedly. *Or just an oversight?*

"Oh, sorry," he explained almost bashfully. "I… have two more of these babies scattered around lower Birchwood."

Carol sat back in her seat. "Get out of town."

"True story." Gabe nibbled on his rapidly disappearing waffle bowl before explaining, "There's this one here in the Birchwood Galleria, the one across from the Cumberland Mall and my newest out near the college. For some reason, that one's giving me the most trouble lately."

"How…how do you do it all?"

"I don't," Gabe insisted. "I have a good management team, but they're mostly new so it's a lot of handholding and mothering by phone."

"Except tonight?" Carol prodded.

Gabe merely nodded, wadding up the last of his crunchy, chocolatey waffle bowl in a trendy little Soft Swerve napkin. She'd done the same, both of them lingering in the soft, muted sugar rush that followed. Carol had never been one for desserts before moving to Birchwood, but her odd hours at the Helpline had her all mixed up, in more ways than one. She wondered how lacking her life might have been if she'd gone to some random drive-thru instead of seeing the neon Soft Swerve sign on her way home earlier that week and pulling in instead.

"Yeah, sorry about that," Gabe said.

"For what? You would have saved me five hundred calories or more if you'd stayed closed."

Gabe crossed his legs and turned toward her. One of his big hands was resting on the table for two beside him, distracting her to no end with his long, slender fingers and the dirty-blond wisps of hair that shimmered up the length of his forearm in the dim neon glow of the empty ice cream parlor.

"And miss all this?" he asked quietly but, Carol noted, not snarkily.

Carol nodded. She wondered how to respond, as Gabe was clearly talking about more than just some trendy soft serve combo before bed. Before she could rush in and say something foolish, however, he smiled that gentle, crooked smile, letting her off the hook.

"You *do* bring up a good point, though."

"I do?" Carol was shocked. After all, she hadn't formed an intelligent sentence since the two had met earlier that week.

"Yes," he insisted, waving that big hand back toward the stylish chalkboard menu above the whirring soft serve machines. "Here I am, slaving over all these fancy new flavors every season and no one ever tries any of them."

"Isn't pistachio and peanut butter one of your seasonal favorites?"

He gave a little tut-tut frown before arguing, "Yeah, from Thanksgiving."

She frowned, staring into the muted dregs of her recently demolished waffle bowl. "I was gonna say, it's not very Christmas-y."

He arched one delicately fuzzy eyebrow. "It isn't, but plenty are. Maybe tomorrow you can try something…different?"

A slight surge of excitement gurgled just beneath Carol's already flushed skin. "What, you mean like a challenge?"

"Yes!" Gabe sat up to his full height. "Exactly like a challenge. That way instead of having the same old thing every night, you can sample all my holiday favorites and tell me what you think of them."

Carol was flattered. More than that, she was excited. It meant a reason to see more of Gabe. An official reason, and one he'd suggested, after all. Something more than just her obsessively wanting to ogle the sexy counter boy every night after work and hoping he'd still be open by the time she clocked out.

"Well, haven't you done focus groups on each one first?"

His guffaw was open and raw, like his big-boned body with all its soft curves and hard angles and ooey, gooey deliciousness. "With who?" he teased, leaning forward as another waft of his manly cologne interrupted the waffle cone and mint chocolate aroma that always permeated Soft Swerve. "Giggling teens after school? Crazy busy soccer moms juggling eight preteens? My ravenous employees who'd all just say 'add chocolate to everything'? No, it's pretty much just me tooling around here after hours, racking my brain for new ideas."

"Sounds lonely," she blurted before she could stop herself. After all, she was only projecting her own solitary career mindset, finely honed from years climbing the corporate ladder.

Their eyes met. He paused before nodding. "It is, actually."

She homed in. "Can I ask, did you study any of this in college?"

"College?" Gabe huffed. "I barely graduated high school."

"Why not?"

Gabe cocked his head, as if to scold her. She blushed and stammered out a reply. "No, no, I get it, barely graduated, I remember you mentioning that, but I help students navigate college applications every shift. Surely a kid with your initiative and ambition could have wriggled his way into a good school, low GPA or not."

Gabe smirked. "I think I hear a compliment in there somewhere." Then he stood, as if signaling an end to a conversation she was hoping was just getting started.

"Well, I just mean..." She followed suit, standing with resignation as her heart fell. It seemed that every night, just when things were starting to go well for her, he'd stand and abruptly signal its end.

"Listen, try one of my holiday specials tomorrow night and maybe I'll answer your question, okay?"

Carol brightened. "Deal!" she said too eagerly, extending a hand.

He considered it only a moment before embracing it wholeheartedly. His touch, as ever, was warm and smooth and utterly intoxicating. Quietly, with eyes full of dubious intent, he winked and said, "And, in return, surely you'll answer a question or two of my own?"

Chapter Eight

Gabe

"Raymond!"

Gabe winced as Jazz's familiar voice cut through the rehearsal space like a heat-seeking laser beam. While the long, thin room was great for acoustics, it was also a natural bullhorn whenever their fearless leader unleashed a predictably unpredictable outburst.

He hazarded a glance at his old pal, Ray, kitted out in his newly-tailored breeches and fine brocade jacket, mutton-chop mustache grown out to perfection and blending perfectly with his round spectacles and crooked top hat. "Sorry, Jazz, I'll get it right this time, promise."

I'm too far away, that's the problem. Gabe strained at the new alignment Jazz had insisted on this year. Usually, Gabe and Ray walked side by side through the ritzy neighborhoods, trendy gallerias and tony shopping malls of Birchwood, allowing Gabe to assist his less acoustics-prone pal. But this year Jazz had laid waste to their usual arrangement, placing Ray next to Mason instead. No surprise, Ray was missing his beats as they rehearsed an old English carol, *Child of Burden*, envisioned as a round but slightly off-kilter thanks to poor old Ray.

"You said that the last three times," Jazz reminded him. "This isn't a challenging carol, Ray. We've sung much more difficult ones in the past."

Ray raised his hand, the collar of his silk shirt stiff beneath his waist-high riding jacket. "Yes, I'm aware, if you could just—"

"Burden," Mason hissed from beside poor Ray, interrupting him. "When I sing 'Burden,' you start the chorus from scratch. 'Child of blessing, child of want, child of need, child of…'" Mason rolled his own hand, clad in a leather riding glove.

Ray brightened, standing an inch higher in his replica riding boots. "Burden!"

Gabe nearly smacked his forehead. "No, Ray," he whispered helplessly, knowing full well the others could hear. "When Mason says 'Burden,' you start with 'Child of blessing,' see? You start the whole thing over again."

"Yes! Yes, I see it now." Ray did. Smack his forehead, that was. The sound reverberated through the rented rehearsal space. The hour was late, as usual, but not for Gabe, who still had a full hour to get back to Soft Swerve, change into his work clothes and whip up a holiday special for his new favorite customer.

"Do you, Ray?" Jazz huffed. "Because you said that the last three times we've tried this and—"

"If we could just go back to last year's positions?" Gabe interrupted hesitantly, knowing that to speak at all was to risk Jazz's full wrath. "Maybe I could help?"

"And how's that?" Jazz huffed, fussing with the flair of the emerald-green bow knotted gaily at her own stiff white collar. It paired perfectly with the satin sash that wound round her Regency-accurate bonnet.

While their fiercest rival, Victorian Voices, had unanimously decided on a winterberry maroon tint to their caroling costumes, Jazz had made a deliberate choice to bedeck her own Mistle Tones carolers in varying shades of pine, fir and emerald colors, as if to distance the two rival troupes all the more.

Gabe continued to sputter out in defense of his old pal. "Nothing, it's just, Ray and I can usually keep each other on cue if we're...closer together. You know, like every other year?"

Gabe glanced over, expecting Ray to look relieved. Instead, he seemed panicked. Gabe frowned. "Make up your mind," he wanted to shout. "Do you want my help or not, you big mutton-chop-wearing chicken shit?"

Jazz broke character, stepping out of line with the rest of them and approaching the whiteboard that Mason had recently cleaned. Tearing the cap off a dry-erase marker, she quickly scrawled four circles on the board. "I'm trying something new this year, Gabriel," she said, marking initials over each circle to indicate their renewed positioning. "Obviously, what's worked in the past hasn't...worked quite well enough now, has it?"

Gabe nodded, adjusting his tone somewhat in solidarity to sound more agreeable. "I want to win this year too, Jazz."

"It's not just about winning, Gabe." Jazz's tone had softened somewhat as well. It was still shrill and stiff, but not quite as high a pitch as when he'd first intervened. "It's about surviving."

Suddenly, Gabe was listening. "If we don't win the Jingle Jangle this year," Jazz announced, speaking to them as a group this time, "I'm not sure this town is big enough for two Victorian caroling troupes anymore."

"Jazz." Mason broke rank as well, standing to face his closest ally. "It's always been like this. Folks enjoy a heated rivalry, and if we're not Number One each year, it would be Birchwood's loss if we left them with only Victorian Voices to satisfy their Olde English carol cravings next year."

"I agree," Ray insisted. "You know my feelings on modernity and how I'd take the direction of this group, but if we're committed to Regency-era carols, dress, the whole nine, then at least we do it with originality and energy. They're just so boring, and if we drop out of the race entirely, then who could possibly stand up to them?"

Jazz offered a rare smile. "We agree on that much at least," she said. "But clearly the judges don't. And unlike the rest of you, I have a reputation to uphold. A business reputation, that is."

Gabe snorted. "What, like I don't?"

Mason turned toward him, nearly as tall but two decades older. Still, his salt and pepper sideburns and carefully coiffed curls lent him a most gentlemanly demeanor despite the current fire in his eyes. "Please, Gabe," he huffed. "Being Number Two clearly hasn't hurt *your* business any. I can't drive anywhere in this town without another Soft Swerve popping up along my path."

"What, like you're able to miss one of Jazz's billboards?" Gabe clapped back. "Or bus benches? Or full-page ads in the *Birchwood Gazette*?"

Across the room, Ray shot him a look that screamed, "Be careful."

He ignored it.

"That's just it, Gabe." Jazz relented, inching closer to touch his sleeve. She was an imposing woman, elegant, sophisticated, whip smart and almost single-mindedly obsessive. Not the warmest woman he'd ever met, but Gabe still had mad respect for her skills nonetheless. "I can hardly keep calling myself 'Birchwood's Number One Realtor' if I can't even win a simple caroling competition."

"Jazz, it's apples and oranges."

"Not to me it isn't." She insisted. "Things come easy for you. I get that. You're young, handsome, charming, in a growth industry. I've staked my claim in a much more challenging profession and it's dog eat dog in this town."

"Please." Gabe huffed. "Property prices climb every year. We're in one of the richest counties in the state, the research park next to the university keeps expanding and hiring, construction is at an all-time high. You think a little caroling competition is going to touch your platinum reputation?"

Jazz's face fell, revealing a smidge of her actual age. "That's just it." She sighed, releasing Gabe's sleeve and returning to formation. "It's always been a 'little' competition to you, right Gabe?"

"You know what I mean, Jazz," Gabe struggled to argue, but the light in Jazz's eyes was gone, back to her old, steady fierceness.

"I know *exactly* what you mean, Gabe. Now, back into formation please?"

Gabe nodded. Why did he always cave to Jazz's many whims and wants? The period dress, the strict policies and procedures, the simmering resentment and gall of her every syllable. Perhaps she was wrong after all. Maybe the Jingle Jangle competition meant more to him than he let on.

Even to himself.

All the same, he wondered if Jazz was on the right track. After all, if nothing they'd been doing so far was working, why keep doing it?

Chapter Nine

Carol

"Carol?"

Carol paused mid-stride from where she'd been wearing a hole in her new office carpet. "Yes?" She blinked her eyes as if to make sure her boss was actually standing there.

"You good?" Rome's voice was firm and assured, the acute opposite to her harried mental state at that moment.

"Mmmm-hmmm," she mumbled, an already bitten-to-the-quick fingernail flying to her mouth. An old, but bad habit. He took another precautionary step further into her office, already warning her with a wagging finger.

"Fine, yes." She pulled the offending fingernail away, letting both hands fall to her sides before crossing them almost protectively over her chest. "I'm…what now?"

For the life of her, Carol couldn't remember whose turn it was to speak, or if either of them had spoken yet at all.

Rome chuckled at her predicament, big smile filling his cherubic young face. He inched the door halfway shut behind him, the way he often did if they were speaking in private. "I just…" He paused, troubling the hem of his ever-stylish rugby sweater, the perfect complement to his trendy caramel-colored corduroy slacks. "You've been in here, pacing, for the better part of an hour. You *sure* you're good?"

She started to lie. Started to bluff. Started to spew the nonsensical lines she'd been rehearsing ever since her phone had rung exactly an hour earlier. Then she sagged instead, crumpling onto the corner of her desk and upsetting a trio of Christmas cards she'd placed there earlier that afternoon.

"No," she admitted miserably.

Rome smiled in self-satisfaction, sinking into the plush leather chair across from her and crossing his legs as if he'd already assumed the role of therapist. "I knew it!" He pumped his fist into the air triumphantly. "Now, spill it so old Rome can make things right."

"Stop teasing," she ordered, although Carol had to admit Rome's sudden burst of youthful enthusiasm and "nothing can be all *that* bad" attitude was clearly just the balm she needed.

"I'm not," he insisted, making himself comfortable across from her desk. "This is what I'm good at, Carol. Helping people. This is what I'm *built* for."

"Yeah, well, I'm not usually in this kind of dilemma, so forgive me if I'm not exactly used to asking for… help."

Rome shrugged casually beneath his maroon and evergreen striped rugby sweater. "First time for everything, girl. Now...spill."

Carol glanced past him toward the busy call center floor beyond. December was creeping into mid-stride now, the phone banks busier than ever as college finals season rapidly approached. She could hardly afford the extravagance of a mid-shift breakdown, but...what choice did she have?

"Promise not to tell anyone?" she asked, already sensing Rome was someone she could trust — and then some.

He scoffed at her concerns. "Like who, Carol? Our eighteen seasonal helpers, most of whom I barely recognize when they start their shift each day?"

Carol shrugged her concerns away. After all, she was desperate. New to town, lured away from her high-powered recruiting job at nearby Kensington State after nearly a decade on campus, she didn't know a sole in Birchwood besides, well...Rome and Gabe.

And she certainly couldn't tell Gabe!

"I have a dilemma," she blurted.

Rome was still enjoying himself. "No shit? Like the straight hour of robotic pacing with your eyes glued to the floor didn't clue me in?"

"Please," she begged. "This is hard enough as it is. It'll be easier if you just...let me finish?"

He mimicked locking his mouth shut and throwing away the key. Carol rolled her eyes at his dramatics, not sure why she'd expected anything less from her charming, if over the top new boss.

"Okay, so..." She shifted to get comfortable, crossing her legs as if she could hide her sudden air of vulnerability. Rome sat up a little straighter, the new leather chair squeaking slightly beneath his movement. "There's this guy in town. I really like him, but...I'm not sure if he likes me back..."

Rome started to roll his eyes, lips parting. She silenced him with a look. He nodded, rolling his hand to indicate she should keep going. "I know it seems immature, sophomoric even. I should know these things by now. But...I *really* like him, and he's so different from any other guy I've ever dated before and I just don't want to scare him off too soon considering our...age difference."

Rome's hands crept to the sides of the wing chair, as if holding himself in place while his mouth struggled not to interject a dozen or more sarcastic comments, witty one-liners or cheesy double entendres. She snickered at his obvious desire to interrupt, enjoying his forced silence as she prattled on like some lovesick teen. "Anyway, we had a kind of a very informal, sort of, maybe date tonight and, well..." She reached into her jacket pocket for her cell phone, pulling up the text thread in question. "Then I got this."

Rome broke his silence to read the message aloud. "Dear Carol, sorry for keeping you on the sidelines so long. The woman we chose in your stead isn't working out so if you're willing, we'd love to give you a shot at being this year's newest addition to...Victorian Voices!"

Rome paused, thick brow furrowing momentarily before beaming and gazing up at her. "Victorian Voices? You tried out?"

She nodded, almost as proud of herself as Rome seemed to be of her. "Why didn't you tell me?"

"I figured after my disastrous audition earlier this week, no chance in hell they'd ever call me back in, so why double the displeasure, you know?"

"But now...they have!"

Carol scowled for the first time all day. "I have a feeling they've gone through more than just one soprano since they held auditions, but it's what I wanted so...yay me?" She did a tentative golf-clap for herself.

Then Rome's face softened somewhat. Handing the phone back, he said, "Don't take this the wrong way, Carol, but I don't see where the dilemma is."

"I called Reginald after our text thread and he said there's a mandatory rehearsal tonight and it's..." Carol's voice trailed quietly off.

Rome nodded with sudden understanding. "At the same time as your maybe-kind of date with Mr. Younger Than You But Still So Wonderful, right?"

"The exact same time," Carol all but moaned. "*Now* do you see the dilemma?"

"Can't you push back the date? Tell New Guy how important this rehearsal is to you?"

"How important it is for me to tromp around in Victorian dress and belt out obscure Regency carols for complete strangers? In public? Are you *mad*?"

Rome frowned for the first time. "Carol, if he's that important to you, he'll understand. If not, then, maybe just hit it and quit it, you know? Get it out of your system and then you're free to carol anytime, anyplace without having regrets?"

"Gross." Carol wrinkled her nose and swept her hand outside the office window where frat-boys and coeds alike toiled while helping their age-appropriate counterparts struggle through Finals Week, currently in high gear. "Now you sound like the kids we've just hired."

Rome chuckled, not denying it. "Just saying, I'm sure he'll understand."

"Would he, though?" Carol thought of Gabe, sweet and goofy and endearing. He probably would, but what if he didn't? What if he laughed and made fun of her and she was forced to admit that literally every man on the planet was exactly just as horrid as her admittedly short, but no less odious list of exes would indicate?

"It's not the plague, Carol. It's caroling. What, you think he's not going to see you out and about town with the Victorian Voices anyway?"

Carol winced. She hadn't thought of that. "Well, yeah, but by then I figure I will have slipped it into conversation somehow?"

Rome arched one thick eyebrow cautiously. "I feel like you're creating a problem here that may not actually exist."

Carol slapped the thighs of her midweek crinkle skirt. "Wow, Rome, congratulations on guessing my emotional middle name!"

He glanced out at the call center floor with a most unconcerned expression. "Okay, so…my two cents?"

"Please!"

"You definitely can't cancel on Reginald," he insisted, confirming her worst fears out loud. "If you really want to be in Victorian Voices, mandatory means mandatory, so…"

Carol nodded sagely. "I get that. I figured, I just…I want both!"

Rome chuckled. "You know, I'm not big on games, but in my experience? Playing hard to get isn't the *worst* way in the world to snag a cute guy."

"I don't want to be that girl, Rome."

"Do you want the boy?"

Carol felt the answer deep in her gut, and even lower, where her fantasies had been swirling ever since she'd first set foot in Soft Swerve. "Honestly?" she croaked. "I desperately do."

Rome sighed. "Then make yourself happy first, Carol. Go to Victorian Voices. Be a seasonal caroler in the most carol-loving town in all of North Carolina. Hell, go on and win the Jingle Jangle Competition while you're at it and then? When the dust has settled and you've ticked all that off your bucket list? Well, your boy will still be there when you've done all you set out to do for *yourself* this Christmas."

Carol nodded with resignation. He was right, of course. Statistically speaking, his words were ninety-nine-point-nine percent accurate. It was that zero-point-one percent that had her still debating what to *actually* do. "I was afraid you'd say that, Rome."

He nodded, standing as if to signal their mid-shift counseling session was over. "It's only advice, Carol," he said from the doorway. "But I think the fact that you're even wavering in the first place means you know which has to come first."

Chapter Ten

Gabe

"Boss?"

Gabe glanced toward Jalise, revising the new Holiday Hours sign on her pink laptop. She sat at the far end of the sales counter, which was brimming with a new assortment of holiday goodies just in time for the rapidly approaching Christmas shopping rush. "Yeah?"

"You good?"

Gabe forced a smile, glancing up from the increasingly populated Mistle Tones group text thread on his cell phone screen. He set the phone down and nodded, then frowned. "I need to ask you a favor."

Jalise glanced up suspiciously from her glowing monitor. "What, even more wacky holiday hours?"

"That's just it," Gabe said, waving his phone as if it explained everything. "We've got our first official caroling gig tonight and...I won't be able to stay late for once."

"Good." Jalise slid her laptop shut with an air of finality. "Then I can quit looking up stupid snowman clip art once and for all!"

Gabe fixed his eyes on his trusty assistant manager. "No, I just...need you to cover for me tonight. When, I mean if, you know..."

Jalise beamed with supreme satisfaction. "You mean if your new sexy librarian MILF hottie shows up?" Her tone was uniquely sing-songy, the cheer evident in her almost giddy expression.

"Stop calling her that," Gabe hissed, glancing around the empty dining room. "You'll forget yourself one day and use it while she's here."

Jalise rolled her pale-blue eyes. "Well, hopefully by then you'll tell her what you think of her and it won't come as such a shock that you've been fantasizing about her day and night."

"Fat chance," Gabe moaned, not disputing a single syllable.

Jalise rolled her eyes, the gesture made all the more dramatic thanks to the large, swooping eyeliner above them. "God, why are grownups so stupid about this stuff?"

"We're not stupid," Gabe insisted. "We just have more to lose than you kids."

"Like what, Gabe? You're gonna lose the store if you don't stay open for Little Miss Pistachio Swirl one stupid night?"

He chuckled despite himself. "What?" she asked, self-conscious.

"Nothing," he insisted. "I just, that's probably better than calling her 'Hot MILF Librarian,' right?"

"Or you could just use her real name, boss."

"Fine, yes, I just…" Gabe's argument broke off, mid-stream.

Jalise took pity and inched closer. "Boss, I know it's been a while for you. You work hard, no time for a personal life. I get all that. But what's the point of being so successful if you don't take time to really enjoy it?"

It wasn't the first time Gabe had heard the argument, and certainly not the first time he'd heard it from Jalise. "I'll have time to enjoy it," he insisted. "Once this new store is up and running, all the kinks worked out, I'll be able to coast for a while."

"Yeah, yeah." Jalise wasn't having it. One bit. "You said that about the *last* new unit, boss. Next it'll be, 'once the holidays are over you can coast for a while.' Then after that it'll be, 'once the spring breakers are gone and we aren't so busy every night, I'll get some rest'. Suddenly it's summer and we're busy nonstop and then, finally…it's the holidays all over again. How long until you look up and find me gone, along with your hair and all your chances of getting with Pistachio Swirl Girl then, huh, boss?"

Gabe chuckled despite the sudden dose of lead in his belly. Or, perhaps, because of it. "Wow, that's…bleak."

"Yeah, well, that's where you're headed, you silly old spinster, you!"

Gabe frowned. "I think spinster is a lady who never marries, right?"

Jalise frowned back. "What's a dude who never marries called then?"

"Not sure," Gabe grumbled.

Jalise slugged him on the shoulder. "Just kidding, a dude who never marries is called a 'Gabester'."

He rolled his eyes. "If you want to prevent that, Jalise, you can simply cover for me tonight and I'll jet over as soon as we're done caroling over at the Pinewood Shopping Center."

"So I've got to work late just so you can get laid?"

"Ja-*lise*!"

"Look, I'm all for it, trust me." Jalise paused in baiting him just long enough to give Gabe a good once-over. "I've been here over two years and despite all these soccer moms throwing themselves at you? Spring-breakers and secretaries? I haven't seen you do a single Walk of Shame yet. Am I wrong? Or am I right?"

Gabe started to argue, to protest, then quickly thought better of it. "I mean…" he hemmed, not exactly regretting it. He'd never been the love 'em and leave 'em type, not even back in high school. Which might have accounted for his less-than-stellar sex life growing up. All the same, they were getting off track here. "Remind me to invest in an HR Department so I don't have to talk about my sex life with minors, thank you very much."

"Who you callin' a minor?" Jalise teased with a quick but effective jab to his shoulder. "You're only two years older than me, pops!"

Gabe eyed the neon clock above the cash register and winced. "So listen, yes or no? I've got to get dressed for tonight and you know how long that takes, so…" He made a toothy-faced grin and waited.

Jalise finally relented. "I'll stay until nine, okay?"

Gabe hugged her. When he finally released her, Jalise took a deep breath and teased, "Now, what would an HR Department say about that, huh, boss?"

"It'd be worth the fine," he gushed, racing from the store and hoping against hope he'd have time to go to the john before buttoning himself up in those stiff, concrete caroling breeches for the rest of the evening!

Chapter Eleven

Carol

"I thought it would be tighter."

Carol turned left, then right, admiring the burgundy sash cinched just under the bustline of her Regency-accurate snow-white gown.

"Most people do." Bertha, Carol's lowkey supporter during her initial audition, eyed the gown with practiced scrutiny, a tug here and a pinch there seeming to satisfy her.

"It's stiff," she admitted, the severe lines and column-like cut of the dress making aerobics out of the question, perhaps, but surprisingly modern given her assumptions about the time period. "But I suppose I'll get used to that part?"

Bertha rolled her eyes and handed over a burgundy-colored spencer jacket, stylish, flouncy and hitting right at the waist. "First time dressing with period accuracy?" she surmised.

"I mean, I've gone to Halloween parties before, but this is…extreme."

Bertha wore a concerned frown. "Don't let Reggie hear you say that," she hissed as Carol began the odious process of clasping the nine brass buttons of her jacket, each authentic clasp more challenging than the last. "He takes all of this *very* seriously."

Carol reached out to tuck the brim of her lacy Regency bonnet on a nearby rack for emphasis. "You think?"

They were behind a trio of rich, tapestried screens, no doubt historically accurate as well, in the corner of the rented Quick Copy office space where Carol had auditioned over a week earlier. Bertha was already bedecked in an identical costume, down to the sash, fitted riding jacket and long, white satin opera gloves. Now she fixed a bonnet to her pale-blonde hair, tying the maroon sash beneath her rosy, plump chins and, with a nod at the hat rack beside them, indicated that Carol should do the same.

"Listen," Bertha said, admiring her own reflection in the full-length mirror behind Carol. "I know it took a while to get back around to you. I know you're coming in last minute, I know you're new to all this, but I can't stress enough just *how* important it is to simply 'grin and bear it' if you want to enjoy the benefits of being in Victorian Voices."

Bertha seemed earnest. Carol nodded, having expected as much already. "I *do* want to enjoy them," she insisted, clutching Bertha's gloved hands almost desperately. "I was really glad when I got the call up, and I don't want to jeopardize it, but…is singing going to be the *only* thing I'm allowed to do here?" Carol nodded beyond the tapestried screens.

"Here, yes," Bertha insisted, squeezing her hand back before helping Carol straighten the burgundy bow beneath her own bonnet. "Out there, yes. Later, if there's time, or before, we can catch up and gossip and bitch and moan, but honestly? If you want to sing the best carols, with the best group, and win this year's Jingle Jangle, it's best to..."

Bertha seemed to struggle to find the right word. Carol didn't have much trouble finding it for her, even if it did roll off her tongue like a wet pebble. "Behave?"

Bertha winced at the accuracy. "Listen, it's not all bad. Just...pay attention tonight. At the faces of the crowd. How raptly they listen. How much they enjoy what we do. How with what we wear and sing and how we sing it, we take them to someplace they've never been before, and leave them wanting to linger there for just a little longer. Then come and talk to me and see if toeing the line a little more and speaking out a little less isn't worth it."

Carol nodded. It sounded a bit like gaslighting to her, but it wouldn't be the first time. Besides, she liked Bertha. Liked her kind, round face. Her shy smile. The way she fidgeted over her bonnet and lace as if even she wasn't convinced by the spiel she was giving Carol.

"Okay, I will," she promised, before turning to admire herself in the mirror. "Oh. My."

Carol had busied herself with applying the pieces of her Regency-accurate costume one at a time—fine stockings of lace, stiff, high boots of leather, the sash and the jacket and the buttons, but now? All at once? The effect was striking. Carol felt like she'd just stepped back in time. Suddenly, all the hours she'd spent down the rabbit hole finding those obscure carols for her audition seemed more than worth it.

"See what I mean?" Bertha began, admiring her look.

A booming voice announced from behind the tapestry, "Ladies? Time's up!"

It wasn't playful or teasing, but downright demanding. Even Bertha had to grit her own teeth before replying out loud in a fussy, "Coming, Reggie dear."

Reggie clapped his large, beefy hands together just on the other side of the changing screen. So closely, in fact, Carol couldn't be certain he hadn't been listening to them chat the whole time. "Well, chop, chop! Poor Felix and I have been ready for ages."

Carol cocked her head. As he continued blathering, Reggie's accent had turned decidedly...authentic. Bertha saw the look on her face and gripped Carol's arm gently. "Oh, yeah, the closer we get to a performance, the more, uhm...British? He gets?"

Carol leaned closer, dread nearly closing her throat altogether. "Are we...supposed to talk like that, too?"

Bertha barely had time to nod before Reggie cleared his throat and announced, primly, as if rehearsing for an off-Broadway production of some long-forgotten Jane Austen play, "Ladies, are we quite ready then?"

Bertha blinked twice, as if rebooting her default language settings, before doing a little curtsy and slipping from behind the trifold screen in all her Regency finery.

"Indeed, gov'nor!" she proclaimed giddily.

Carol, still hidden, shook her head, gritted her teeth and whispered to her own shocked reflection in the full-length mirror, "What the *hell* have I gotten myself into?"

Chapter Twelve

Gabe

"Twelve and twenty pence for some..."

Gabe's voice soared as the crescendo of the Victorian carol reached its peak, the others joining in as their voices blended across the courtyard of the tiny shopping center on the outskirts of town. "Fourteen for another!"

They ended on a clipped note, Jazz's velvet gloved fist held high to indicate a clean cutoff. The crowd, uncertain how to respond — was there more to it? Would there eventually be something Christmassy to latch onto? Was it all going to be this incredibly *boring*? — mumbled and shuffled and, hearing no further lyrics, clapped. Weakly.

Gabe couldn't blame them. It was an odd carol, short and clipped and far from Christmassy, but it was Jazz's new flavor of the month and they'd been practicing it nonstop all week. It had its charms, no doubts. Brevity, for one. But it was also deep and rich, showing off Gabe and Ray's lower range while showcasing Jazz and Felix's rich falsettos and competing high notes.

All the same, Gabe had been against it from the get-go, and with good reason. Just like the new arrangement Jazz had insisted upon, where Gabe was no longer singing side by side with Ray, it was simply more chasing of Victorian Voices and trying to outdo their dry, historic obscurity. But Gabe had been trying to behave and toe the line, so he had gone along with it, singing with gusto, smiling for the rapidly dwindling crowds and giving it his all.

He knew how crowds would react to the song, an obscure, droll and depressing carol aptly named *Empty Pockets*, and here was the proof, live and in person. Another two or three of the listeners drifting away to continue their Christmas shopping while Jazz turned and instructed the Mistle Tones on their next ill-advised carol. "And we'll move on to *Storm Carol* in three, two, one..."

Gabe steadied his nerves, took a breath and plunged into the next song, another dry and dusty hymn plucked from obscurity in Jazz's endless quest to out bore Victorian Voices, note for note and lyric by lyric.

"Brave the storm and gray the sky," Gabe sang, low and deep as beside him Mason trilled an octave higher. "Choir singing from on high..."

Beneath the heavy top hat clenching his brow, Gabe scanned the thinning crowd as he sang, "Organs chiming in each church, robins nesting in each birch..."

Gabe was proud of their harmonies, sung sweetly and carefully, as always. He was proud of his troupe in general, dressed to the nines and ready to wow crowds with their discipline and grace, well-honed over their several holiday seasons together thus far. Yet, as the dry song rang on, note for boring note, he ached to break free and sing something the crowd actually *knew*.

He could sense in their anticipation, in their disappointed faces, in the way they leaned forward, ears pricked up, to hear a lyric they recognized or a note that was familiar, that they wanted to enjoy the song, rather than just...*endure* it. If only Gabe and the rest of the troupe could pick that very moment and launch into, say, *God Rest Ye Merry Gentlemen* or even *Good King Wenceslas*, both still period accurate, how quickly the crowd would perk back up. And grow. And smile and clap and cheer when they were through.

It hadn't always been this way. When he'd first joined the Mistle Tones four years earlier, Jazz had been much more casual about their song choices. About the troupe in general. When they met to get ready early each December, it would be an informal gathering of four old friends, chumming it up about what they'd eaten on Thanksgiving and how soon to put the tree up and, "oh yeah, which songs would you like to sing this year?" That was about the sum of it.

But with each crushing loss to Victorian Voices during the Jingle Jangle Competition every Christmas Eve, Jazz had grown more serious about their song choices the following year. Their wardrobe choices. Their pitch and their collaboration. Where they should have responded, in Gabe's humble opinion, to Victorian Voices' choice to go deeper into history by embracing modernity, Jazz had chosen to follow their lead rather than branch off and do something brave and perhaps even enjoyable.

Now, as predicted, the crowd thinned all the further, dwindling to a few hearty, polite souls who gave a far more generous than they deserved golf-clap when the song finally — some might even say *mercifully* — ended.

Even then, before having to endure another soul-crushing non-Christmas carol from, say, the last century, the crowd dispersed completely, leaving the Mistle Tones facing a large Christmas tree in the shopping center's courtyard.

Jazz glanced around for any strays that might wander by before fixing on a grin and announcing, "Well, this might be a good time for a break, huh, gang?"

Her taut tone and forced smile made Gabe feel for her, however briefly. She tried so hard, and wanted all of this so badly, yet every choice she made seemed to take them further and further away from the reason they'd started Mistle Tones in the first place — to provide free and enjoyable entertainment to the crowds of tiny little Birchwood every Christmas.

Perhaps it was the business owner in Gabe, young as he might have been, that found him thinking in terms of return on investment. After all, why give so much of their time, freely and oh so willingly, to wind up with such pitiful results? Still, as they amicably drifted apart for the next ten to fifteen minutes, Gabe wandered toward the cozy little café he'd had his eye on since they'd gathered around the courtyard Christmas tree earlier that evening.

"Don't say it," Ray grumbled as he joined him.

Gabe chuckled, secretly relieved for a little company after rattling around alone in his brain all evening. "Say what?" he asked innocently as they joined the queue at the popular little kiosk.

Ray craned his neck, stretching the confines of his high, stiff collar to make sure Jazz and Mason weren't lurking nearby. "Say what I know you're about to say."

"If you already know what I'm about to say." Gabe said, taking off his heavy felt top hat to massage his aching forehead and stretch his sore neck. "Why should I have to say it?"

"You don't, okay?" Ray moaned. "I get it. I can see the crowds getting bored midway through each new song."

"So how do we say something without, you know...saying something?"

Ray glanced his way, a pained expression on his jowly face. "Maybe she'll finally come to her senses," he suggested, inching closer as the line dwindled. It was nearly eight, and they still had another half-hour of caroling to go before Gabe could call it an evening, race to the store, change out of his costume and into his work duds before Carol showed up for her nightly waffle bowl. He tried not to look as impatient as he felt.

"Do you really think that's gonna happen?" Gabe asked, his tone bordering on hopeless.

"It *is* the holiday season," Ray teased, brightening before he took his place at the kiosk's crowded sales counter. "The time for miracles, remember?"

Gabe rolled his eyes as Ray ordered, expertly and deliciously—a frozen hot cocoa-mocha and gingerbread cookie. "I'll have the same," he intoned when it was his turn, not surprised that Ray would offer to pay for his, too.

"Maybe next time," Gabe chuckled, offering his card instead.

"You always say that," Ray grumbled as they took their orders and found a quiet table for two near the towering Christmas tree. "Just because I'm not some local ice cream parlor magnate doesn't mean I can't still afford to buy you a coffee now and then, okay?"

"I know that, Ray," Gabe insisted. "And I'm far from a magnate."

"Yeah, well, you don't work in some stereo store in the mall, either."

"You don't just *work* there," Gabe reminded him. "You're a manager there, remember?"

"Oh, how could I forget?"

Gabe chuckled. "Don't blame me," he teased, savoring the first sip of sweet and savory frozen cocoa. "You know my offer to come and run the newest Soft Swerve with me still stands."

"What?" Gabe teased, gingerbread crumbs gathering in his thick handlebar mustache as he nibbled his oversized cookie. "And listen to that canned instrumental eighties crap all day?"

"Hey!" They shared an amiable chuckle. Gabe knew he'd wear his old friend down one day, but he'd learned early on that hiring friends wasn't always a great fit. At least, not until they were good and ready. They nibbled and sipped, seeking late night nourishment for their last round of musty, dusty old carols.

"So what do you think our chances of winning are this year?" Ray asked.

Gabe frowned. "Not good, if this is the best we have to offer."

Ray nodded, then shook his head. "We have to stay positive," he insisted.

"I'm trying, bro, but…"

"Listen, Gabe, maybe the judges will be into it this year, you know?"

Gabe gave his old friend the benefit of the doubt. "Listen, I hope they are. I really do. But if the crowds this year are any indication, well…"

"It's only our first gig of the season," Ray pointed out, glancing at the half-empty shopping center. "The crowds are still thin and that Christmas magic just isn't in the air yet. Just promise you'll give it some time before you give up on us winning this year, okay?"

"Of course I will," Gabe said. "Winning would be nice, but it's not the reason I do all this." Gabe waved his hands over his ridiculous costume, frilly and fussy and dated, but not entirely without its charms. "You know that, Ray."

"I know, I know, I just..."

"I'm here, aren't I?" Gabe said, brightening. If only for Ray's benefit, that is. "A guy can voice his opinion, right? Doesn't mean I'm not Team Mistle Tones for life, you know? I mean, you guys would have to kick me out to get rid of me, you know that."

Ray chuckled almost mechanically, avoiding his eyes, and Gabe wished he had noticed the dry, hollow sound...before it was too late.

Chapter Thirteen

Carol

"Ready now, pets?"

Reggie beamed, songbook in hand, freshly pressed like the rest of theirs, looking for all the world as if they had been bound in the finest leather. In this case, Carol reasoned, pleather would have to do. And a good thing, she reasoned, straightening her bonnet as they prepared for their first actual gig together. Between buying the era-accurate costume, all the many and expensive accessories and, now, the personalized songbook, she was nearly into the troupe for a quick grand!

One by one the members of Victorian Voices rang out as they stood in the employee breakroom of the Pine Crest Retirement Home.

"Ready, guvnor!"

"Ready, guvnor!"

Finally it was Carol's turn, her throat a lump as she struggled to play along with this cringe-worthy and sudden turn of events. "Ready, guvnor!" she squeaked, struggling to match the fake cockney accents of her counterparts and, from the look on Reggie's face, failing.

Miserably.

He frowned, relinquishing the Sherlock Holmes-era pipe from between his pursed lips and waving it at her solemnly. "Come, come now, lass," he scolded in his best BBC-worthy impression of a tony English lad. "We can do a far sight better than that, shan't we, pet?"

Carol struggled not to cringe. This was like bad — really bad — regional theater, only she was actually a part of it and couldn't simply bail during intermission. With Bertha encouraging her from the sidelines, Carol summoned whatever dignity she could muster, gathered the frills of her ankle-length skirt, endured a mock little curtsy and dug deep to intone, in her finest faux-British accent, "Ready, guvnor!"

A quick glance found a smile creeping to Bertha's face as, at last, Reggie broke off a grin of his own from between a stylish tweed-colored goatee. "There, there," he said, clipping the pipe back between his teeth with an audible *click-clack* sound as his smile broadened, pushing back plump, rosy cheeks. "I say, bravo!"

They all clapped, while Carol could feel her face turn a bright shade of almost painful burgundy to match her frilly brocade jacket. She did her ridiculous curtsy thing anew as they turned to follow Reggie toward the breakroom door.

"Now," he said, turning and still clearly in character, "chins up, pinkies out, smiles bright and remember — mind what we covered in rehearsal and we're sure to have a jolly good show on this bright December eve!"

Carol's heart was pumping, while she nodded eagerly and clapped her gloved hands as their fearless and oh-so-cheesy leader turned and, with great aplomb, shoved wide the double doors of the employee breakroom as if walking onto a Broadway stage. Beyond them, their host for the evening, the retirement home's director, Lacy Tinsdale, struggled to hide a bemused and somewhat alarmed smile.

Carol knew just how she felt. Victorian Voices was… a lot!

"My, my," she said, hand rising to her collar as if she didn't know what else to do with it. "You certainly do make an impression."

"Indeed," Reggie gushed, bowing at the waist, his ample backside straining against his camel-colored breeches. "Now, if you'll show us the way to your wards, mum, we are prepared to dazzle them with delights of the hearts, minds and ears."

His English accent bristled, wavering here and there as poor Lacy struggled to keep up with its amateurish changes in pitch and, no doubt, period accuracy. "Ah, yes, our…wards?"

Carol stifled a chuckle, admiring the way Reggie skillfully found a way to communicate with someone not quite under his spell. "Yes, m'lady," he enthused, waving a walking stick bedecked with the head of a gold elephant clutched in his clammy fingers. "Those entombed here in your house of respite."

Jesus, Carol nearly snorted. This guy! He was like a random English-phrase generator, few of them making sense in context and even less helping their poor client understand him! She wanted to inch forward, clutch the poor girl's arm and do a quick interpretation, but no doubt that would result in immediate termination and, after all she'd been through, was it really worth it?

Lacy stiffened slightly all the same. "If you're referring to our 'residents,' Mr. Archibald, they're… just this way."

"Ah yes. Quite." Reggie ignored the small slight, rising to his full height and tugging on the hems of his ill-fitting livery jacket in reply. "But please, dear, 'Reggie' will suffice for the duration of our musical engagement. No need bringing formalities into the equation, quite right!"

Carol busied herself with straightening her bonnet, if only to avoid listening to their fearless leader butcher history with his bumper-sticker cockney sayings and fill-in-the-blank British-isms.

"Uh, fine, Reggie?" Lacy's voice was as uncertain as her expression. She waved a hand toward a long, sterile hallway covered in plaid wallpaper and appropriately relaxing golf prints throughout. "The residents are waiting and we've really been looking forward to this all month long."

"As have we, madam," Reggie insisted, sounding nearly sincere as the caroling troupe followed in their footsteps. "A finer establishment we've not yet encountered in these strange parts."

"Well, yes," Lacy stammered. "We're just grateful for the last-minute cancellation in your schedule. We weren't sure we'd booked far enough ahead this year."

"Quite right," Reggie blathered. "Dreadful business, that women's group canceling on us at the last minute like that, but how else to explain the weaker sex's delicate disposition, eh pet?"

Lacy paused in front of a closed door. The hallway was wide as Reggie gave the signal for Victorian Voices to assemble, a little half-twirl of his cane summoning them like a conductor's baton, which brought them all to attention. Carol leafed through her songbook to the first carol, her beloved *Birch Tree Blessing*, the choice flattering her to no end.

A quiet knock brought the door open, revealing an older gentleman in a powder-blue bathrobe, eyes keen as he stood there expectantly. "And a good morrow to you, bright gent," Reggie announced in his cockney gobbledygook. The older man was rightfully confused, wincing at the inappropriate volume in the otherwise quiet hallway this time of night. "On this fine holiday even, we shall make you merry with voices gay. And, troupe?" Reggie turned from berating the wide-eyed retiree to address his equally browbeaten carolers. With a practiced ease he nodded at each caroler in turn as they began to sing the old tune, "Birches stand, alone and white, a silent army on this night…"

Carol's voice held true, blending perfectly with the rest of her troupe as the carol rang out in the once quiet hallway. "A crisp and quiet moon above, bare branches still below, the birches sing their carol sweet, snow drifting to and fro…"

The older man, confused at first, soon warmed to the carol. He wasn't alone. Doors squeaked open one by one as the hallway's residents heard the old Regency tune and clearly wanted more. Victorian Voices eagerly obliged, a balm in the darkness as their voices merged to continue the carol. "Birches dancing, roots like feet, rise and join the carol sweet, dancing midst the forest glen, abandoned by the sons of men…"

Carol leaned into the song, warmed by her troupe mates, encouraged by Reggie as his hands swayed, conducting their highs and lows, signaling them softer, louder, then softer again, beaming around his non-smoking pipe as they clicked into a cohesive unit at last. Too soon the song was at an end, Carol warmed by the round of applause scattered up and down the once-quiet hallway.

For the first time all night, the bundle of nerves at the back of Carol's neck eased, her shoulders lowered and her belly loosened. *This is fine.* She reveled in the still thundering applause as Reggie gave her a silent wink of approval. The frilly bonnet, the lace, the silk, the expense, even the cringe-y mockney accents, was suddenly all worth it. She had found her place, at last. And for once, Christmas in a new town was starting to feel, well…like Christmas.

Now, if she could just make her feelings known to Gabe, it would be a holiday miracle indeed!

Chapter Fourteen

Gabe

"Why don't you just leave that stuff on, Jesus?"

Jalise was chuckling from outside the breakroom, Gabe struggling to undo his fifteen layers of Regency-accurate attire to swap out for his far less demanding, and far more comfortable, Soft Swerve duds. He struggled with untying his cravat before gasping fully for the first time all night.

"What are you, crazy?" He gulped, tugging on his faded blue T-shirt just before drifting through the breakroom door breezily, as if shedding a fifty-pound rucksack after a ten-mile hike. "She's not ready for all that yet." They both looked back at his breeches and boots, top hat and silk gloves, carefully hung up hither and yon so as not to suffer a wrinkle or a smudge, lest he earn Jazz's ire.

Again.

Jalise frowned. "It *is* a bit much," she admitted, following him to the sales counter as she gathered up her own things before bailing on him for the rest of the night. "But if it's important to you, I'm sure she'd be down, boss."

Gabe considered the notion, but not for long. "Maybe, one day, if it even gets that far, but for now...let's keep it strictly modern, shall we?"

Gabe pictured himself as he consorted with the rest of the Mistle Tones around town, their stiff heels clattering on cobblestones and driveways, top hats waving with every fresh round of applause. Then pictured Carol stumbling upon him in all his mid-Regency-era garb, emerald-green cravat at his high stiff collar and frilly brocade vest buttoned up tight. Even though he was now safely tucked into his workaday garb, the very thought made him shiver.

Jalise chuckled, sliding a denim backpack over one shoulder. "So you mean, if Carol shows up one night and you're not here, I can't divulge your secret identity as a medieval jester out there performing for Lord and Master?"

Gabe bristled. "Is that what you think I do at night?"

Jalise chuckled. "No, I just like to see those pretty nostrils flare whenever I use the wrong time period — that's all."

Gabe relaxed, glad he wouldn't have to lecture her on the fine, forgotten art of caroling troupes once more. His gaze inevitably landed on the clock above the soda machine. "Should I even ask, or..."

Jalise's disappointed face was enough of an answer for him. "Sorry, boss. She was a straight-up no-show tonight, but...there's still time, right?"

Gabe chuckled, pouring himself a soda to soothe his dry throat. He'd forgotten how thirsty caroling for three straight hours could make him but, now that the Mistle Tones were up and running and the holiday season was finally in full swing, he was getting reacquainted with the sensation all over again.

"Only if you're in the mood to mock up another set of new holiday hours," he teased. "After all, we're five minutes past closing time according to your latest."

Jalise rolled her eyes. "You could probably use a break from each other, boss," she teased, swinging the front door open. "Besides, if you keep joining her in double swirl cones every night, you're bound to outgrow your breeches by the night of the Jingle Jangle Competition!"

Her rich laughter filled the air long after Jalise was gone, revving up her motorcycle and racing off into the night. In her absence, Gabe almost welcomed the silence that followed. No teasing. No caroling. No awkward clapping or self-congratulatory preening or the rustling of songbook pages or the cold silence that greeted the conclusion of another ill-advised carol to a cluster of would-be fans expecting *Jingle Bells* or *White Christmas* and not, for example, an old-timey warbler like *The Bishop's Hen* or *Saint Easton's Midwinter Feast*.

He scrubbed the thoughts, even the sounds, away, comforted by the neon glow of the empty dining room as he set about shutting it down, once and for all. With his gaze ever glancing toward the row of plate-glass windows that fronted the ice cream parlor, he emptied the last swirl machine, counted the till, readied the next day's deposit and, eventually, reached for his keys to close the store.

Even so he lingered, drifting across the polished linoleum floor tiles toward the door as if, perhaps, Carol might come screeching into the parking lot at that very moment and find him there, pining like some lovestruck teenager.

Outside, the mid-December air was brisk against his flushed skin. After a night encased in Regency-era garb, trousers tight and collar stiff, Gabe felt practically naked in his casual work attire of cargo pants and soft, pale T-shirt. He lingered with the door lock, the Birchwood Galleria long since shuttered for the night. Even so, the grounds were merry with winking Christmas lights on every available branch or bush, canned Christmas carols waltzing through rock-shaped speakers near the many wooden benches that dotted the cobblestone paths of the trendy outdoor shopping center.

The seasonal splendor made him admire his own shop even more keenly, realizing that in his rush to win favor with the Mistle Tones, he'd done little to spruce up his own business for the rapidly approaching holiday season. He considered opening the store back up. After all, there was a box in storage, winking lights and bottle-brush trees and fuzzy soft snowmen galore just waiting to be plundered, but a sudden weariness came over Gabe that prevented him from doing so.

There would be time enough the next day, killing the silent hours until the Mistle Tone's next gig and, hopefully, the briefest of visits from Carol. Gabe wondered, as he slid into his van for the quick drive home to the nearby Century Arms apartments, what Carol might have done that night to prevent her from stopping by.

And why it hurt him so much that she hadn't.

Chapter Fifteen

Carol

"So how was it?"

Carol glanced up from scanning a spreadsheet of performance hours, smiling at the prep-school cut of Rome's burgundy sports coat. All that was missing was the golden crest across the left pocket and he'd be all settled in at Gryffindor.

"Which part?" She lay the spreadsheet back down on her desk before stretching. "The caroling or the pining?"

Rome's face fell. "Damn, you didn't make it before closing?"

Carol shook her head. "Not even with his fake extended holiday hours."

Rome cast a calculating glance toward her. "Okay, well, at least you ticked off the 'playing hard to get' box," he teased, rushing to assure her. "Even though I know you didn't want to."

Carol glanced out of her office window, admiring the late-afternoon sun cascading across the treetops just outside the fifth-floor office suite. "I'm not sure I thought this through all the way," she admitted.

"Which part?" Rome mimicked her playfully, sinking into the buttery leather of the wing chair across from her desk. "The new job, the old-timey caroling troupe or your ice creamy dreamy boy toy?"

Carol pursed her lips and sighed. "All of the above, I suppose." All the same, only one of those line items made her heart race and her pulse quicken, and she was pretty sure Rome knew which one that was. After all, her pitiful ass certainly wasn't hiding it from anybody.

"You wouldn't have bitten off more than you could chew if you had," Rome insisted wisely.

"I suppose," she conceded with a quick glance in his direction. "After all, I've never been afraid of a challenge before."

"Softening in your old age, perhaps?" Rome joked, face wary lest she might take offense.

She forgave him the cheeky retort. Softening, indeed. "Perhaps," she conceded wearily, not sure if she was up for another night of mock cockney accents, musty olde English carols and locked ice cream parlor doors. "Can I ask you a question?"

Rome wriggled even deeper into his favorite chair, as if settling in for another involuntary therapy session. "Shoot!"

Carol lingered by the window, enjoying the late afternoon warmth on her face as she gazed at the half-empty parking lot below. "Did you know that Victorian Voices was so...authentic?"

Rome's expression froze for a moment, as if his brain was uncertain how to proceed. Then his youthful face broke into a series of guffaws that saw more than one of the call center operators from outside Carol's office glancing up from their phone lines to see if he was all right. "What, you didn't Google them first?"

Carol shook her head. "I mean, I've seen troupes before, frolicking in the mall or gift shops or whatnot, looking goofy in their outdated garb and faux-fur muffs and kerchiefs. I knew about the bonnets and the lace-up boots. I just…am I supposed to stay in character every time we go out on a gig?"

"Only if you want to stay in the troupe, Carol."

"I mean, I joined it, so obviously, but…" Carol frowned. "It certainly adds another layer of complexity to an already high-stress gig."

Rome nodded. "After they rejected me, I YouTubed a bunch of their rehearsals because obviously Reggie's going to post that stuff, and that's when I first found out that, yes, he expects his troupe members to speak Olde English until after the Jingle Jangle Competition."

"Jesus." Carol was not amused. "And you didn't warn me?"

Rome reminded her, "I didn't even know you were going to audition until after you'd got the spot, Carol."

She nodded. "Maybe that's why I was called in to replace the soprano before me. She wasn't up to the fake cockney accents being used around the clock."

"And the soprano before her," Rome pointed out cautiously.

Carol stared at the rapidly blurring numbers on her long-forgotten spreadsheet. Then she smirked. "I wonder what it would take to make me the *next* ex-Victorian Voices singer."

"Stop." Rome's voice was firm. "You went to all this trouble, Carol. You're so close now. What, nearly two weeks from now and it'll be the competition? You're telling me you can't play nice for twelve whole days?"

"Nice is one thing," she said, peering back out through the windows of her office as if planning her escape. "Pretending to speak cockney for three hours a night is a whole other thing altogether."

Rome considered the notion. "Why not invite your boyfriend along to watch?" he teased, face already breaking into a grin that was as contagious as it was wide. "That would surely make the nights go by faster."

"And let him see me groveling in front of Reggie?" Carol's tone was pure venom. "Curtsying half the night and apologizing the rest? He'd go running as fast as he came, and I wouldn't blame him one bit."

"Well, he's gonna have to find out sometime, right?" Rome paused. "I mean, you've been here long enough to realize that Birchwood is as small as small towns get."

Carol hadn't considered it until that very moment. "I mean, I suppose. The later the better, frankly."

"You mean, in all your late-night swirl spooning it's never come up?"

"Why would it?"

Rome shrugged. "I mean, it's high caroling season. Doesn't he wonder why your hours are so wonky lately?"

"We hardly know each other's schedules. And I'm already at a disadvantage when I walk in wearing my business duds after work every night. I should strut in with my bonnet and opera gloves and pointy boots and let him get a gander of my nursery rhyme attire?"

Rome didn't argue the point. "Still, Victorian Voices plays the most coveted venues in town. Malls, shopping centers, gallerias. He's bound to see you out and about at some point while doing his Christmas shopping."

"Righty-oh then," Carol adopted her mock-English tone playfully, even going so far as pretending to tip her dowdy old bonnet. "That's when I'll lower me brim and raise me songbook, pet!"

Rome winced and bolted from his chair. "Uggh, if you wanted to get rid of me so you can get back to work, you could have just said so."

"Pip, pip," Carol teased, watching Rome scramble from her office at warp speed. "Jolly ho and all that. Be a good lad and check on the wastrels for me, eh guvnor?"

Carol was still chuckling long after Rome had gotten suddenly busy scurrying about the maze of cubicles outside her office. But before long, her laughter died and desire replaced it. After all, how the heck was she ever going to woo her little ice cream hottie if she was stuck in 1798 England until Christmas Eve?

Chapter Sixteen

Gabe

"Is that...is that...peppermint sauce?"

Gabe turned to find Jazz hoisting the edge of his frilly red-and-white-striped scarf dismissively, nose already turned up at even the slightest hint of impropriety.

"No," he said at first, before conceding, "I don't think it is, anyway?"

"It *absolutely* is!" Jazz was incensed, her nostrils flaring and carefully manicured—though hardly period accurate—eyebrows arched for good measure. "It's not just peppermint sauce, it's...green peppermint sauce?"

Gabe glanced around the room, finding Mason and Ray with their eyes downturned. "Most peppermint sauce is?" he explained in a clipped tone, struggling to keep his patience in the face of one of their fearless leader's pointless tirades.

Jazz was adamant. "Gabe, you can't go out there like this."

"Seriously?" Gabe had just rushed from work, somehow managing to change into seventeen gaudy-ass pieces of period-accurate Victorian garb without spilling chocolate sauce and yogurt mix all over himself in the cramped breakroom of Soft Swerve. One microscopic splotch of peppermint cream on his Christmas scarf and he was suddenly unpresentable? "I'll just tuck it in, sheesh."

"Tuck it in where?" Jazz fumed, circling him like a fashion designer taking notes before he stumbled onto the catwalk. "Your cravat, perhaps? Just like they did in the days of yore?"

Gabe frowned, unable to hold his tongue a moment longer. "Frankly, the scarf covers up the cravat, so I'm not sure that's quite how they did it back then, anyway, but...sure."

Jazz took a step back as if he'd actually slapped her, instead of just spitting some cold, hard truth. Ray slid closer, mutton-chop sideburns bristling as he whispered, "Gabe, cool it, bro. It's just a scarf."

Gabe could hardly believe his ears. "Are you...why are you telling *me* that?" he hissed, as if Jazz wasn't standing a mere two buttoned-up boot paces away. "Tell *her* that!"

"Tell me what?" Jazz whipped around, mid-pace.

"That it's just a scarf." Gabe huffed, tufting up his tasseled scarf hems for good measure. "That I can go one night scarf free, without the Official Victorian Caroling Society finding out and issuing a cease-and-desist order before our third song."

Jazz fluttered her own scarf, tousling Ray's for good measure. "It's not *just* a scarf, Gabe," she insisted, as if scolding a toddler on how to brush his teeth. "It's...it's...solidarity. With the rest of us. Who are wearing scarves. Why? Because the client requested them, that's why."

Gabe could suddenly see her point. "If I can just have five minutes, I'll get the stain out and—"

"We're already five minutes late because you had to wait for your relief to get to the store—"

"She was doing a makeup test at school because I had to ask her to cover for me yesterday—"

Jazz turned on her heels, pointing toward a regal mansion where a local magnate's Christmas party was already in full swing. They were in the pool house, as spacious as Gabe's whole apartment, getting ready. Or so Gabe thought. Jazz clearly thought otherwise. "Bet that as it may, Gabe, the client's been waiting long enough. We'll just have to be a trio tonight."

Even Ray froze in mid-nod. "Wait...what now?"

"You heard me, Ray," Jazz fumed. "If Gabe can't learn to be a part of the troupe, then maybe a night on the sidelines will remind him what it's like to actually be part of a team for a change."

Gabe clucked his tongue. "A real team would come together to create a solution," he explained, tapping into his inner business owner and the many ooh-rah pep rallies he often gave his staff before particularly busy shifts. "A real team would work together to help one of their own. A real team would understand and make necessary allowances. That's what a real team would do. But this isn't a *real* team anyway, right, Jasmine?"

Jazz's nostrils flared overtime despite her managing to utter a cool, calm, even calculated response. "No,

Gabe? Is it not? Please, by all means, explain to me what Mistle Tones is if not a team."

Gabe started to do just that, then stopped himself. Ray was behind her, pleading with him to stop. Even Mason wore an expression of caution, whether for his own self-preservation or Gabe's. Either way, Gabe bit his tongue, counted to ten and did just that.

Well, almost.

"Some other time, I suppose," Gabe insisted, tossing his scarf back around his neck with a flourish for good measure. "After all, I'm on probation for tonight. Isn't that right, Jasmine?"

Jasmine's ooze of a smile was nothing if not triumphant. "Indubitably, sir."

Mason cleared his throat, making a rare interjection from the sidelines. "If I may," he began, pausing as if to choose his words carefully. "Our client ordered four carol singers, not three. Wouldn't it be better to put on our best, scarves or not, and perhaps leave this fight for another day?"

Ray's rotund body sagged with relief. "Yes, yes," he said, straightening as if the matter had already been decided. "Quite right, chap. Jasmine, don't you... agree?"

Gabe watched the war of emotions flit across Jasmine's taut, chiseled face. Not because he was interested in the outcome, necessarily. Mentally, he'd already checked out. Still, enjoying her indecision was always a welcome diversion from her usually confident war dance. Her eyes flitted coldly past Gabe toward the floor-to-ceiling windows that lined the spacious pool house, scanning the winding path that led to the glittering, holiday-bejeweled mansion just above.

"They *were* rather insistent on the full Mistle Tones experience," she mused quietly, as if to herself. "It is rather unique, the predominantly male voices punctuated by the lone female…"

Jazz let her voice trail off, giving Gabe time to call utter BS on her rationale. After all, the only reason there were three men as opposed to the usual two was so that Jasmine could have the spotlights, solos and every high note to herself!

Rather unique, my ass, Gabe thought huffily as he awaited her final decision. *More like rather narcissistic!*

"Well then," Mason said, practically whispering in Jasmine's ear. "There's your answer." Then his gaze, cool and calculating, fell on Gabe. "I'm sure Gabe has learned his lesson this time, right, Gabe?"

Gabe's gaze flitted momentarily to Ray—his old friend seemed to be begging him via ESP to just toe the line! Gabe swallowed his pride and, for once, did just that. "Oh, I'll never store my costume in the breakroom at work again, that's for sure!"

There were nervous twitters all around. Even Jazz's icy exterior defrosted, if only for a moment. Then she pulled herself together, as if remembering this was one of her "teachable moments," as she called them. "Well then," she said, scanning Gabe up and down as if they'd just met. "I suppose it's up to us to give it to them, right, gents?"

Smiles all around, but Gabe knew, in that moment, that the Mistle Tones needed him more than he needed them. He just wasn't sure what to do about that information yet.

Chapter Seventeen

Carol

"Cloppity-clip, clippity-clop, careful when the horses stop!"

Carol stood, burying her blushing face behind her leatherbound songbook, struggling to endure the indignity of her current predicament. They were dressed in full livery, rehearsing their new carol in the dressing room of the Birchwood Parks Department. The song was called *Last Carriage Home* and Reggie had sprung it upon them just that afternoon while loading into the Victorian Voices van for the ride to their nightly gig.

He stood before them now, pale, pudgy hands aloft, pinching and squeezing his way through their third full rendition of the song. "Stop, stop, stop," he wheezed, face flushed with the effort. "Bertha," he scolded, wiping sweat from his indubitably large brow with a period-centric handkerchief. "I'm not getting enough 'clop' from you. And Felix? *Way* more 'clip'!"

Carol couldn't help but snort at the ridiculousness of it all. Naturally, Reggie heard, directing his ire toward her next. "And you?" he all but sneered, giving Carol's Regency garb a good once-over as if to find a single stitch or button out of place. "Have you ever actually *heard* a horse-drawn carriage before, Carol?"

Suddenly, it was Felix's and Bertha's turns to snicker. "Of course," Carol rushed to add, ever the attentive pupil, eager to please even when asked to imitate a horse and buggy, of all things. "It's just...hard to recreate in real time."

Reggie beamed, as if she'd just given him the perfect answer. "Which is why we're rehearsing it once more," he scolded, holding his elephant-tipped cane aloft to begin anew. "Now, from the top — "

"It might help," Bertha interjected almost forcefully — well, for her mousy little ass, anyway, "if you reminded us of our roles again?"

Reggie beamed at the opportunity to lecture. It was his love language, apparently. "Quite right," he tut-tutted, lapsing back into role play as he assumed the tenor of a Victorian headmaster. "Felix, you are the wheels, chugging along down the path toward the storied old manse back home." As if that wasn't enough, Reggie imitated the childish "clippity-cloppety" sounds they'd been muttering for the last fifteen minutes. "And, Bertha, you're in the driver's seat." He gave a playful little wink and mimicked cracking the driver's whip. "Crack-slap!" he encouraged, adding the sound effects as well. "Slap-crack!"

Bertha perked up, as if proud of the role she'd be playing. "Quite right," she gushed, doing a little curtsy as the linen crêpe folds of her Victorian gown scraped the rec room linoleum.

"I'm almost afraid to ask," Carol said. "And I am?"

Reggie scanned their faces gaily, as if thoroughly enjoying the moment. "Why, Carol," he all but oozed, twirling the ends of his handlebar mustache like a true silent-movie villain. "Isn't it obvious? You're one of the horses!"

Carol endured the subsequent snickers, feeling the blush rise and fade from her face. She should have suspected as much, of course. Still, curiosity prevailed. "And you, Reginald?" she asked, placing a profound emphasis on their fearless leader's perfectly dull name.

"Why?" Reggie beamed, as if he'd been waiting to answer the question all evening. "I'm the passenger, of course! Now, from the top..."

As the Victorian Voices put their latest Victorian-era carol through its paces, Carol endured the indignity once more. It wasn't just the thoroughbred noise-making that bothered her so. Although, of course, she wondered why the troupe needed a soprano to make neighing sounds! It was Reggie's insistence on mimicking an actual horse and buggy that chafed all the more. They congaed around the rec room, dodging folded-up ping-pong tables and stacks of chairs, hands on each other's hips, clipping and clopping as if enjoying playtime during kindergarten. All the while Reggie guided them, face a mask of winces and pinches, smiles and frowns, squeezing a fist for more "clompity" and swiping his cane severely for less "clippity."

At last they'd circled the room once more, their lively little human carriage coming to the front gate of the fictional grand old manse with one last neigh and even a high-pitched "whinny" for good measure.

Good God, Carol thought to herself, frowning internally. *I'm even thinking like a horse!*

Reggie was smiling, a rarity after any rehearsal, let alone one involving so many moving parts. "You know," he enthused through a wide, sloppy grin. "I was on the fence about introducing a new carol this late in the season but, my word, you three have hit this one out of the park."

"We have?" Bertha doubted out loud.

"Indubitably," Reggie crowed. "Even our reluctant horse back there pulled it out at the last second."

Despite the inevitable sting of one of Reggie's backhanded compliments, Carol found herself beaming with pride. Felix and Bertha turned accordingly, offering her tiny little golf-claps, muted all the more by the silk gloves on their hands.

"In fact, I'm so encouraged that, well…chuck it all." Reggie pulled a roll of paper from his jacket pocket. It was a vibrant shade of burgundy, his jacket. Brilliantly tailored and featuring a myriad of buttons and layers, and how Carol had missed the rolled-up sheaf of paper inside his side pocket was beyond her. Reggie unrolled it like a scroll, revealing it to be sheet music.

"God, please, no," she whispered to herself, fanning her flushed face with the leatherbound songbook that was her nightly prop.

"Fact is," Reggie blathered, as if to himself. "You all have impressed me so much with *Last Carriage Home* that I'm tempted to fold another carol into rotation."

"This late in the game?" Bertha cautioned, as if reading Carol's mind. The older woman cast a worried glance Carol's way. Felix, too, shuffled from foot to foot as they still stood in their carriage-like, single-file line.

"I wouldn't ordinarily," Reggie confided, inching closer as he waved the sheet music threateningly. "But I was going over our scores from last year's Jingle Jangle Competition and, well, the only category we earned less than ten points on was something called 'Varied Voices'."

Felix raised a gloved hand. "But isn't that category for ranges, like alto, soprano, et cetera?" he asked cautiously.

Reggie nodded without incident, a rarity indeed. "I thought so too until I went to the Jingle Jangle website and realized it was actually referring to our song choices, which upon further reflection, lack more than their share of frivolity and sound effects."

"Sound effects?" Carol couldn't help herself. She'd already spent half the evening making clattering wheels and clomping hoof noises. What was next? Raccoons? Wait, did they have raccoons in the early 1800s?

Reggie, for once, ignored her scoffing tone. "Indeed, so I did some homework whilst burning the midnight oil after last night's performance and found another rare chestnut I think will be perfect to round out our 'varied voices' category and lock us in for this year's win!"

Bertha risked another side-eyed glance at Carol before offering, "Should I dare ask…what, uh, sounds we'll be making on this one?"

Reggie beamed with pride, peeling off a sheet of music and passing it to each of them. "You're in luck,

Bertha," he boasted, handing the last of the sheets to Carol. "This one's called *Bird's Carol* and —"

"It's just bird noises," Felix lamented, waving his heavy, off-white sheet of printed stationery in the air.

Reggie rolled his eyes, gesticulating wildly with his own sheet music. "Did I stutter? *Bird's Carol*? Anyone?"

The three remaining carolers grumbled, considering the chirping, bleating, tweeting, peeping noises printed where lyrics usually flowed. Reggie, unperturbed from his perch at the front of the line, directed them to stand, one by one, next to each other. "As if you're perching on a branch," he explained once they were all queued up. He raised his hands, the left balled into a fist while the other held his trusty elephant-tipped cane, ready to guide them to and fro. "Now? Let the chirping begin…"

Carol girded her loins, clearing her throat as her first "chirp" of the evening began. Her only silver lining was that, for once, the event at the Recreation Center, chirping or no, would be done by seven. Hopefully, even allowing for changing in and out of her caroling costume, that would leave her plenty of time to indulge in her favorite late-night treat.

Oh, and a pistachio and peanut butter swirl, too!

Chapter Eighteen

Gabe

"Can I help you, sir?"

Gabe stood in the doorway of his newest storefront, Soft Swerve number three. It looked much like the other two stores, clean and sterile with white-tiled walls, boasting pink and blue neon signage shapes like cones and spoons and featuring a giant chalkboard over the sales counter boasting his carefully crafted holiday specials. So why was his new manager-in-training, Carlton Rothchild, standing on a ladder in the middle of the store on a random weeknight?

And how the hell had he *not* recognized his own boss?

"Sir?"

Gabe instinctively went to steady the ladder, realizing only too late that Carlton was merely hanging a glittery cardboard ornament from between two ceiling tiles. "Carlton, it's me. Gabe."

"No way!" Carlton glanced down, gripping the rungs of the ladder as if to steady himself. "Oh, wait…it *is* you!"

Gabe stood aside as Carlton ambled down the ladder. Gabe suddenly remembered he was still in his caroling garb, and did a playful little bow at the waist, feeling as always the tight grip of his vest clutching at his chest and the top-heavy weight of his woolen top hat. The one with the wide, emerald-green sash.

"At your service," he teased in the mock-cockney accent he and the rest of the Mistle Tones troupe sometimes adopted while caroling.

"Is this…are you…" Carlton glanced around, pushing wire-rimmed glasses up his skinny nose as if awaiting the rest of some theater brigade to come storming through the ice cream parlor doors during intermission during a local production of *A Christmas Carol*, perhaps. "Is there some costume party you're taking a break from?"

Gabe chuckled, the tension he always felt when caroling under Jazz's iron fist rapidly disintegrating now that he was back on his home turf. "No, I'm a caroler during the last few weeks of December. With the Mistle Tones?"

Carlton was new to town, a recent hire fresh from getting his MBA at Carolina State. Overqualified? Sure, but eager just the same. "Sorry, I'm unfamiliar."

"Probably for the best," Gabe groused, inching behind the counter to pour himself a soda as Carlton slid the ladder back into the breakroom. "We go around town, caroling for malls and retirement homes, that kind of thing."

Carlton was still bemused as he struggled to take in the enormity of Gabe's elaborate costumery. "In, uh…that?"

"We sing older carols," Gabe explained between huge, gulping swallows of soda. "Nineteenth, sometimes even eighteenth-century English Christmas songs. People kind of expect the Victorian look when we do."

Carlton stifled a smile. He was reed thin and wispy, looking much older than his twenty-seven years. "Can you sing something for me?" he asked, deadpan.

Gabe nearly spit out his soda. "Like hell I will," he teased, hoping his newest manager wasn't easily offended. They hadn't spent a ton of time together since Carlton had been hired on back in the fall, mostly because the guy was good at his job, a self-starter who only asked questions when they were absolutely necessary. Gabe liked that about a manager, and hoped to hire more of the same in the future.

Carlton nodded, as if it had been a rhetorical question in the first place.

"How's it been tonight?" Gabe asked, if only for something to take the onus off his ridiculous getup and his new manager pretending to want to hear him sing something while he was wearing it.

"Busy earlier," Carlton explained. "There was some volleyball tournament just getting out and two busloads full of kids all wanted the candy cane supreme twist."

"Nice," Gabe enthused. "We're not selling as much of that at the home store as we should."

Carlton gave a quick nod to the gently humming swirl machines behind the sales counter. "Yeah, well, we'll probably run out of mix tomorrow if this keeps up."

Gabe made a mental note, shifting easily in and out of business mode. "I'll get extra when I do my order tomorrow."

Carlton nodded. Gabe noted there were candy cane flecks on his work smock and a couple of chocolate smears on his left sleeve, signs of an eventful winter's day.

"When's the last time you had a break?" he asked. Far from a taskmaster, Gabe preferred the "less is more" approach to business ownership, making sure his team was well-looked after, whether it was supplementing their health insurance, approving schedule changes at the last minute or, in this case, giving his hardworking managers an unexpected break whenever possible.

Carlton's smile was weak but hopeful. "Stacy called out for her mid-shift and no one else could cover so late in the day, so I've been alone most of the evening."

"Why didn't you call me?" Gabe tut-tutted.

"Did they have cell phones in Regency-era London?" Carlton teased, reminding Gabe he was still all gussied up for his latest caroling gig, disastrous as it may have been.

Gabe chuckled. "I guess you're right." He'd been meaning to just stop in and give Carlton a pep talk after not seeing him all week. After all, the store was on the way home from his gig at the Miller Mansion earlier that night, so why not? But now he could do more than that and, with time to spare to get to the home store before Carol usually showed around the nine o'clock hour, radiate a little holiday cheer for his newest manager as well.

"When does your closer show up?" Gabe asked, releasing one of his stiff collar buttons and feeling ten pounds lighter in the process.

They both glanced at the clock above the soda machine at the same time. "In about ten minutes, why?"

"Why don't you scoot a little early tonight, huh, Carlton?" Gabe offered.

Carlton's face brightened like a Christmas bulb flickering to life. "You mean it?"

Gabe tipped his top hat obligingly. "Sure. I mean, I'm here. I need to spend a little more time at this store anyway, so why not kill two birds and give you an early night in the process?"

Carlton was already whipping off his work apron and hanging it on the back of the breakroom door before Gabe could change his mind. "I *do* need to get my daughter some stocking stuffers," he said, blowing Gabe's mind. Carlton hardly looked old enough to buy beer, yet he already had a wife and three-year-old girl waiting on him at home.

"Well then," Gabe murmured, holding open the front door for him. "The night awaits. And while you're at it?" Gabe glanced around the store, seeing plenty of opportunity for more decorations. "Why not pick up a little tinsel and a few strings of lights? Just keep your receipt and do a paid-out tomorrow when you get in, okay?"

Carlton was already on the move, a blur of waving hands and a nodding head rapidly disappearing from view as a strange new shape took focus in Gabe's peripheral vision. At first, given the velvet trusses and clattering boot heels, he thought it might even have been Jazz, following him all the way from their mansion gig for a little heart-to-heart after their dustup earlier that evening.

But the shape was all wrong. Where Jazz was brisk and haughty, trendily bony and narrow top to bottom, this Regency lady was all woman—legs for miles and curves to match, generous tresses of rich auburn hair pinned up beneath a rich maroon bonnet as she sashayed ever closer to his newest Soft Swerve store.

He still stood in the open doorway, so entranced by the vision of feminine beauty that he didn't have the good sense, or better manners, not to stare. Only when she glanced up, the lights from a cozy Christmas display illuminating the delicate features of her instantly recognizable face, did Gabe do a double-take and splutter, most involuntarily, "C-C-*Carol*?"

Chapter Nineteen

Carol

"Gabe?"

Carol stopped dead in her tracks, Christmas lights winking in the merry bush beside her as, somewhere unseen, Christmas carols faintly whispered along the trendy cobblestone path she'd been focusing on. Her Regency-era "slippers" might have been authentic as hell, but they were also wafer thin. As a result, she felt every ridge, bump, crack and seam of the cobblestone pathway beneath them. But suddenly, hearing Gabe's voice, she glanced up with a vengeance.

Even then, heart pounding at the sight of him, Carol struggled to make peace with the vision that met her probing eyes—tall and rangy, Gabe looked the very part of the young English dandy, kitted out in camel-colored breeches, a sumptuous plaid vest over a silk shirt with ruffled sleeves and a felt coat of splendid forest green. A seasonally stylish evergreen cravat hung loosely from his high, open collar, while a stiff top hat sat jauntily atop his delectably dirty-blond stubble. If it hadn't been for the neon Soft Swerve sign above his head, Carol might have fantasized that she'd just stepped into the pages of a racy Victorian romance novel.

"Are you...mocking me?" Carol's hand flew to her collar, clutching at unseen pearls as she struggled to take it all in. And by "all," she meant the enticing bulge below his last row of brass buttons. She wondered, idly, naughtily, if, like Carol, Gabe had bypassed the restricting undergarments of a bygone era to flow more, uh, naturally down there. Either way, she struggled to take her eyes off the enticing package that was catnip after several years of involuntary celibacy.

"How...why...would I do that?" Gabe stammered, looking as shocked as she did, if not more so.

Carol took another step forward, shaking her head so that the lavish bow that held her single braid in place rasped across the back of her own high-waisted jacket. "I have no idea, I just...whatever are you wearing?" Despite how much it cringed her out during their nightly caroling sessions, somehow the mock-Victorian accent she detested had crept into her daily life.

Somehow, Carol found the nerve to drift past him into the empty ice cream parlor. From behind, still lingering in the doorway, Gabe's voice was low and vaguely reverent. "I could ask you the same, Carol."

Hearing her name on his tongue, so softly whispered, did naughty things to Carol's already trembling, decidedly empty belly. She had reached the sales counter, so similar to the one she normally shared with Gabe that she had to remind herself this wasn't their usual store. He did a double-take as well, then frowned. "But before we get into all that, may I ask why you're cheating on me?"

She took an involuntary step backward. "I beg your pardon!"

Gabe slid one long, single finger beneath the brim of his impressively authentic top hat to reveal the jauntily crooked smile hiding in the shadows underneath. "I meant, why on earth are you at *this* location? And so early? Why, it's barely past eight."

"Obviously to avoid seeing you like this," Carol gushed, waving her suddenly trembling hands down the velvet lapel of her burgundy riding jacket.

"By coming to one of my stores?" Gabe had already breezed behind the sales counter, casually scooping up one of her favorite chocolate-rimmed waffle bowls in his big hand. Despite the stiffness of his period-accurate garb, he spoke even more casually, more effortlessly, more breezily than he usually did. The tone, the cheeky smile, the jaunty cut of his tight little ass in those snug little breeches, made her wonder if they'd somehow crossed some threshold they'd been teetering on up until that very moment.

And if they had, how had she missed it?

"I mean, it's not our *usual* store," she explained. "Listen, if you must know, we did a show at the Community Center just up the street and I haven't eaten since lunch and I saw the sign from the road and immediately started salivating and... Wait, are you..."

Gabe held up the unrecognizable cone proudly. "Trying new things, remember?" he reminded her, handing over the bowl-shaped waffle cone. "Peppermint and mocha supreme, just like you promised to try for me."

Carol struggled to keep the disappointment out of her voice. "Shit, that's right!"

"I mean," Gabe teased, as usual swirling a second bowl for himself. "It's been so long, even I almost forgot."

"Sorry," she gushed, boldly slithering her tongue along the swirled ridges of her holiday-inspired cone. "Between work and, well..." She ran her free hand down across her Victorian garb once more. "My ice cream habit's taken a serious dent."

Gabe merely nodded, looking all of nineteen as he dug into his own swirled cone, a tempting blend of mint green and rich, sumptuous dark chocolate. Their blending of appreciative "Mmmms" and "Yumms" was almost shameful in their shared enthusiasm. "So, just to be clear?" Gabe pressed his hat a tad higher up his head, all the better to gaze back at her with those dreamy gray-brown eyes of his. "You were planning to get your soft-serve fix, just...not at my store?"

"But this *is* your store," she reminded him, the sudden influx of creamy, swirled sugar making her sound more confident than she actually felt. "Right?"

"Technically, yes." He paused to lick a dab of soft serve from his bottom lip and, for the life of her, she'd never noticed how utterly, kissable-y plump they were. "I meant...*our* store?" he finished.

Carol was flattered by the terminology. She'd wondered if Gabe ever thought of her even a fraction as often as she thought of him. His quick turn of phrase, so natural and endearing, made it clear that he had at least a time or two since their last meeting.

Carol nodded. "Here's the thing..." She paused, licking ice cream from her lips as Gabe seemed to watch her every move. Or, she thought was far more likely, tried to reconcile her Victorian-era dress with her usual business-casual attire. "I didn't want to come off like some giant pig when I stopped by your, I mean...*our* store later tonight, so I...thought I'd swing by this one and pre-game a little."

Gabe chuckled, apparently enjoying the awkwardness of her confession. "So, after a double swirl holiday cone here, at this store, what were you gonna order later? At *our* store?"

Carol shrugged. "I obviously hadn't thought that all the way through," she admitted. "I just, things were so bad with Victorian Voices tonight, I just needed a little soft-serve therapy, you know?"

"You're in...Victorian Voices?" Gabe's voice was a notch above reverent, sprinkled with a tone of...disappointed, both sounds swirled together like the soft-serve combination in her bowl.

"Isn't it obvious?"

Gabe shook his head. "No, I mean, it should be, I guess. You just never mentioned it before."

"Me?" Carol was full of just enough sugar, cream, chocolate and pent-up desire to grow cockier by the minute. "Have you checked a mirror lately, *guvnor*?" What the hell, she decided to throw in a little mock-cockney accent there at the end.

Gabe's blush was sudden. And sexy. Too sexy by far. "I thought, I mean, I wasn't sure if you'd...think it was cool or not?"

"Think *what* was cool?" she prodded. After all, if Carol had to admit to her nerdy little Victorian caroling secret out loud, the least Gabe could do was return the favor.

Gabe balled up the last of his waffle bowl in a pink and blue Soft Swerve napkin before tossing it in the trash beside him. "That I'm in the Mistle Tones."

Carol nodded. "Our biggest rival," she purred, suddenly turned on. After all, if the sexy Victorian getup wasn't enough to make the much younger Gabe irresistible, to say nothing of the lack of undergarments beneath it, secretly caroling with her troupe's biggest enemy was one more notch scratched onto her taboo bingo card.

"I mean, I didn't know," he insisted. "You never said and, well…"

"You never asked," Carol pointed out.

"Neither did you." Gabe's retort was playful, his gaze busy dancing all over her Regency costume.

Carol nodded, withering delightfully under his close scrutiny. "Fair enough, I mean, I never would have guessed that you would be interested in, well…" She trailed off. Her words were truer than she'd intended. The hell was her sweet little nightly ice cream treat doing strolling around in Regency garb caroling every night? Had she misjudged him or, perhaps, not thought past his pretty boy persona to what mysteries might lie beneath?

"Nor I." Gabe's voice, slow and thoughtful, made it clear that he was probably thinking the same thing.

Carol sank onto one of the neon barstools at the sales counter. Between working all day and caroling all night, she couldn't remember the last time she'd simply…relaxed. Then again, admiring Gabe's lean, slender body and the way his authentic period costume clung to it was far from relaxing, but still.

"How long have you been caroling?" she asked at last.

Chapter Twenty

Gabe

"This will be my fourth season with the Mistle Tones."

Carol nodded as Gabe reached for a bottle of water beneath the counter. He handed it across and she took it. She twisted the cap effortlessly before wrapping her full, burgundy lips around the clear bottle top. He watched her drink, imagining what her kiss might taste like, those lips full and damp against his own. "Have you always wanted to...carol?"

Gabe frowned at her playful tone, feeling more ridiculous than ever in his full regalia. "See, now, that's why I never tell anyone."

"I'm asking seriously," she insisted, big green eyes full of curious intent, batting luxuriously beneath her own bustling bonnet. "I just, between all your locations and your eighties New Wave playlist at each one, all this modern neon and clean, white floor tiles, I just...didn't peg you as a lover of ye olde English Christmas carols, that's all."

"I'm not, per se," Gabe confessed. "I just, I was in chorus in high school, did karaoke at my favorite dive bar in my spare time and then I had to quit all that when I opened my first store. Then someone hung an ad for the Mistle Tones on our bulletin board in the breakroom and, well...I thought it might be fun to dip my toe back into performing."

"And is it?" Carol prodded.

Gabe hemmed long enough to answer her without saying anything. Then he did anyway. "The singing is fun," he said pointedly. "When the crowd is into it and the Christmas lights are swinging overhead and we're all in tune and vibing, there's honestly nothing like it."

"I'm glad," Carol said.

"Trouble is," Gabe explained, "that only happens now and then. And this year? Not quite yet."

Carol nodded all too soon. "I wish I could disagree with you," she blurted. "I just, the ad for Victorian Voices pushed all the right buttons, you know? And my audition, I thought, was the closest I've come to enjoying singing since I was in our college acapella group. And then, well..."

"You met Reggie?" Gabe commented. The look on her face told him that he was right.

She seemed surprised by the realization. "You know...Reggie?"

"Everyone in the Mistle Tones knows Reggie," Gabe groused. "We know he's a blowhard and a bully, a bad winner and an even worse ally to the caroling community. We've seen, and heard, him in action and, honestly? I wish there was room for another female voice in the Mistle Tones because I'd poach you in a heartbeat, if only so you don't have to deal with that pompous man baby for another single note."

Carol blinked several times, lustrous, long lashes working overtime in reply to his quite sudden and even more unexpected outburst. "Sorry," he gasped, nearly out of breath. He hadn't thought of Reginald Carver the Third since the big, bloviating oaf had hoisted the Jingle Jangle trophy the year before and, suddenly...whoosh, it all came rushing back. Gabe made an apologetic face before asking, "Too much?"

Carol smiled with understanding. "I mean, you're not wrong but like you said, I joined Victorian Voices to carol, not kowtow. I get Reggie's game. I've met men like him all my career. I can handle him."

Gabe nodded. Carol smiled, reached across the counter and patted his hand mildly. "I figured a successful businessman like you could too, right?"

"Of course you're right." Gabe smiled, feeling the heat radiating off of her flesh as it rested gently against his own. "It's just...I auditioned for him, too. Auditioned for him first, actually. Before the Mistle Tones, I mean."

Carol chuckled slyly, taking her hand away. "So *that's* it."

The echoes of her touch throbbed along the top of Gabe's hand long after Carol dragged the digits away from his burning flesh. "That *is* it."

"How'd it go?" Carol pressed, wriggling atop her puffy pink counter chair to get comfy. Gabe did as well, sinking onto an old rattan barstool the team used to count receipts at the end of the night.

"It went well, I thought. It was *their* flyer I saw on the bulletin board," Gabe recalled ruefully. "Same one I still see today... Music notes along the border..."

"Sprigs of era-accurate holly in each corner?" Carol finished for him.

He nodded, marveling that they felt so similarly about something they'd never shared with each other before. It made him wonder what else they might have in common. "That's the one. He probably just copies and pastes the same one every year, buys the holly and music notes stationary in bulk. Probably uses it as a tax write-off, the big fraud." Gabe took a breath and continued. "Anyway, I found a couple old chestnuts I figured they hadn't heard before, went in and—I thought, anyway—nailed the audition."

"Lemme guess—Reggie disagreed."

"With extreme prejudice," Gabe recalled bitterly. "Afterward, me standing there like an idiot with this crumpled sheet music in my sweaty hands, the rest of the troupe sitting there silently judging me, Reggie takes a breath and announces that my performance was 'subpar,' my song choices 'blasé' and, for good measure, added that he thought I simply couldn't 'deliver the kind of nightly performances necessary to win a major award'. So…"

Carol's face had fallen sympathetically. "Ouch. I'm…sorry you had to go through that, Gabe."

"I'm not," Gabe insisted, only partially fibbing. "I mean, I'd rather know upfront what kind of person I'm dealing with than soldier on for four long years pretending he isn't what he is."

"Still, that was some pretty harsh language to use with someone who just wanted to sing."

"It was." Gabe looked up, nodding. "I mean, just say I'm 'not a good fit'. Just say 'don't call us, we'll call you.' Something. Anything." He paused to wave tired arms around the ice cream parlor floor. "I mean, when

I'm interviewing kids for a summer job here, I know in five seconds whether they're going to be a good fit or not. I still hear them out, let them down easy. Tell them I just filled my last position or I'll keep their application on file, you know?"

Carol rumpled her pretty face. "I don't think Reggie has that kind of grace in his DNA."

"My mom always said, when someone shows you who they are, believe them. I guess I've seen who Reggie was since that day, so…"

Chapter Twenty-One

Carol

"And Mistle Tones?" Carol pressed quietly. Perhaps more cautiously than she ever had before. She couldn't help herself. Something about the depth of what they were talking about, the sudden discovery that they both shared a secret love of caroling, gave the empty ice cream parlor a kind of intimate nature.

Gabe noticed, eyes following up her arm to meet her curious gaze. "Once Reggie shot me down," he confessed. "I was absolutely committed to caroling, full stop. I would have bought a cheap Santa costume online and stood on random street corners belting out *Jingle Bells* at that point, if only to prove to Reggie he wasn't the only one who knows how to draw a crowd. Luckily, I saw the Mistle Tones performing out in the commons one evening…"

His face warmed at the memory. "I waited until they were through and then approached one of them. Turned out to be a gal who was leaving and she gave me one of their cards. I waited a few days until I figured they were starting to replace her and hit them up. The rest is history."

Carol smiled. "It's funny, because after I auditioned, Reggie ghosted me. Didn't say nasty things like he did to you," she rushed to add, as if out of some misguided loyalty she didn't really feel. "Just gave me a kind of 'don't call us, we'll call you' shrug and then never did."

"So...how did you get in?"

"Same way you did, I suppose. Whoever they hired instead of me must have chafed under Reggie's, uh, particular way of doing things. And the girl he hired after her. Eventually, I suppose, he ran out of applications to consider and hit me up out of sheer desperation."

Gabe grinned. "You would have been my first choice," he gushed, a rare burst of flattery from the usually far more restrained ice cream parlor magnate. "But ever since that last girl left the troupe the year I joined, Jasmine prefers the Mistle Tones to have just one female singer."

Carol nodded with more understanding than she should have. "As you might imagine," she said, "Reggie doesn't have the kindest things to say about Jasmine."

Gabe snorted, a kind of deep-seated growl that, paired with his turn-of-the-century Victorian doodads, made him sound like a sexy pickpocket on the streets of a far distant London. "You think?"

"But clearly, you prefer her since you're still in the Mistle Tones."

Gabe hunched his broad shoulders, made even broader by the clingy cut of his sumptuous green jacket. "I mean, it was kind of out of the frying pan into the fire, but at least we can contain our simmering animosity to a dull roar until it's time to sing."

"And then?"

Gabe smiled broadly. "Then I suppose it's all worth it."

Carol wriggled deeper into her comfy neon-pink stool, feeling as if she'd finally found a kindred spirit. "I guess that's why I put up with Reggie's shenanigans." She sighed richly. "The troupe itself is quite good, if I do say so myself, and we're even better when we're performing for a crowd."

He nodded. "I'd like...to hear that. I mean, I'd love to hear you sing. Honestly."

"Well, show up one time," she teased, blushing at the very thought. Singing was a private indulgence, something she did for herself, and obviously strangers, but she couldn't remember the last time someone she cared about had heard her sing. Not the way she did with Victorian Voices—but loud and proud, carefully and passionately. Suddenly, the very thought of singing in front of Gabe embarrassed her. To say nothing of the thought of him listening in as she sang the horse or bird parts of Reggie's latest two carols! Gabe? Watching her shrug her shoulders and piston her arms and chatter out "Clip, clop"? Why, she'd rather die.

Quite literally!

"Back at you," Gabe challenged, crossing his arms over his chest in a cocky, jaunty fashion.

"But what would your fearless leader think?" Carol teased.

"What would Reggie?"

Carol shuddered at the thought. "Would he recognize you, do you think?" she pressed. "I mean, it's been four years, right?"

Gabe's face fell beneath his stylish top hat, making Carol regret the offhanded question. "That's the thing," he mused, sinking back into his barstool as if the cozy, flirty vibe had just been broken. "To him, I was just another wannabee Jingle Jangle winner but, to me, his words still sting."

"But why, Gabe?" she pleaded. "I mean, look at you! Big business owner, VIP around town, and you're going strong, caroling in our closest competition. What should something that big blowhard said four whole years ago still matter to you when you've accomplished so much since?"

Gabe answered, reluctantly at first, but didn't quite look back at her. "I think because, at the time, I'd just lost my mom..."

She yearned to reach out again, but he was sitting too far back, hunched into himself as if forming a protective shell. "I'm sorry, Gabe, I didn't mean to..." Her words trailed off, Carol uncertain what, exactly, she hadn't meant to do. Or say.

"Not your fault," Gabe insisted, making brief eye contact before breaking it again. "Not Mom's, either. She had a weak heart. Always had. Hereditary, I suppose, not that she ever did anything to help herself, but...anyway, it took a lot of courage for me to go to that audition. I think, in a way, I'd hoped it might be therapeutic for me. Singing again. *Winning* something after so much loss. And then, well..."

"It was the opposite of that," Carol finished for him, through gritted teeth. She couldn't help but picture an even younger, more vulnerable, less sure of himself Gabe standing there, music sheets in hand before a bloviating, gloating Reggie.

"Did he know?" she pressed when the silence had grown heavy and still. "About...what you were going through, I mean?"

Gabe made a pained face. "No, of course not. Nobody knew except the families I stayed with until I finally graduated high school. And those were just a few and not exactly in Reginald's, uh...social circle, shall we say?"

"But still..."

"I guess it just taught me to be kind," Gabe explained almost stiffly, as if he was already busy stuffing all the emotions back wherever he hid them when she was around.

Carol frowned. "I doubt you had far to go to learn that lesson, Gabe."

He smirked, brightening. "Maybe not, but after that, I decided that the only thing worth doing in life is making yourself and others happy." He turned, nodding toward the store where they sat. "That's why, when the old owner was thinking of selling, I used most of Mom's life insurance to buy him out. I thought, what better way to make people happy than ice cream, right?"

Carol smiled, warmed by the recollection, no matter how bittersweet. She couldn't remember the last time a man had opened up to her so eagerly, so willingly, so thoroughly...so quickly.

"And caroling, of course?" she nudged, guiding him back to the hopefully happier present.

He blushed, then grinned. Mission accomplished. "And caroling. Of course."

"And so, remind me since I'm new, Victorian Voices wins this Jangle Spangle contest *every* year?"

Gabe frowned. "It's the Jingle *Jangle,* and not every year, but every year we've been competing against them. I know that much. Smug bastards that they are."

All the same, his tone was lighter now. More playful, like the jaunty look in his clear gray-brown eyes and the way those plump, pink lips kept trying to curl up into one of his dazzling smiles.

"And this year?" she teased. "Think you can take us on?"

Gabe nodded, both of them leaning forward as if they'd just discovered they liked the same movie and couldn't wait to dissect all the best parts together. "I think we're better this year than we've been in the past, yeah."

Carol squirmed anew. "Oh, a little friendly competition, huh?"

He chuckled, face brightening in a dozen delectably different ways. "For once," he exclaimed, glancing past her to the wall of windows at her back. "I wonder what Reggie might think, were he to happen on us here, canoodling like this."

"Consorting with the enemy," she murmured in that vaguely British accent she inevitably, perhaps even involuntarily by this point, adopted whenever discussing Victorian Voices.

Gabe got the hint, tucking the brim of his felt top hat with two fingers before easing into a thick, cockney brogue. "A right proper scandal, eh, pet?"

She giggled. It sounded so much more natural coming from him, especially with the way his long, rangy body seemed ready-made for the clothes of the period.

"Aye, matey!"

Carol rocked back and forth on her padded counter stool as Gabe stood at last, unfurling from his own barstool like a solid mile of ooey, gooey taffy. He jerked a jaunty thumb back toward the row of swirling ice cream machines behind him. "Another round then, love?"

Carol stood as well, skirt all a twirl as she patted her full belly. "In this gown?"

They were still laughing, teasing each other in varying degrees of bad to worse "mockney" accents when a trio of teenage girls walked in, sports jerseys and flushed faces sweaty after what looked like a strenuous volleyball game. Gabe and Carol froze, mid-pantomime, as one of the girls glanced around the empty store then, pointedly, at their past century fashion choices.

"Are we, uh...interrupting something?"

Chapter Twenty-Two

Gabe

"How did you come by this?"

Jazz studied the sheet music to *Birch Tree Blessing* suspiciously while Gabe rocked back and forth on his sneakers. He shrugged casually in his faded jeans and Soft Swerve hoodie, feeling ten pounds lighter when not bedecked in woolen trousers and knee-high stockings.

"I thought we were always supposed to be on the lookout for old, buried chestnuts of yore, right?" Gabe avoided her eyes, afraid that she might somehow decipher the fact that Carol had turned him on to the long-forgotten song before leaving the ice cream parlor the night before.

Jazz frowned while she studied the carol with the rest of the troupe. Gabe couldn't tell her, of course, that it was one of the songs Carol had used to audition for Victorian Voices and, since Reggie had already phased it out of rotation for the rest of the season, she'd passed it on to him as a "thank-you" for all the free soft serve he'd been feeding her since they'd first met.

"Has potential," Jazz said, in that dismissive way she had when what she meant to say was "thanks, but no thanks."

"I think so." Gabe brightened all the same. He'd given himself a pep talk in the parking lot before leaving the work van, promising himself he'd be diplomatic, pleasant, understanding and even *patient* during today's rehearsal. So far? Jazz was already threatening to make him go back on his word and they'd barely gotten started.

He looked across the rehearsal space to find Ray, hoping for a little nod or God forbid a smile of encouragement. Instead, his portly friend stood staring at his grubby size ten sneakers, the name tag still clinging to his ill-fitting blue Hydro-Phonics work shirt. He must have left straight from the store, a custom stereo installer based out of the Birchwood Mall.

Before Gabe had the chance to wonder why Ray couldn't, or wouldn't, look him in the eye, the sound of sheet music rustling drew his attention back to Jazz. She was setting the oft-neglected eighteenth-century Christmas carol Gabe had brought as a peace offering aside on the podium next to her. For a few moments, awkward silence filled the rented storage space, outside sounds filtering into the usually bustling garage—a random leaf blower a few units down, the beeping of a delivery truck backing in just a little farther away, bare tree branches creaking in the gentle December breeze.

"Listen, Gabe…" Jazz's voice was calm, sending him immediately into high-alert status. Jazz was high-strung, wiry, energetic, lean and efficient. Calm? Not a chance. Calm meant bad. Even worse than bad. Calm was not good. Calm was, well…threatening. "We've been meaning to talk to you ever since the other night…"

"About that," Gabe blurted, forcing an apologetic smile to his face. "I was out of line. Totally. I enjoy singing with you guys so much," he said with a practiced ease, though what he really meant was "singing with *some* of you guys." Instead, he forced himself to continue his apology tour, despite the apparent lack of interest on Jazz's taut, pinched face. "Sometimes I forget that this is actually a job. I acted unprofessionally and…it won't happen again."

Jazz inched to her full height. She, too, had come straight from the office, bedecked in a stylish business suit that somehow managed to add a much-needed few pounds to her painfully thin frame. Her fashionable heels slid along the bare concrete storage unit floor in the process. "Well, you're right about that part at least."

Gabe cocked his head with caution. There was something about her tone, a warning bell just starting to go off. "Right about…which…part?" he stammered, hating — absolutely *loathing* — the supplicating tone in his wavering voice.

"It *won't* happen again, Gabe," Jazz announced at last, crossing her long arms over her flat chest. "Because we've decided — all of us together have decided — that it's best to finally…part ways."

Gabe stiffened. No wonder wimpy-ass Ray couldn't look up from his stupid lame-ass non-skid standard-issue stereo-store sneakers. Locking eyes with Jazz, he asked bluntly, "What does that mean, exactly?"

"You're going to make me say it?" she huffed.

"I guess so, Jasmine." Gone was the bootlicking sycophant Gabe had promised to be after his solitary pep talk in the van. Back was the business owner used to dealing with rude customers, insolent teenagers and pushy salespeople. This time when he spoke, his voice was deadpan, deep and defiant. "Define 'part ways' for me."

"You're being let go," Jazz blurted, stepping away from the safety of her podium to pace in front of him, high heels clacking with every fresh syllable. "Fired. Dismissed. Sacked. Axed. That plain enough for you, *Gabe*?"

"Not quite," he replied coolly, lowering his eyelids threateningly. "Now tell me *why*."

"Should I have to?" Jazz grunted, clearly taken aback by Gabe's sudden defiant streak. "Should any of us have to explain why your unprofessional attitude has made working with you this year all but insufferable?"

"Insufferable?" Gabe had heard enough. He held up a hand, as if to silence her, then nodded, as if for himself. "Okay then, well…thanks for the pep talk and, oh yeah…" Hanging off to one side, on trendy rolling racks as if they were at some high-end fashion show, Gabe's caroling costume hung, freshly laundered after their latest performance. "Thanks for *this*."

"Gabe?" Jazz said. Perhaps she had thought she could use it for his replacement.

"I paid for it," he insisted, snatching the clothes off the rack as the launderer's plastic crinkled and snapped in the process. "I'm keeping it."

"Whatever for?" Ray asked, rousing to speak for perhaps the dumbest of reasons.

Gabe shot him a look that made it clear the silent stereo salesman should have kept his mutton-chop mouth shut after all. "I dunno, Ray," he huffed, hating the way it made him sound more like Jazz than he cared

142

to admit. "Maybe I'll use it when I audition for Victorian Voices."

"Nice try," Mason scoffed from the sidelines, his default stance, looking fussy in his cheap bank teller's suit. "They're already booked for the year."

"Maybe next year," Gabe spat. "Maybe the year after. You think you're the only caroling troupe in town?"

"The only one worth joining," Jazz pointed out, and rightly so. Gabe stopped, not sure why, just shy of the rental unit's opening. "But, Gabe, a word of advice?"

"Oh please," he pretended to beg. "I can't wait to hear it."

Jazz ignored his histrionics. "No troupe is going to hire you if you don't watch your mouth."

This, he realized. This was why he'd lingered at the door. The chance to clap back at Jazz's flagrant gaslighting. "You're wrong about that, Jasmine," he said calmly. And, Gabe felt, quite rightly. "You're wrong about a lot of things. I believe it's out of love for the music, fair enough, but a lot of it comes from a love of winning. Everything I've said, every argument we've had, every gripe or concern I've vocalized? This year or any other year? Has been to help this troupe, to help *our* troupe. None of it has been unreasonable. Not my suggestion for more comfortable shoes, lighter, more breathable hats or even to sing more recognizable songs. I believe that, objectively speaking, those are all valid concerns that got shut down, probably because someone other than yourself suggested them. I believe you're a passionate leader, but not a particularly *good* one. Or, at the very least, not a fair one. And now? I'm the one being punished due to your lack of leadership skills. Period."

"Gabe," Jazz called out behind him, but Gabe had turned at last, speeding across the threshold, sneakers slapping against the cold parking lot concrete, jacket and breeches, vest and cravat dangling from the accordion-like hangers tossed over his shoulder.

Footsteps sounded behind him. Not high heels, but the *flap-slap-thwop* of grubby white sneakers. Ray's, it turned out. "Gabe," he called out, reaching the van moments after Gabe had slung the costume across the passenger seat and swung the door shut dramatically. "Gabe, I'm...I'm sorry."

"For what?" Gabe asked. He was done groveling, even to his so-called friend.

Ray's eyes were pained, his jaw slack, his expression grave. "For making it unanimous, I guess?"

A rush of air coursed from Gabe's lungs, gushing out in an involuntary grunt. It was only appropriate, he supposed, since he felt literally gut-punched.

"You didn't even try to keep me?" Gabe asked. "*You*? Of all people?"

"I tried," Ray insisted and, God love him, the poor guy was too sweet to lie. But weak, also. At least, weak-willed, especially in the face of intimidating, gaslighting, glamorous, bossy, brassy Jasmine "Jazz" Radiance. "But not very hard, Gabe. And not hard enough, clearly."

Gabe sank back against the side panel of his van. The same van where he'd spent five minutes pep-talking himself silly before walking into an ambush and getting sacked instead! "It's not your fault, Ray."

Ray's matted hair and limp, lackluster mustache made it clear he probably hadn't slept much the past few days, making Gabe wonder just how long this plan had been hatching in the first place. "But it kind of is, Gabe. I mean, I should have spoken up for you more."

"Maybe," Gabe agreed. After all, why let the poor shmuck off the hook entirely? "But it wouldn't have mattered, Ray. Not to Mason. Not to Jazz. You would have been outvoted either way, so it's smart for you to go along to get along, you know?"

"But us," Ray squeaked. "I mean, I genuinely like you. Care for you. And most of all? I just plain enjoy singing with you."

Gabe softened. "Me too, Ray. These last few years? You're the main reason I kept coming back every December. Maybe...maybe one day we'll both join a troupe where *all* we have to do is enjoy singing together and not play politics the whole time."

"Yeah, but until then?" Ray pressed. "What will you do now? This season?"

Gabe shrugged. "Not a clue." He sighed heavily. The adrenaline from being fired, canned, axed out of nowhere was wearing off, leaving Gabe more weary, shocked and hurt than he dared admit.

"Will you join another troupe?" Ray asked, a dash of hopefulness bringing a smile to his wan face.

Gabe chuckled. "What other troupe?" he joked wryly, sliding a hand in his front pocket to snatch his car keys. "You know there are only two troupes that matter in this town. Jazz was right about that much, at least."

"Yeah, but there *are* other troupes," Ray reminded him, as if he'd rehearsed his little peace offering in advance. "The Merry Gents? The Silver Belles?"

"The Merry Gents are four brothers," Gabe reminded him. "Actual brothers, so...no shot there. And the Silver Belles? As in, the six ladies from the same retirement home? I'm...not sure I fit the target demo there, pal. But thanks for trying."

Ray nodded, risking a glance over his shoulder as if Jasmine might appear in the rental unit's doorway, hissing him back inside with a penetrating glare from her beady brown eyes and a curling gesture from one of her long, bony fingers.

"There's always the shower," he said, before extending a hand.

Gabe shook it eagerly. "We still on for drinks this Friday?"

Ray slid his hand free and took what looked like an involuntary step backward. He took another glance back at the open storage unit before demurring. "I…probably shouldn't. All things considered, you know?"

Gabe squared his shoulders and slid out his keys. "I don't, Ray. But you do you. Maybe one day, when you finally find your balls, you can reach out and we'll catch up. Until then, best of luck with everything, okay?"

He didn't wait around for a response, but walked behind the van then toward the driver's-side door. He figured he'd see Ray giving a weak little wave in the rearview mirror as he backed out, but the parking lot was clear.

Ray had already scurried back inside.

Chapter Twenty-Three

Carol

"Orchards bare this time of year, and only children linger here..."

Carol paused, halfway through the rehearsal space door, hearing the familiar lyrics of the *Orchard Carol* trill out of a young woman's mouth. *Another* young woman's mouth.

She stood, much as Carol had only weeks earlier, quivering and rigid in front of a self-satisfied Reggie, bloated and ready to burst out of the seams of his off-the-rack leisure suit, his preferred ensemble when not dressed to the nines as a mid-century reveler and human random cockney word generator.

The others ignored her — Carol, that was — entranced with the young woman's rendition of the self-same carol she'd auditioned with. Letting the door shut quietly behind her, Carol listened as the young woman's voice oozed another few lines. "Frost upon the midnight ground, angel's feet don't make a sound.

Whisper phrases heard by none, glad their work is finally done..."

There was a wobbly old desk chair by the front door, long since abandoned. Carol sank into it, perched on the edge as the strange young woman finished the carol with gusto. "Orchard carol, sung this day, here's your merry takeaway. Celebrate, the time's at hand, peace and joy upon the land..."

Reggie clapped uncharacteristically, his big, hammy hands slapping together as Carol cringed from the sidelines. The others followed suit, Bertha more reserved but Felix pantomiming his hero with an enthusiastic round of applause, the whole effect something dry and brittle in the end.

"Penny, is it?" Reggie asked in that presumptuous way of his. Carol assumed he knew good and well it was the poor girl's name. It was just his way of indicating how much more important he was than everyone else. *Me? Remember names? Darling, it's your job to remember* mine! Carol held back a smirk just the same, picturing Gabe's pinched face whenever the man's name was mentioned. "I would just like to say that you did that song justice."

Young Penny tucked a dirty-blonde strand of hair behind one blushing ear and did the same little curtsy Carol had done earlier that December. "Thanks for letting me borrow it," she said. "I've never heard it before."

"Just a little discovery of mine," Reggie blathered, as if *he'd* been the one to spend countless hours online looking it up instead of poor Carol herself. "We like to keep our listeners on their feet."

Carol rolled her eyes so hard she wasn't quite sure how they didn't stick all the way in the back of her head. "And I must say," Reggie oozed insincerely, "I've never heard anyone sing that song quite the way you just did."

Carol clucked a wicked tongue at that one. After all, as far as she knew, she was the only one who'd ever sung that song.

Penny nodded and, awkwardly, handed the sheet music back to Reggie. Or tried to, at least. "Keep it," Reggie said with a bombastic little wave of his hand. Then he winked glaringly, sprinkling in a little of the patented mockney accent to come. "You'll need it to rehearse, m'lady."

Penny clapped her hands excitedly. "You mean it?" she squealed predictably, as if she'd just snapped off the perfect selfie and couldn't wait to share it with her BFFs.

"If you get the call, that is," Reggie cautioned with a playful wag of his thick, sausage finger. One that clearly intended she would. Carol sat up as Penny gathered up her things and scuttled toward her. They shared a glance, cautious and guarded, before Penny rushed through the door and out into the world.

The door shut on an awkward silence, one Carol was in no rush to fill. Ridiculously, humiliatingly, she waited to be addressed and, in due time, Reggie glanced her way. "Oh, Carol," he lied through his teeth, his all but yawning tone indicating that she was less than an afterthought by this point, "I didn't see you sitting there."

"I gathered," she said, standing and scanning Bertha's and Felix's faces for some clue as to what in the hell was going on. Not surprisingly, both were busy staring at their shoes.

"You're early," he announced, flouncing the cuffs of his tacky work suit.

"Nope," she said, striding toward him. "I was actually running a few minutes late. You said rehearsal started at six, correct?"

Reggie avoided her eyes. "Did I?" He sighed dramatically, as was his wont. "Shame, I didn't necessarily want you to see that just now."

"See what?" There was a chair in front of Reggie. Directly facing him, in fact. It was the way he preferred to arrange auditions, though few ever sat while they sang. She sat there now, glad she'd come straight from work and was still dressed in her business suit. Such armor, she felt, was about to come in handy.

Reggie glanced over at her. "Why, see your *replacement*, of course."

Carol kept her expression placid, though inside her heart raced. "Is that so?" Somehow, she managed to keep her voice sounding even.

Reggie nodded, looking disappointed that perhaps she wasn't dissolving into a hand-waving whirling dervish of panic and surprise. "Indeed it is." Their eyes locked for a tense moment before his flicked to where the rest of the troupe sat silently in little fold-up picnic chairs, a sad little audience of two. "Felix, would you do the honors, please?"

"Of course."

"And Bertha?" Reggie's smile was thick and moist and damp. "The lights, if you would?"

Carol clucked a quiet tongue. *Lights? Honors?* She kept her cool externally while inside she wondered if, perhaps, the Feds were due to bust down the door at any moment. She was up to date on her taxes, at least according to her accountant.

So what else could all the hubbub be about?

The desk chair under Reggie squeaked as he turned sideways to face a screen covering the wall behind him.

Where did that come from? Behind her, Felix fiddled with a humming slide projector. She recognized the sound from her old high school health classes.

Briefly, as she'd turned to admire the circular slide berth, Carol caught Bertha's eyes as she returned to her seat after turning off the lights. Before she sat, Bertha winced and mouthed the words "I'm sorry." It didn't exactly help Carol's already skyrocketing blood pressure.

"As you'll recall," Reggie announced, drawing Carol's attention back to the front of the room, "recently we held a mini-concert at the Birchwood Regional Recreation Center."

Carol glanced around the room, then back to Reggie, still admiring the wall screen in profile. "Are you... talking to me?"

Reggie glanced sideways. "Obviously."

Carol resisted the urge to roll her eyes. "Then yes, I recall."

Reggie's impish gaze glanced past her before he nodded at Felix. A slide clicked into place. Carol smiled, relieved, seeing only the cluster of branchless trees behind the Rec Center sign, bedecked in winking Christmas lights that somehow lost their magic in the still photograph beamed big as life onto the screen in front of her.

"Look familiar?" Reggie asked in a smarmy voice.

Carol finally lost her well-practiced patience. "Yes, Reggie, Jesus, we were just there and, even if it didn't look familiar? Look, there's the sign right there!" She read it out loud, if only to give him a taste of his own redundant medicine. "The Birchwood Regional Recreation Center."

Behind her, Bertha chuckled dryly. At least, Carol assumed it was Bertha, since she'd never heard Felix laugh. Ever. Not once. For his part, Reggie shrugged and inched even further into his seat. "Yes, well, you'll recall also that we wrapped up our rather lackluster, I should say — performance — shortly before eight?"

As if to prove it, and clearly no longer needing any prodding from Reggie, Felix did the little *click-click* sound and another slide appeared on the screen. This one showed the Victorian Voices troupe mingling with a clearly adoring crowd. Carol caught sight of herself, in full Regency regalia, nodding reverently toward a group of women who were admiring the authenticity of her elbow-length opera gloves.

Carol frowned at the still photo, crossing her legs and wondering where this could possibly be going. "If you say so."

"I don't have to say so," Reggie practically oozed, voice positively dripping with superiority. "The camera doesn't lie."

The word "camera" made Carol cock her head. "Speaking of, who's taking these pictures anyway?"

"I am, obviously," Reggie snapped. Carol regarded the slide still glowing on the wall screen. Indeed, Reggie was conspicuously absent.

"But why?"

Reggie sighed so heavily she felt the wave of his breath wash over her. "If you'd ever bothered to follow any of our social media accounts, you would know that I like to update them after every performance. This one," Reggie noted with an absent wave toward the wall panel, "was no exception."

Carol sagged with relief. "Okay, fine, well if this was your elaborate way to get me to follow our socials, mission accomplished, I mean — "

The *click-clack* of Felix's overactive slide machine interrupted the gushing relief of Carol's voice.

Suddenly, the innocent "meet and greet" of the previous slide gave way to the neon glow of a store sign. A very particular, very retro, very *recognizable* store sign.

"Look familiar?" Reggie asked as Carol's posture stiffened subconsciously.

"Obviously," Carol bluffed, hoping this was the carousel's last slide. "Soft Swerve. It's a local institution here in Birchwood, am I right?"

Reggie's dry, humorless chuckle was low and superior sounding. "That's one way of putting it." He was still smarming when the slide changed from Soft Swerve's charming exterior to the ice cream parlor's even cozier interior.

But that wasn't *all* the camera caught, of course.

Carol stifled an "Oh" as she saw herself, midway to the sales counter, but couldn't help blushing at the sight of sweet, young, taut, sexy Gabe grinning at her from behind the counter.

"Care to explain?" Reggie asked in a tone that made it clear no explanation was necessary.

"Explain what?" Carol bluffed. "That I got hungry after skipping lunch before three straight hours of nonstop caroling? Guilty as charged, I suppose?"

"Guilty indeed," Reggie murmured as Felix click-clacked to another incriminating slide. This one looked far more intimate. Carol and Gabe canoodling across the counter as they sat discussing, of all things, their respective caroling troupes. As embarrassing as it might have looked on camera, Carol was at least grateful that the slides didn't have sound!

The awkwardness of the moment passed as, click by clack, slide by slide, Gabe and Carol shared a quiet, awkward dance around the ice cream parlor. But midway through the horror show, something dawned on Carol and she turned from the screen to find Reggie studying her carefully.

"Why did you take these?" she asked bluntly.

His fluttering eyelids and puffy pink lips made it clear Reggie was surprised by the question. "Why wouldn't I?" the big man huffed. "I thought I was getting some candid shots of one of our troupe members enjoying a snack after performing. Instead, I got, well, the performance of a lifetime."

"Hardly," Carol scoffed, nodding toward the intimacy of the photo displayed on the wall behind him. "I mean, you don't consider this an invasion of my privacy?"

Reggie seemed to pounce on something in her retort. "I consider this a disgrace," he spat. "And, what's more, a spit in the face of our code of conduct."

"What code of conduct?" Carol asked.

"The one you signed when we brought you on."

Carol quickly recalled the two page "contract" she'd signed earlier that December. No chewing gum while performing? Check. Must remain in period dress at all times while performing? Check. Nowhere had she seen "must not flirt with the cutest guy ever to wear Victorian breeches."

"Refresh my memory," she said instead.

Reggie met the challenge with aplomb, reaching beside his chair to a file folder and slipping forth what appeared to be a contract. Flipping the first page over, he scanned the second until he read aloud, "Members of Victorian Voices will refrain from spending inordinate time in the company of other caroling troupes while in period dress."

Carol waited for more, assuming there was some big bombshell she might have missed. "That's it?" she clucked, half-expecting Reggie to shake his head.

He nodded instead. "Well, yes," he insisted. "Isn't that enough?"

"For this kangaroo court, maybe," Carol spat. "But hardly grounds for…what exactly *is* this anyway?"

Reggie stood abruptly. No little feat considering his advanced age and considerable girth. "This, Carol, is you consorting with the enemy." He tapped the pull-down projection screen for emphasis, sending the cute-as-could-be image of Carol and Gabe blurry for a moment. "This is you betraying our trust. The trust you vowed to uphold when you signed these very pages."

Reggie waved them at her predictably. She rolled her eyes at last. "Okay then," she said, standing to her full height and towering over him by a good three inches in her standard workplace heels. Okay, okay, she *might* have stood on her toes a bit just to exaggerate the height difference just a smidge. "I mean, we could have gone about this a bit less dramatically, no?"

"Dramatically?" Reggie sounded thoroughly insulted.

"Not just this penny-ante pantomime," Carol insisted, waving a hand at the slide on the screen. "But the whole asking me to show up at the exact same time you were auditioning my so-called replacement. Petty much?"

"A mere scheduling mishap," Reggie fibbed.

"Be that as it may, Reggie, point taken. I'm out. Fine, I get it. Can't say I'm surprised with the way things have been going around here."

"As in?" Reggie sounded suspiciously curious.

Carol ignored him, glancing around the room. "Let's face it," she said directly in Bertha's direction. "I was never really made to feel welcome here, right? I mean, hard to fit in with the three founding members already a well-established team. But it makes me wonder..." Carol purposefully left her sentence unfinished.

Eventually, Reggie bit. "Wonder *what*, exactly?"

Carol paused just long enough for an impatient vein to start pulsing on one side of Reggie's damp forehead before sighing and asking, "Why you can never be satisfied with any of your newest members?"

"Of course we can," Reggie insisted. "If they're up to snuff, that is."

Carol rolled her eyes. "So all this time nobody, including me, has been 'up to snuff,' as you call it?"

"Of course they have," Reggie insisted, waving a hand to six consecutive Jingle Jangle trophies he'd proudly displayed on a shelf over his desk. "Obviously."

"Then why do they never stick around?" Carol pressed, even as she reached down to pick up her work satchel. "Why do you have the same ad running every year if folks are just so happy to join you?"

Reggie puffed out his chest. "Not everyone is lucky enough to make the cut year after year, Carol. And this year? Looks like you're the unlucky one indeed."

Carol paused at the door, staring at Bertha while addressing her boss. Make that, *former* boss. "That's where you're wrong, Reggie," she said slowly, turning her attention back to him. "You...have just done me the biggest favor you could. Matter of fact, I feel like the luckiest carol singer in all of Birchwood, North Carolina."

Reggie huffed as she pulled the door open wider. "You won't be feeling so lucky when we win for the seventh year in a row, Carol," he bluffed predictably. "And you're sitting there in the audience, watching it all happen from the sidelines."

Carol paused in the doorway. She hadn't been going to give him the satisfaction of an outburst, a challenge, let alone a threat. Not even a little. But something about that row of trophies gleaming above his big, fat, stupid head and, of course, Reggie's smug, plastered-on grin inspired her.

"Who knows, Reggie?" she teased. "Maybe instead of joining together this year, we'll be facing off together?"

"Fat chance," he was still blathering as she inched through the door at last. "Not a troupe in town is going to hire you after being fired from Victorian Voices!" he shouted behind her as the door swung shut on more than just his voice. She was almost surprised that he hadn't added the old "You'll never work in this town again" caveat to his parting words!

Carol waited until she was at her car to sag into the driver's seat, hands trembling as she clutched the wheel. She didn't want to admit it, of course, but in a tiny town like Birchwood? Reggie was probably right.

Chapter Twenty-Four

Gabe

"No. Way!"

Carol sat at her favorite booth, idly dragging a spoon through one of Gabe's new holiday swirl cone creations. He thought the gingerbread and white chocolate combo might cheer them both up, but hadn't been prepared for her sudden, very un-cheery bombshell.

"Yes way," she retorted, lips curled into a curious smile. "I mean, it's ridiculous, of course. He did me a favor, I know that in a rational sense, it's just...the part that really hurts? I've never been fired from anything before. Ever."

Gabe gave her a quick once-over, resplendent in a cream-colored business suit that seemed tailor-made for her feminine curves and long, sultry body.

"No," he concurred almost reverently. "I imagine you haven't."

"I haven't," she insisted, sitting up a little in the neon pink booth as if to prove it. "And even if I know in my heart it's for the best, I'd have preferred it if I'd made the choice to leave rather than have it thrust upon me, you know?"

Gabe shook his head, still in disbelief. "And he had pictures? Of us? In here?"

"Not here," Carol corrected, glancing around the small but stylish Soft Swerve dining room. "From the other night. When I was performing near your other store."

Gabe recalled the occasion. Intimately. "How creepy," he observed.

"Right?"

"I mean, why?"

"Because...Reggie." Her reply was blunt. "Honestly? He's probably been trying to find a reason to get rid of me since I first joined."

Gabe thought of the Victorian Voices flyers that perennially went up, and stayed up, around town through the months of November and December. "He's definitely got a turnover problem."

"Not if you're a kiss-ass," Carol replied and Gabe couldn't help but laugh. "Well, am I wrong?"

"No, it's just...I guess I've never heard you cuss before?"

"Yeah, well," she grumbled adorably. "Now that I'm unemployed, expect to hear a lot more of that shit!" They both chuckled at her sudden outburst, the sound of their joint laughter echoing off the otherwise empty dining room walls.

Then Gabe smiled, if only to think that he might hear more of Carol doing anything, cussing included. Cussing in particular, since she was so very good at it.

As she struggled to finish the last of her holiday edition swirl, Gabe wriggled deeper into his side of the booth. He was flattered that she'd come to him with her news. Come straight from rehearsal, it would seem, cheeks still flushed and nostrils still flaring — sexily — with righteous indignation. Then he wondered, idly, what might happen now that neither of them were carolers anymore.

As if reading his mind, Carol pushed her waffle bowl away and regarded him almost shyly. "I'm sorry," she said.

"For what?"

"Just…rushing in here and blathering on about my problems this way."

"I'm glad to hear them," he blurted before correcting himself. "I mean not glad, glad, just…you know what I mean."

"I do," she said, in a way that made it clear she actually might. "I just, I've only been in town a few months and in all that time, between getting settled and acclimated at work, I didn't have anyone else to tell."

Gabe was surprised, if still flattered, to hear it. "No one at work?" he pressed. "Or a neighbor? Someone at the gym?"

"My supervisor's a sweet guy," she said. "But with work and training me and his own life and the holidays to boot, well, he's got his hands too full for all my personal mess."

"It's not a mess," Gabe assured her. "You just got unlucky enough to hook up with the most dysfunctional caroling troupe in Birchwood."

She shrugged then nodded his way, the simple attention never failing to send his pulse racing into overdrive. "Too bad Mistle Tones wasn't hiring," she teased, obviously unaware. "I would have tried there first."

Gabe swallowed and took the plunge. "Don't be so sure," he blurted.

But Carol was too smart for that. "Meaning?" she probed, those wary green eyes fixing on his as she leaned a smidge closer.

"Well, I didn't want to leapfrog onto your current sitch, but...they let me go today, too."

Carol looked visibly shocked, rocking back into her booth seat so fast the leather squeaked beneath her. "No shit."

"Believe it," he insisted. "I mean, I wasn't necessarily surprised—Jazz and I have been butting heads for years and I suppose she finally got fed up with it."

"What reason did they give?" Carol probed. "Please tell me you didn't have to endure some embarrassing slide show as well!"

"Nothing that dramatic," he insisted. "But I thought I'd made enough of an impression on my troupe mates that it wasn't so...unanimous."

Carol regarded him thoughtfully. "I don't really see you as a troublemaker," she noted.

"I'm not," he insisted. "Honestly. But I also can't watch us lose year after year, for simple, easily rectified reasons, and keep my mouth shut about it."

Carol used her spoon to swirl the melted ice cream in the bottom of her waffle bowl. "Not to sound snobbish," she began, "but I find that, oftentimes, folks that aren't overly successful in business don't take constructive criticism particularly well."

"Indeed," he agreed. "None of the things I said were personal. We were all capable singers, and we *did* sound good together. Better than good, in fact. But every time I tried to suggest a simple, agreeable, objectively reasonable way that we could sound even better? Immediate shutdown. And not just a shutdown, but a gaslighting shutdown that had me feeling guilty for even bringing it up in the first place."

Carol nodded eagerly. "I guess we shouldn't be surprised." She sighed, pushing her bowl away.

"No?"

She regarded him evenly, as if they had been discussing last quarter's sales report instead of being fired from competing caroling troupes on the very same day. "I mean, small town, not a ton of competition. It's no surprise that Reggie and Jazz would be egomaniacs who run their respective troupes like micro-cults."

Chapter Twenty-Five

Carol

"Micro-cults."

Gabe nodded, looking boyish and charming in his faded powder blue Soft Swerve tee. Though what she would have given to catch sight of him in those tight-fitting, form-hugging breeches of his just one more time! "I like that."

"I don't." She huffed. "I mean, the whole time I was being shown slide after slide I just kept thinking how unnecessary and childish it all was."

"Yes," Gabe commiserated, leaning forward so that Carol could get a whiff of his by-now familiar scent, a uniquely personal combination of spicy cologne and a lingering hint of sweet chocolate chip mint. "Just rehearse, perfect and go sing. That's all anybody wants, honestly."

"You can see it in their faces," Carol agreed, struggling not to lean forward as well. But she was already vulnerable, wounded by the slight from her own caroling troupe and more susceptible than usual to a sexy young man's charms. "The audience, I mean. They want to be entertained. They want the simple pleasure of being surprised by this cheerful little group of singers on some random weeknight, infusing a little holiday cheer into their shopping trip or office party or wherever it is we'd be playing next."

"Just such a missed opportunity," Gabe groused, sinking back into his chair. "And the carols they choose, year after year."

"Not sure what it was like with the Mistle Tones," Carol reasoned, "but Victorian Voices? It was like they were bound and determined to pick the most unhinged, absolutely non-cheery, anti-audience carols they could find."

"I get you don't want to sing *Jingle Bells* every night, but once? Just once? Something the crowd can recognize and vibe to?"

They both nodded. Carol was flattered that, perhaps in response to her obvious turmoil, Gabe had forgone his usual chair at the table nearby to sit in the same booth with her!

Progress? she wondered as she struggled not to also admire the lean, sexy physique that rested so casually against the opposite booth bench. He wasn't wearing a hat tonight, she noted. Not his spry Victorian top hat or his trusty Soft Swerve ball cap, allowing her to appreciate the way the muted neon colors of his store played with the sexy dirty blond stubble atop his adorable little head.

"I'm sorry," she said at last, afraid the comfortable silence might stretch long enough to allow young Gabe to read her sinful little mind. "That that happened to you, I mean."

"Same here," Gabe replied. "I was hoping Reggie would behave himself this holiday season."

"I honestly don't think he can," she said. "And if I thought the girl he replaced me with was some mega talent, maybe I could have left on better terms."

Gabe cocked his head. "You already met your replacement?"

Carol flushed. "Oh yes," she said through gritted teeth. "He made sure to audition her just as I was showing up for rehearsal."

"Gross."

"Indeed."

Gabe growled to reiterate just how gross it was. As if she didn't already know. "No," he insisted. "That's, like...really gross."

"Yeah." She chuckled dryly, as impressed with his unlikely bout of histrionics as she was curiously amused by it. "I know. I was there."

"No, like, abusive gross," he gushed. "Psychotic gross."

"Don't forget narcissistically gross," she teased.

"But wasn't everyone else showing up too?" Gabe pressed, as if hoping for a sign that maybe Reggie wasn't the worst person on the planet. All evidence to the contrary, of course. "Like, maybe the audition ran long?"

"Oh no," Carol assured him. "He made sure to tell everyone else to get there before I did. That way I'd be sure to get the message that they were all in on it."

"Gross," Gabe repeated. "Nothing worse than an ambush."

"It's the sign of a weak leader," she noted as professionally as possible. "Not man enough to fire me without a crowd, so he made sure all his allies were there with him."

"Or he just enjoys humiliating people with an audience," Gabe pointed out.

"That tracks," Carol agreed. She glanced out of the window. A van was pulling up and narrowly coming to a stop before a passel of preteens slid from the side panels as if they were a dozen or more clowns emerging from a car in some lively circus act. Assuming they were headed straight for Soft Swerve, she stiffened and balled the last of her waffle bowl into her cheery pink napkin.

"Well," she said, standing before she had the chance to wear out her welcome. "I'm sorry for us both, I guess."

He nodded and stood to accompany her. But this time, Gabe reached out to take the trash from her hand and throw it away for her. Another first? "Guess it's back to singing in the shower," she said with a nervous laugh, fingers still tingling from where Gabe's had glanced against hers.

"Funny," he said, following her to the trash can where he deposited her half-eaten waffle bowl. "That's just what one of the members of the Mistle Tones said."

"It's too bad this town is only big enough for two real caroling troupes," Carol sighed, holding open the door just as the van full of tykes poured into the store like refugees from a sugar-fueled slumber party, looking to get their next fix before they inevitably crashed.

"You're not wrong." Gabe chuckled with a wink, holding the door open for her as she trundled quickly past, lest she be tempted to linger another moment longer. "At this rate, the only way we'll be able to carol responsibly is if we start a troupe of our own!"

Chapter Twenty-Six

Gabe

"God, what *are* we listening to?"

Jalise stood staring up at the glowing monitor above the condiment station. Usually it was muted, set to playful, colorful, childish nature, animal or sports cartoons, a subscription feed designed for a moment's distraction while snatching up extra spoons or napkins before taking a seat.

"It's December eighteenth," Gabe pointed out, centering a snowman window cling to one of the six floor-to-ceiling panes facing the curb outside. "I'm trying to get a little spirit up in this place."

"With this?" she pointed to the screen in question, currently playing out a scene from one of Gabe's childhood favorites, *Marty's Merry Wonderland*.

"Sure, why not?" Gabe asked. "Customer Channels, our infotainment company, has a holiday site and one of its dozen or so Christmas feeds is retro cartoons from the eighties and nineties. I thought it might cheer us all up."

"Can I mute it?"

"No, you can't mute it," Gabe spat. "I literally just *unmuted* it. The hell?"

Jalise smiled contentedly, never happier than when she'd gotten under Gabe's skin enough to make him cuss, a more common occurrence than he'd cared to admit. "Damn, okay, how do you really feel, boss?"

"I feel like I've neglected the holidays," Gabe admitted, moving on to the next window cling, a series of three oversized snowflakes this time. "And now that I'm out of the Mistle Tones, I'll have more time to rectify that."

"Oh God," Jalise moaned, crossing her arms over her work smock as she stood watching a scene from *Marty's Merry Wonderland*. "You're going to be insufferable for the rest of the year, aren't you?"

"Probably," Gabe conceded with a curious little smile, the cheesy cartoons and sarcastic camaraderie suddenly cheering him. "So...sorry in advance."

She turned from the screen, watching him finish centering the middle snowflake. Once she'd seen the open decoration box and three windows left to fill with holiday merriment, Jalise joined him. "It really does suck," she said, dusting off a pastel-pink bottle-brush tree to put in the napkin holder on a nearby table. "I mean, all the years you've been with them. The practice and rehearsals? The Jingle Jangle? What are you going to do for fun now?"

"Bug the shit out of you, probably."

Jalise snorted, straightening another bottle-brush tree that had been bent somehow in the storage box while hiding away in the breakroom all year. "I'm serious, boss." Her soft, gentle voice indicated she actually was. "You love that stuff."

He began applying a jolly red Santa cling to the next window over and nodded. "I do. Yesterday I was so pissed off I couldn't really absorb it but today? It's really bumming me out. Especially because we had that big gig at the mall I always enjoy."

"They'll be missing you for sure," Jalise assured him, centering the now fixed tree beside another pile of napkins.

"That's just it," Gabe conceded as he smoothed out Santa's big rear so there were no bubbles or ridges to annoy him as he stared at it for countless hours from across the dining room. "I honestly don't. They'll do just fine and move on and I'll be a footnote by the time the Jingle Jangle rolls around next week."

"I don't believe that," Jalise insisted, joining him at the window and standing conspiratorially close. Coming from an emotional cyborg like his typically frosty assistant manager, Gabe appreciated the gesture more than he cared to admit.

"What?" he asked as she reached past him.

"It's crooked," she pointed out, un-clinging the cling only to re-cling it more accurately this time.

He smirked, sensing it hadn't been that at all. Not really. "Oh. Sorry."

"It's okay," she said, all business again as she reached for the next window cling on the sheet between them. "You're upset. Why don't you watch some of your childhood memories and let me finish, huh, boss?"

He sank into the nearest booth without argument, an unexpected — and most unwelcome — weariness suddenly overtaking him. "You don't mind?" It turned out to be a rhetorical question. He wouldn't have been able to get up again so soon even if she had.

Jalise's smooth, oval face broke into a sly little grin. "No, boss. You earned it, all right?" Her voice, and her expression, were both uncharacteristically gentle.

He glanced past her at a second monitor, synced to the first but twice as big, still playing *Marty's Merry Wonderland*. The sight of Marty the Mule, wearing his dapper little Christmas cap between his two fuzzy ears, made Gabe smile in a way he hadn't in years.

"What's got you so happy?" Jalise teased, finishing with the window clings and moving on to place the rest of the pastel-colored trees in the equally trendy napkin holders.

"I just haven't seen this one in a while," Gabe admitted around a sudden and quite unexpected lump in his throat. "My mom and I used to watch this together every year."

Jalise glanced up at the flickering TV screen above them and smiled at last. "Yeah, mine too." Her voice was uncharacteristically even and calm, almost wistful. "She loved the song at the end."

"Mine too," Gabe replied, smiling as Jalise sank into the booth bench across from him. "I got headaches as a kid," he confessed, not sure why but also not sure why he wouldn't. "And to help me sleep at night, she'd sing it sometimes, even when it wasn't Christmas."

Jalise was looking at him funny. "What?" he asked.

She shrugged her big, broad shoulders and flashed him a wry, curious smile. "Dunno, I guess I just never thought of you as a kid before. Or having a mom, for that matter."

Gabe's sudden burst of laughter was clipped and raw. "How do you think I got here, weirdo?"

She wrinkled her long, smooth nose. "Not sure, I thought you just sprung up in that Soft Swerve shirt a ready-made, grown-ass man."

Gabe snorted. "Sometimes I wish I had," he admitted without elaborating. "Would have saved a lot of pain along the way."

Jalise shrugged. "Yeah, but you would have missed growing up with Marty Mule."

"There's that." Gabe sighed as they settled in for the big finale. As if on cue, it began, Marty the Mule settling in between Santa's reindeer after proving himself more than worthy to help guide his sleigh one cold and windy night. Then, as the sleigh lifted off and drove into the cold, dark Christmas Eve sky, the soft, sweet, silly strains of the cartoon's theme song began, followed by the iconic words, "Clop, clop, clop and neigh, neigh, neigh, Marty mules the day away." The song continued, almost harsh and tinny as a grownup where, as a child, it had always been so soft and sweet. "And when the snow is heaviest, put Marty in the lead, for his heart is twice as big and he eats just half the feed!"

Gabe found himself mouthing the rest of the song, about a tiny mule who thought he was a reindeer. But he wasn't alone. Glancing over at one point, struggling to keep the tears from his eyes, Gabe noticed Jalise singing along with the chorus. "Marty Mule was merry, Marty Mule was gay, Marty Mule, the little mule that saved our Christmas Day!"

"What?" She snorted when he caught her look of pure, childlike joy and carefree singing. "You think you're the only one who knows this song?"

"I thought you wanted me to turn it off," Gabe reminded her as the credits rolled.

Jalise stood wearily, back to sorting through the last of the Christmas decorations. "Naw," she conceded at last. "You can keep it. It's kind of sweet. Besides…" She jerked a furry white bottle-brush tree at the glowing monitor. "I kind of want to see what golden oldie comes on next."

Chapter Twenty-Seven

Carol

"You wouldn't mind?"

They stood in Rome's office, a surprisingly dowdy blend of framed degrees hanging from tweedy bamboo-covered walls and bookshelves full of old software boxes and business books. She'd thought her stylish supervisor might surround himself with more trendy things, movie posters or framed sports jerseys or some such macho nonsense.

Either way, the office didn't match the man, currently bedecked in a stylish maroon business suit, tailor-made to hug Rome's squishy body and, as *GQ* as it all was, down to the camel-colored dress shoes, the whole ensemble failed to impress as much as another one of his trademark scarfs, wound jauntily around his broad shoulders.

"Why would I mind?" Carol insisted. "I'm the one who told you, Rome."

"I know," he whined, pacing the long row of floor-to-ceiling windows that fronted his corner office. "It's just, they canned you, Carol. Like...only the other day. Shouldn't I at least wait until the body is cool to step over it?"

She frowned at his imagery. "There was no love lost there, trust me. And you were the first person I thought of when I got over my pseudo-grief to realize that now Victorian Voices has an open slot."

Rome looked genuinely surprised. "Me? Why me?"

Carol cocked her head. "Because you said you auditioned for them years ago. I thought...closure?"

Rome's smile split his kind, cherubic face in half. "It would be nice," he agreed, still pacing. Carol sat in an uncomfortably stiff chair across from his boxy wooden desk.

"Right?" she encouraged. "Plus they've got gigs lined up for days and the girl who I heard audition? A little sharp, if you know what I mean."

Rome nodded conspiratorially from halfway across the big corner office. "Still, they usually put an ad out for a girl."

"Yeah, but like I said—desperate times call for desperate measures."

Rome stopped pacing to be dramatic. "Wow, thanks."

Carol frowned. "You know what I mean. If you sing half as well as you dress, you're in like Flynn."

Rome inched closer until he sank into the large, padded chair behind his desk. "Funny thing is," he mused. "I don't even think it's about talent with them. It's about how much ass you can kiss, how quickly and how eagerly."

Carol nodded so hard she almost strained her neck. "I wish I'd learned that lesson a little sooner."

Their eyes met across his cluttered desk. "No, you don't," he insisted, tone no longer hesitant. "I don't know you well, Carol, but well enough to realize you don't suffer fools gladly. Nor should you. If you're out of Victorian Voices, it can only be because Reggie didn't think you were licking his boots long or hard enough."

"And you?" Carol sighed, almost wishing she hadn't told Rome about the sudden opening in Birchwood's most popular caroling troupe. "Is that what you want?"

Rome nodded toward a shelf in the corner. It wasn't grand or overly ornate, but it contained a variety of trophies, ranging from horseback riding to various sports to a variety of other extracurricular activities. "I'm a collector, Carol. I have interests and hobbies that make my life more agreeable and for those? I like to excel. I like to wow. I like to win!"

Carol smirked knowingly. "So you want a trophy for your shelf there?"

Rome nodded at the shelf again. "There is an opening there on the end I've been saving."

"For Victorian Voices?"

Rome scowled. "For the Jingle Jangle, obviously," he all but snapped. "If shining Reggie on for the next week or so is what it takes to bag that particular trophy and cross that accomplishment off my bucket list, well…"

"So what are you waiting for?"

Rome glanced down at his phone sheepishly. "Reggie hasn't called me back yet."

"Why, you little stinker?" Carol chided, wishing she was closer so she could have slugged him on the shoulder. "You already reached out?"

"I mean, the flyer's still in the breakroom, I needed coffee, why not kill two birds?"

"I only suggested it at lunch," she reminded him.

"The early bird, bro," Rome insisted with a wag of his finger. "The early bird."

Carol stood up from the uncomfortable chair. It was barely midday, another long afternoon shift stretching out for hours and hours on end. It wasn't that she didn't enjoy her new job. She did. Rome was a godsend, the kids who manned the phone bank were all sweet and endearing, the work was rewarding and the hours mostly agreeable. She just enjoyed her late-night soft serve visits more.

And somehow? They never came soon enough.

"Will you miss it?" Rome asked as she lingered near his door.

"The boot licking?" she teased. "No. The caroling?" She nodded shyly, as if just realizing it for herself. "I actually will."

"There are other troupes, you know?" he said with a face that said, *no, there really aren't.*

Carol shrugged. "Like you said, this late in the game? I'll just stick to singing along with the car radio for now and maybe next year? I'll start auditioning with those other troupes a little earlier."

"That's the spirit," Rome said. She wasn't sure what to say next, or how quickly to leave, until the ringing of a nearby phone set her in motion. It wasn't the landline on his desk. Rome's eyes lit up, seeing the number on his cell. "It's them," he mouthed, nervous again.

She chuckled from the doorway, giving him a thumbs up sign and mouthing back "Good luck!" before inching quietly away, shutting the door behind her.

At least someone is excited about the holidays, she thought, beginning another twisting turn through the cubicles that lined the call center floor.

Chapter Twenty-Eight

Gabe

"It's good. Honestly!"

Carol sat with her pink plastic spoon halfway to her mouth, as if uncertain whether to eat another bite or possibly hide it in a napkin when Gabe wasn't looking.

"Are you just saying that?" he asked, back to his usual seat at the next table. He'd enjoyed their time together in the same booth, but the intimacy of being that close to the object of his affection had been nearly overwhelming. Besides, Gabe wanted a little distance between them in case she turned down his offer and bolted for the door the first chance she got.

"No, seriously," she insisted too kindly. "The gingerbread really offsets the, uhm…is that…plum pudding flavor?"

Gabe frowned, suspecting as much. "You can't even say that with a straight face," he chided.

"Well," she admitted, putting the spoon back down in the chocolate waffle bowl she favored. "It's honestly hard to say the words 'plum pudding' with a straight face, in any context, let alone in relation to…ice cream?"

They shared a quiet chuckle. "I know, I know," Gabe admitted sheepishly. "I think I got caught up in all the seasonal offerings after Thanksgiving and just went haywire when the flavor catalog came in."

"Did you order them all?" Carol inquired, subtly pushing her bowl a little farther out of reach.

"Not all," Gabe replied. "I mean, the mince pie flavor was a little off-putting."

"But plum pudding wasn't?" she blurted as if forgetting that he was sitting right there.

Gabe snorted, staring at his lap. "Guess not."

She gripped his wrist from across the small space that divided them. "Sorry," she said, squeezing once more before letting go. "You were very sweet to let me try it."

"If you want to go back to pistachio and peanut butter swirl," he promised, his eyes searching hers, "I'll be glad to make you another one."

"Honestly? I'm enjoying the holiday flavors you've put together for this season."

"Just not plum pudding?"

They shared another laugh, more conspiratorial this time. She glanced down into her waffle bowl, dragging her spoon through the dregs of her uneaten Plum Pudding Pizzazz Swirl Special. "I guess in all the hubbub of moving to a new town, the new job and then caroling, I forgot to stop and enjoy the season."

"Same," Gabe agreed, waving a hand toward the newly decorated ice cream parlor. From the pastel bottle-brush trees in each cozy little napkin holder to the vibrant holiday window clings to the new snowflakes hanging, glittery and bold, from between the ceiling tiles overhead, the place finally had that Christmas feel it had been missing until that very day. "I suppose getting axed was a blessing, in some ways."

"Only some?" Carol teased, those big green eyes probing as she risked a glance across the booth they shared.

Gabe heard the offering of a quick segue in her voice, and finally saw the opening he'd been waiting for. "Actually," he began, shifting in his seat as if bracing for the inevitable, "there *was* something I wanted to ask you."

Carol froze, from the expression on her face to the hands poised atop the table in front of her. "Yes?" Even her voice was cautious, to say nothing of her wary emerald eyes.

"It's nothing bad," Gabe insisted, sensing her reluctance. Or perhaps feeling his own. "It's just that, I miss it, you know?"

"Caroling?" she prodded.

Gabe nodded. So did Carol. "Me too." She sighed. "More than I cared to admit. The other day? I was just pissed. But today? I'm thinking of what songs they're singing and how many people are clapping and how left out I feel about it all."

Gabe nodded. "Same," he agreed. "And it sucks that there are only two real troupes to choose from in all of Bergen County."

Carol replied cautiously, "Indeed."

"So I was wondering, if you were interested, I mean…maybe we…could…" Gabe was the one to freeze this time, the words halting midway across his tongue.

"We...could...?" Carol all but made a hand-waving motion to jump-start his interrupted proposition back to life. "We could *what*, Gabe?"

He exhaled, shoulders collapsing as he hunched into himself. Staring at the ground, he forced himself to ask the question that had been simmering alone inside his brain all day. "Start our own troupe?"

Carol sat back in her bench seat. A slow pause followed, one Gabe was sorely tempted to fill with useless words, excuses, reasons and more. Somehow, he resisted. Then...a smile, slowly creeping across her face. "The thought *had* crossed my mind," she confessed.

He sat back up. "Really?"

"Sure, how could it not? I mean, the odds of us both getting canned on the same day? Why, it's almost like they're begging us to start a troupe together, right?"

"They totally are!" Gabe agreed, wriggling excitedly in his seat. "I mean, I want it to be about more than just revenge, but popping up on the same holiday circuit as them, living our best lives as a duet and giving the crowd something to actually sing along to? Could you imagine?"

Chapter Twenty-Nine

Carol

"Duet?"

Carol perked up, wanting to make sure she'd heard him right. Gabe's face, at once so eager and boyish, eased into a flat line. "Sure, I mean…" Suddenly, his voice was cautious and muted.

Carol rushed to reassure him. "No, I just wasn't sure…is that even allowed?"

Gabe nodded a little more enthusiastically. "I spent a bit of time this morning checking out the Jingle Jangle bylaws on their website—which was really stimulating reading by the way—and there's nothing that says you have to have four singers to be in the competition. Or even three. You could do a solo act and still win, technically speaking."

Carol was nodding, if only to herself. "Wow, I guess I just never thought of a troupe as anything less than four."

"That's what they want you to think," Gabe insisted. "They want this town locked into thinking a certain way. There can only be troupes of four. They can only dress in Regency garb. They can only sing dusty old fart outdated carols that nobody knows anymore or, for that matter, even wants to."

"Jeez, Gabe, how do you really feel?"

"But you know what I mean, right?" Gabe insisted.

"Of course I do."

Gabe's enthusiasm faltered. "Why, did you have others in mind?"

Carol did, of course. Rome, for one. She knew her sweet, talented new boss was as eager to sing as she was, but the selfish part of her wanted Gabe all to herself, even as the unselfish part wanted Rome to sing in a nice, welcoming, non-dysfunctional troupe. Fortunately, Victorian Voices had snatched him up in a heartbeat, soprano or no. And if what he really wanted was a trophy for his Wall of Fame? Then he'd be more likely to get it with the six-time-running champions in town and not some new startup who only had a few days to rehearse before the big competition.

"Not specifically," she fibbed all the same. "Why, do you?"

Gabe merely shrugged, pausing as if maybe he had a Rome of his own in mind. Then he shook his head. "The only other carolers I've ever known were in the Mistle Tones. And your troupe, obviously."

"*Ex*-troupe," she reminded him.

"Ex, right." Gabe admired her openly, but not in his usual horny adolescent way. "What, you never thought of it yourself?"

Carol shook her head. "Going out on my own? No, not really."

"Why not?" he asked.

"I guess I just never thought in a million years you'd go for it, that's why."

"And now?" Gabe pressed. He'd shifted in his chair, inching closer to the edge of his seat by degree. He wasn't alone. She'd turned in her booth, toward the edge where she could face him, legs crossed and arms over her chest protectively.

"Now?" she confessed. "I'm kind of excited."

"Yeah?"

Carol nodded. "You're serious, though, right? You're not just hopped up on plum pudding and gingerbread swirl?"

"Not even a little," Gabe admitted. "In fact, I don't think I've eaten all day."

"What? Why?"

"Been too nervous, I suppose," he confessed.

"Nervous about what?"

"That you'd say 'no,' I guess."

She struggled not to make too much of that, then immediately made everything out of it. "And now? That I'm on board, I mean?"

He screwed up one eyebrow deliciously. "*Are* you, though?"

"Yes," she insisted, more fervently than she'd hoped. After all, the thought of doing more with Gabe than just spending a few minutes in his ice cream parlor every night was making her near delirious by this point.

Gabe seemed to relax back into his seat. "Then I suppose I'm not nervous anymore."

Carol nodded, vaguely breathless, her throat taut with sudden tension. "Do we have to register or something?" Now that this cockamamie idea was sounding more and more like it might actually come to fruition, the business side of her was beginning to take over.

Gabe shook his head, already one step ahead. Now why wasn't she surprised? "Not until our first paying gig, then we're automatically in the running."

"Which is when, exactly?" Carol's voice fell flat. "I mean, seems like Victorian Voices and the Mistle Tones have all the business in this town locked up tight. And there's barely a week until Christmas as it is. How are we ever going to crack that stranglehold?"

Gabe glanced out of the window at the parking lot beyond, a curious smile curling up one side of his ridiculously addictive smile. "It just so happens the Birchwood Galleria has been trying to book one of them all December and both troupes have been blowing them off. I told them I had a solution and if they could wait until Saturday night, I'd have a brand-new troupe that would be well worth the wait."

Carol froze once more. "*This* Saturday night?"

Gabe chuckled. "That would be correct. Why, that gonna be a problem?"

"Not getting the evening off—my supervisor already knows about my extracurricular activities, it's just...Thursday. Today is Thursday."

Gabe sagged a little into himself again. "I'm painfully aware."

"I mean, we don't even have a name yet, we don't have any songs, what are we going to wear..." Carol trailed off, mid-panic attack.

Gabe stood just then, smirking as he strode across the black-and-white tiled floors of the dining room. He clicked the deadbolt into place, then turned the neon "Open" sign off before sliding a handful of dimmer switches on the wall into the "off" position. Almost immediately the dining room took on a surreal quality, lit solely by the neon signage throughout the place and, drawing her attention to the wall across from where she sat—a long, wide monitor showing retro Christmas cartoons, of all things.

"Yeah, about that..." Gabe chuckled, returning to the sales counter and scooping ice into a cup.

"Which that?" Carol asked, watching his every move. Although they'd barely changed positions, being in the closed store with him felt far more intimate than she might have imagined.

"A name, of course." He poured himself a soda. Or, knowing Gabe, poured her one out of habit. "Grape or orange?"

"Water, if you don't mind?"

He snapped his fingers and frowned, as if mad at himself for forgetting. "Of course," he muttered, reaching for one out of the cooler beneath the register. "Working with teenagers, I always forget what it's like to socialize with adults."

Chapter Thirty

Gabe

"Are we...socializing?"

Carol lingered, half-in, half-out of her booth seat, long legs primly crossed in her mint-colored business suit. Gabe chuckled, midway across the dining room floor with their drinks.

"Of course not," he teased. "This is work, obviously. And hard work, at that."

She beamed that winning smile, lighting up her face all the way to her luminous green eyes. Her hair was back in a ponytail, no braid this time, just loosely gathered, little sprays of auburn hair framing her elegant, eager face. "Indeed."

They each drank slowly, Gabe still standing as he paced beneath the flickering TV monitor, hoping to draw her attention to it. He sipped his orange soda, lost in thought, until Carol cleared her throat and said, "You were saying...about a name?"

He paused, mid-pace, beaming. "I was, wasn't I?"

"You were, weren't you?"

He enjoyed her playful vibe, watching as she wriggled deeper into the booth seat beneath her, every ripple of her sensual body a sight to behold. "Do you...have any thoughts?" he offered cautiously.

"About a name? For our caroling duo?" Her voice was pure syrup, to match the radiant glow in her eyes and the sensual ripple across her skin. "It's your idea, Hot Shot," she teased, making him wonder if she was this playfully bossy at work, figuring she probably was.

"Why don't you start this brainstorming session?" she suggested.

"Okay, well, I was hoping to stay as far away from Victorian Voices and the Mistle Tones as we possibly could."

She nodded eagerly. "Agreed."

"But something musical and Christmasy at the same time," Gabe hemmed, afraid to throw out the first idea.

Carol frowned. "Yes, agreed and...your idea was...?"

Gabe rolled his eyes. "You're really gonna make me go first?"

Carol smiled. "Not if it's going to cause you creative paralysis, Gabe, no."

"It's not, I'm just...embarrassed."

"About what?" Carol chuckled. "We're about to start singing together, in public, for a crowd of strangers, big as you please. Choosing a name for all that should be the least embarrassing thing we do for the next week or so."

Gabe blushed and nodded and paced and said, "You're right, you're right. Okay, so...how about...the Candy Canes?"

Carol's smile didn't quite reach her eyes this time. "That's a good start," she offered.

Gabe snorted. "How diplomatic of you to say so." Then he sagged with relief, realizing he'd done his part to at least prime the old creative pump. "Okay, your turn now."

"That's it?" Carol laughed. "That's all you got?"

"For a *start*," he reminded her.

Carol clucked her tongue and rolled her eyes. "Touché, sir. Okay, so how about...the Regency Revelers?" Gabe noticed her wincing in advance, and with good reason.

"Not bad," he hedged his bet. "But that brings up a good point—are we going to *be* Regency revelers? Is that... This is really our chance to break free and do our very own thing, right from the start."

Carol nodded. "You're right," she agreed. "I was hoping to avoid all those musty old evergreens, frankly."

"Same," Gabe practically gushed with relief. "Most of the time I was cringing inside, knowing the crowd was restless to hear something, anything, they recognized."

Carol nodded emphatically, her sensual body rippling delightfully with the effort. "So that's agreed then, no Victorian or Regency shenanigans, yes?"

Gabe was tempted to reply with some cockney BS along the lines of "Right, pet," but didn't want to trigger her. Or himself, for that matter. The very thought made him shiver. "Okay then, my turn?"

Carol nodded, beaming. He frowned and racked his brain. She waited patiently until she clearly could wait no more. "Was 'Candy Canes' all you thought up?" He could tell she was struggling to hide the impatience in her voice.

"I mean, I did a lot of the groundwork first, okay?"

Carol gave him an approving wave. "You did, you did, so I'll go twice then, all right?"

"Yes please!"

Her frown was delectable, smooth brow furrowed just a touch, lush eyelashes fluttering as her brain fretted double-time. "I'm leaning toward the Mistle Tones style of pun rather than Victorian Voices, don't you think?"

"It always sounded so blunt to me," Gabe agreed, forgetting it was Carol's turn to brainstorm next. "But since we're steering away from the Regency era into more modern times, what about...the Holly and the Ivy?"

Carol sat up at last, giving him a slight sense of encouragement. "There *are* just two of us this time," she agreed. "But maybe Holly and Ivy might roll off the tongue better?"

Gabe nodded, then frowned. "Yeah, but...which of us is which? I'm not comfortable being either."

"Too macho, huh?" Carol teased so quickly she seemed to surprise even herself.

"More like too awkward," Gabe compromised. "But I like the two-word playoff, what are some others?"

Carol thought briefly before spitting out, "Pine and Dandy?"

Gabe nodded appreciatively. "Better, better..." he murmured, vaguely noncommittal. "Let's circle back to that. How about...the Snow Flakes?"

Carol's eyes widened. "You know, something like that could be good if we keep caroling after the holidays, like for New Year's parties and whatnot?"

"So we'll keep that in the bank, too," Gabe rushed, not wanting to lose momentum. "Snowflake Serenades?" he riffed, enjoying the brisk back and forth. "Frosty Friends? Comfort and Noise?"

Gabe paused to wet his whistle with a fresh gulp of orange soda. "Wow," Carol mused, watching him sip from a pink-and-blue-striped straw. "You're really good at this."

Gabe swallowed. "Yeah?"

She nodded. "Really, keep going."

He frowned. "You just don't want to play along," he groused.

"Not true," she said, even as a rich blush rose to those hollow cheeks. "I just suck at this."

Gabe frowned, but wanted to nail their name down so he could move on to their song choices. "Fine, what about...food names next?"

"Food names?"

"Yeah, you know, we already did Candy Canes to no big fanfare, but what about other holiday food groups, like... Gingerbread? Eggnog? Toffee?"

"Maybe if we added a 'the' to them," Carol suggested from her seat on the sidelines. The gloves had finally come off, he supposed.

"You think?"

"Two words, remember?" she cautioned, all business now as her lenient smile grew more severe. "*The* Gingerbreads. *The* Eggnogs. If we're going to really give the others a run for their money, let's not be too different from them?"

Gabe frowned. "I thought we were being totally different from them?"

"We are, silly," she cooed, her dulcet tones touching him in places that yearned to be caressed even more.

"But on the surface, at a glance, we should all fit together. So...two words. Now...go!"

"Fine then," Gabe growled, digging deep for another round of brain sauce. "I'm just going to riff on two-word food pairings and you stop me when you hear something you like, okay? So...Figgy Pudding?" He paused, but Carol's face remained a blank slate so he kept going. "Mashed Potatoes? No, duh. Jesus. Sugar Cookies? Hot Cocoa?"

"Yes!" Carol stood at last, all curves and angles as her whole body shimmied under the tailor-made business suit.

"Which one?"

"Hot Cocoa, obviously." She approached him, heels clacking on the tile floor. "It just...trips off the tongue, you know?"

"You think?"

"I do, Gabe." Her voice was lower as she approached, just above a purr, as if to readjust due to their sudden proximity. "It's got all the energy where those other two are just...static. Boring. Flat."

"Hot. Cocoa." Gabe gave the words a spin, feeling the energy roll off his tongue. "It does have a vibe, huh?"

"Totally it does," Carol agreed. "A punch, a ring, pizzazz, even. Just think about it from a crowd's perspective. Victorian Voices? Dull, blasé, old, musty. Even the Mistle Tones, though cute and punny, sounds like your grandmother's favorite polka band."

Gabe chuckled at the implications. "Never thought of it that way," he mused, admiring the way Carol leaned back against the sales counter, so casually yet so elegantly. Like she was the one who owned the place, not him. "But yes, cute enough, but Hot Cocoa really brings the heat."

Carol squinted. "No pun intended."

"Oh, yeah, no...sorry."

She waved it away. "Plus, if we do keep singing after the holidays, for Boxing Day, say, or those folks who don't take the tree down until the first week of January, or churches...heck, we could keep going all winter with that name."

Gabe nodded. "It's settled then."

Carol seemed surprised at his definitive response. "Yeah?"

"Sure, why not? To keep going is just to tempt ourselves into finding more names we like and then we'll never decide on one."

"True. So...next?"

Chapter Thirty-One

Carol

"Outfits, I guess?"

Gabe sank into another chair with what seemed to her some kind of reckless abandon. It wasn't his usual chair, per se, over near the booth where she typically sat. Or even the chair closest to where she was standing at the sales counter. Just some random-ass chair, for no particular reason.

It was so freeing — the whole store to themselves, the gentle glow of neon against the chill, black night just outside the wall of windows overlooking the empty parking lot. And her new partner, so young and full of energy, hopping from booth to chair to pacing back and forth before sitting back down again, like a kid on, well...Christmas morning.

"What?" he asked, as if noticing the fresh waves of pleasure crossing her always too expressive face.

"Nothing, just...we *are* doing modern carols, right?"

"I thought we were doing clothes first?" Gabe pressed, boyishly curious, adorably eager and creatively all over the place.

"Right, but it will depend on what carols we're singing, I suppose."

Gabe looked at his feet sheepishly, a far cry from the cocky young savant who'd brainstormed them into the sassiest caroling troupe name in just about ever. "What's wrong?"

He patted the table where he sat, nodding above her. She turned, even as she backed into the chair beside him. There, on the flickering monitor, was a Christmas cartoon. But not just *any* Christmas cartoon. She looked closer, recognizing the sad, worn little teddy bear from her youth. "Bear Buddy?" she asked, risking a glance from the heartwarming old cartoon to her heart-pounding new singing partner.

"*Buddy Bear Wakes for Christmas*," he corrected her.

Carol risked a glance away from the way the neon bathed Gabe's chiseled face in even sexier shadows to admire the fuzzy little teddy bear rubbing his black button eyes on the TV screen above them.

"I *love* this one." She sighed in contentment, warmth spreading like a fuzzy wool blanket all over her inner child. "Wherever did you find it?"

He wagged a periwinkle-blue bottle-brush tree before sliding it back in the napkin holder between them. "When I finally realized I hadn't done any decorating and started to care about the season again, I ran through our list of pay-per-view channels and found this. *Retro Reels*, it's called. It's just a running feed of old and sort-of-old Christmas cartoons to play when the kiddies get out of school this week and the place starts getting busy."

Carol nodded, admiring the old-school illustrations and cheesy one-liners as Buddy Bear talked to all his stuffed friends. "My dad would watch this with me every Thanksgiving weekend," she recalled. "Seemed like it always came on around then."

"Before it played all Christmas long," Gabe pointed out, as if remembering watching it a time or two himself.

"True," she murmured, still mired in the memory of a long-distant father, snuggled up in her childhood bedroom until she fell asleep in his big, strong arms. Those were the good years, of course. Before the divorce and the ugliness, the blame and the alimony, the child support and bitterness. One year her father had watched *Buddy Bear Wakes for Christmas* with her and the next? He was living halfway across the country with his former secretary from the bank, not even sending so much as a Christmas card. All the same, the fuzzy teddy bear and all his stuffed friends, even the cheesy canned music, warmed her heart. "That must be why I remember it so well."

Gabe nudged her arm lightly. "Do you remember the songs?"

"All of them," Carol enthused with a vigorous nod. "They were so cheesy, even back then. But also? So catchy and singable at the same time."

As if on cue, Daisy Doll patted Buddy Bear on the head and broke into one of them. "There oh there, sweet Buddy Bear," she crooned, slightly offkey now that Carol was older and could recognize such things from a decidedly more adult, even professional, perspective. "The day is finally done. Just focus on the Christmas lights, much brighter than the sun."

The world fell away as the scene played out, dragging her back to a simpler, more innocent, sweeter and more childish time. "The holiday will soon be here," sweet little Daisy Doll crooned, taking a bow from one of the nearby Christmas presents and wrapping it around Buddy Bear's neck like a scarf. "And with it lots of cheer. And from each gift we're given a smile from ear to ear…"

Carol turned to Gabe as Buddy Bear and Daisy Doll danced around the room, lit only by a towering Christmas tree. "Thanks," she said through a lump in her throat. "I needed this tonight."

His smile was soft, his voice low as if to let her keep listening to the once-familiar tune. The tune she could still recite, word for word, as if it had been buried in her brain for years, just begging to come back out and cheer her up just when she needed it most.

"I think a lot of people need this right about now," he said, nodding with his cute little face and stubbly hair toward the clumsily animated dancing scene on the big flat screen above their heads. "Don't you?"

She nodded in agreement, both of them glancing up to the screen as the scene played out, the song ending and the cartoon returning to its usual childish holiday antics.

"I do," she agreed, turning back to him with a dawning sense of apprehension. "Is that…is there…some reason you showed me this? Now? Tonight?"

He nodded. "We won't have much time," he pointed out. "To rehearse, I mean. And sure we *could* do *Jingle Bells* and *Silent Night,* and maybe we even will, as filler. But for now? To start? I think…I think that I should keep watching this channel and come up with a list of ten to twelve cheesy little tunes to sing. The kind parents and kids can share together. The kind they haven't heard in years. Until…"

"Until we sing them for them," Carol finished for him. "Again."

"Again."

Chapter Thirty-Two

Gabe

"You've sure given this a lot of thought, huh?"

Carol stood at last, stretching wearily as she ground her hands into the small of her back. Gabe knew the feeling. The anger, the hurt, the betrayal of being fired from his old caroling troupe had left him emotionally and physically drained, as had the double-rush of excitement over starting their own. Now, suddenly, with the agreement struck, the name sorted and the carols coming together, weariness dogged him as if he'd never slept before.

He saw Carol's eyes flitting toward the door and nodded. "It means a lot to me," he insisted, still lingering beneath the flickering glow of yet another childhood Christmas cartoon.

She stood close, as if unable — or perhaps unwilling — to move any nearer to that door. "The caroling?" she pressed, nudging his shoulder with her own. "Or the winning?"

He shrugged, the echo of her touch humming through his whole body. "Would it be gross if I said...both?"

"Not gross," she insisted. "Just...natural, I suppose. I mean, I've always believed that if you're not in it to win it, what are you doing there in the first place, right?"

Gabe grinned, relieved to have found a kindred spirit in a town that had always felt so foreign to him, even though he'd lived there his whole damn life. "I mean, I didn't start an ice cream parlor to fail, right?"

She beamed. "And look at you now."

Gabe's confidence, usually in such vast supply, dimmed slightly. "This is different though, I suppose."

Carol nodded as they drifted toward the door at last. "Which part?" she teased, ponytail swishing across her back with each step. "The two days to rehearse? The brand-new songs? The no clothes yet? The staggering stage fright?"

Gabe was still nodding when she turned at the door, glad he wasn't the one talking because she would have taken his breath away. She was radiant as the dimly lit neon cast dramatic shadows across her already evocative face.

"Well, now," he struggled to calm her, willing his voice not to crack like some horny teenager. "You let me handle the songs. Maybe, for your homework, you could brainstorm some outfits?"

A small smile perked up one side of her lips. "Ooooh, I like that. And rehearsal? I mean, at some point we're going to have to come to grips with the fact that we have to sing in front of each other."

Gabe gulped. "Well, and *with* each other, too."

"Right, so…" Carol hadn't reached for the door yet. Nor had he. They stood very close just beside it. He'd thought of this moment, where they'd rehearse. His place? Her place? A part of him enjoyed the neutrality of Soft Swerve — plenty of room, nice lighting, and snacks and beverages ever at the ready. But he hadn't thought of starting a caroling duet for all innocent reasons, obviously. At some point, he knew — or, at least, Gabe *hoped* — they would move things away from the professional and closer to the personal.

But now? He caved at the last minute. "I have a storage space," he blurted before he could chicken out. "Just at the edge of town. Extra chairs and tables, holiday decorations, nonperishable stock items. It's just past the high school, out on Deacon Lane?"

Carol reached for the door, a dubious look on her face. "Perfect for rehearsing," she mused, hand on the door but not quite pressing it open. "Or a place where no one can hear you scream?"

Gabe flushed. "Somebody's been watching too many *Forensic Case Files* lately."

She held up her free hand, so close it could have brushed his cheek if she'd wanted. "Guilty as charged." Then she reached for the door handle, pushing it open. "I can't get off until after seven." She sighed, avoiding his eyes.

"Same," he lied. With his status, he could get off any time he wanted to. "Is that gonna be too late?"

She shook her head. "I come here later than that," she reminded him, giving the empty dining room a quick once-over. "But I'll be hungry and I imagine you will, too. Chinese takeout okay?"

"You buying?" he teased.

She rolled her eyes and inched a little farther through the door. "Least I can do for all the free soft serve you've been giving me."

He followed her out into the courtyard, Christmas lights still winking in the crisp night air. "Looks like my investment paid off, though," he suggested, unable to help himself.

She turned, halfway to her sleek luxury sedan. "Yeah, how's that?"

"I mean, you agreed to this crazy idea of mine, right?"

"Was it yours?" she sassed him over one shoulder, slinking away to her car in that form-fitting business suit.

He followed her to the curb. "Well, I mean...yeah?" But suddenly, Gabe wasn't quite so sure.

"Or did I lead you there, scoop by scoop?" She let the question hang in the air, slipping into her driver's seat and turning on the engine with little more than a purr. He waved foolishly, watching her back away without another word, secretly wondering if she'd been right all along.

And not so secretly flattered that she had.

Chapter Thirty-Three

Carol

"Twig the tree swings merrily..."

Gabe crooned, his back still to her, his deep, rich voice a welcome surprise in the vast confines of the spacious storage space he rented on the outskirts of town. "Dancing underneath the lights," Carol sang, the high to his low, the yin to his yang. There was no sheet music to hold. No leatherbound songbook to consult. They were both going on full memory overload, their inner children providing the words they'd thought they'd long forgotten. "Seeing all the Christmas sights..."

She waited anxiously for the next verse, hearing the squeak of his stylish sneakers on the varnished floor as he turned toward her.

"Dancing with his roots undone." Gabe's moist lips parted as he sang, Adam's apple bobbing sexily as he eyed her doubtfully. "Skipping toward the setting sun…"

His voice dimmed as if to match the dancing Christmas tree in the cheesy retro carol. She golf-clapped and squeed as his gaze met hers, almost begging for acknowledgment. "So good," she squealed, shoving his shoulder lest she wrap him in her arms and eat him up whole. "So. Frickin'. Good!"

He nodded bashfully, hands digging into his jeans pockets as if she wouldn't see them tremble there. Spoiler art—she did. "Yeah?"

"Gabe, honestly, you can quit asking that. Okay? Three songs in and we're a perfect fit."

He grinned, chin finally up. "We are, aren't we?"

"I mean, I think so." Carol waved toward the open storage shed door, parking lot empty in the quiet night. Above them, lit only by the half-full moon, trees stood awkwardly on the side of Bald Mountain, the scenic crest that overlooked quaint, charming Birchwood, North Carolina. It was the last shed in the row, though "shed" hardly matched the aesthetic. Crafted to look like individual cabins, with roughhewn faux-log siding and forest-green accordion garage doors, Cozy Cabins Storage might as well have been a four-star Airbnb.

Gabe nodded, a dashing smile creeping to his cautious face. "Then that's all that matters."

"I mean, there's still the crowds to think of," she mused, knowing the poor guy's nerves had been on edge all night. "The clients. Not to mention…the competition?"

But Gabe's confidence had returned. "Screw them," he huffed, looking almost unrecognizable in faded blue jeans and a stylish taupe pullover that flattered his broad shoulders and lean, tapering torso. "Mark my words, stage fright or not, Hot Cocoa's going to give those other duds a run for their money this week."

Carol arched her back, pressing firm hands into the small hollow just above her equally casual crinkle skirt. "How can you still have stage fright when you've been doing this four times as long as I have?"

"Bad word choice," Gabe corrected himself, inching closer to the humming cooler in the corner. It held a vast array of non-dairy soft serve mixes and, thanks to Carol's quick thinking on the drive over after work, a six-pack of Samurai, her favorite Asian beer. "I meant, afraid of *you*."

Carol snorted as he opened the cooler and snagged two of the frosty green bottles, clanking against one another as he slid them from the bright red box with one big hand. "Afraid of what?"

He turned, wearing that bashful grin. "It's just so intimate, don't you think? Singing together? A duet?"

Carol's stomach growled, as if suddenly giving itself permission to crave her attention now that Gabe had called an unofficial break. She reached inside the bag from Hop Sing's and offered him a crinkly wrapper full of egg rolls. He grinned just as eagerly as her stomach had growled, trading her an ice-cold beer for one of the still-warm egg rolls.

"Surely you had plenty of those in high school chorus?" she offered, watching him dig into the egg roll with gusto. She couldn't blame him. Though she was scolding him now, however playfully, Carol's nerves had been on edge all day. Now that she'd heard their chemistry for herself, she was ready to make up for lost time.

"Yeah, but you already knew those girls," he groused, Adam's apple throbbing as he swallowed a mouthful of egg roll with cold Japanese beer.

"You don't know me?" She pretended to be offended, waving her own egg roll for emphasis just before she took her first, sumptuous, much-needed bite. "By now?"

"Sure, on the surface," Gabe agreed. "But I was worried you'd think I wasn't good enough."

"Oh my God." Carol was stunned. Not too stunned to finish her delectable egg roll, of course, but stunned just the same. "What kind of girl do you think I am?"

"Not a mean one," Gabe assured her, inching closer to root around in the sack of takeout for a pair of chopsticks and a pint of lo mein. "Just a demanding one."

"Demanding!" Carol nearly threw her beer bottle at him.

Gabe ducked all the same, just in case. "Okay, okay, wrong word choice."

"Again," Carol reminded him.

"What I meant to say was," Gabe assured her while plucking open the top of the familiar red-and-white takeout container. Then he paused. "Are there two of these?"

She chuckled. Even when he was insulting her, Gabe was still the ultimate little charmer. "Yes, that one's chicken, I think. The other's pork?"

He smiled. "Okay if I scarf this one?"

Carol nodded. "That's...why I brought it."

He chuckled, sensing her growing ire. "What I meant to say," he mused aloud, all while slithering lo mein noodles through his thick, dreamy lips, "was that you were coming from the six-time, county champion caroling troupe while little old me was just in the sloppy seconds category, that's all."

"No, you weren't," Carol challenged. Something about the cabin-like storage shed, the savory egg roll and dry, cold beer had her feeling downright...frisky. "You were lowkey calling me a boss bitch, weren't you?"

"N-n-never!" Gabe's jaw hung slack, lips shiny from savory noodle grease as she struggled not to wonder what they might taste like at that very moment, sweet and savory, wet and slick, hints of hops and barley and soy sauce and chives. "I just meant, maybe I wasn't up to par. That's it."

"Well, you are," she huffed, snatching up one of the two orders of sweet and sour chicken from the takeaway bag. "And anyway, I'm no expert on all this caroling stuff. You are, remember?"

Gabe sank onto a stack of cardboard boxes marked "floor tiles," nibbling his takeout between full-lipped drags of beer. "Oh yeah." He snorted. "I forgot."

"Besides," she reminded him, finding a stack of folding chairs and sinking into one across from him. "I think we sound great together. Don't you?"

Gabe sank his chopsticks into the half-empty takeout container, sliding it to one side. Gripping his beer atop one knee, he gave her a level gaze. "I do, actually. It's all...all..."

She waited him out, nibbling a warm wedge of pineapple before washing it down with another sip of beer. Carol wished she was closer, close enough to slide a cautious, but reassuring hand atop his own. "All what, Gabe?" she asked instead, as gently as she might have gripped his hand.

"All too good to be true," he blurted, as if getting more than he'd bargained for off his chest. "Don't you think?"

She did, actually. But she didn't want Gabe to know that. "Explain," she said, as she might to one of her new employees at the Homework Helpers hotline.

Gabe chuckled, seeming to relax by degree. "What did you call yourself earlier?"

She knew exactly what he meant. "Boss bitch," she said in a playful clipped tone.

He nodded. "Yeah, well, you're kind of being one right now."

Carol chuckled. "If it works, so be it. Now…spill."

"I'm just saying, what are the odds you walk into my store just as December starts? And we have this thing between us, whatever it is, and you get recruited into Victorian Voices, and I already sing for the Mistle Tones and we get canned on the very same day and we like the same cheesy cartoon theme songs and we actually sound really good together? I mean…"

"Too good to be true indeed." Carol sighed wistfully. "I mean, when you put it that way."

"Well, how would *you* put it?" Gabe asked with a wave of his half-empty beer bottle.

Carol struggled to answer. Then she smiled and all the struggling went away. *Funny how some virtual stranger can make me feel so at ease.* "It's almost Christmas, Gabe. Isn't that enough?" His curious expression made it clear that, no, it certainly wasn't. At least, not for him. "I mean, even though we're grown now, we can still have a little of that Christmas magic, right?"

He nodded at last. "That what this is?" he asked, taking in her crossed legs, hiked crinkle skirt and all-too-clingy sweater. "A little Christmas magic?"

She paused a beat before answering. "It's whatever you want it to be, Gabe."

Chapter Thirty-Four

Gabe

"Me?"

Gabe was surprised his voice hadn't cracked. "What about *you*?"

Carol shrugged, shoulders rippling beneath her slinky maroon sweater and causing the clingy material to glance across her small but striking breasts — they were so evident he wondered if she'd skipped wearing a bra to rehearsal altogether.

"What *about* me?"

Gabe chuckled. She was being cheeky and he dug it. All of it. From the casually brushed-back hair to the flouncy crinkle skirt that kept hinting at the bounty of her smooth, creamy thighs to the effortlessly casual sandals and the entirely sexy picture. He waved beyond her, to the majesty of Bald Mountain just beyond and the rolling green hills and forested vacant lots that dotted the landscape just past the Country Cabins Storage property line.

"Isn't this all magical enough for you?"

She sipped her beer, following his line of sight before settling her gaze back on him in a most unsettling way. She'd been flirty before, back at Soft Swerve. Or, if not flirty, at least cocky. Coy. Sublimely confident in how she looked or, perhaps more to the point, how Gabe looked *at* her.

He'd never been shy about ogling her, though he'd thought he was being slick. She was just such an exotic creature in his world, so full of brittle, tweaked-out soccer moms herding their kids in and out of the store, or the brusque and bossy businesspeople who came and went from the local office complexes or the surly teenagers looking for a little sugar rush to sweeten their days.

Or nights.

A goddess in a business suit, swooping in during the store's quietest hour, filling the already gaudy ice cream parlor with a radiance all her own. And now, here she was, casual and flouncy, braless and open, raw and urgent and only a few sexy feet away.

"You're right about one thing," she conceded, sighing and standing abruptly.

He couldn't help but sound surprised. "I am?"

She smiled, perhaps at his stupidity. She was always doing that, giving him a look that felt more like a pat on the head. "This is…a lot."

He chuckled. "Which part?" He grunted, shifting awkwardly off the stack of boxes where he'd been sitting. His days were so full now, between brainstorming and working, shuttling between his three stores and doing the schedules and staffing up for the busy winter break that was just around the corner. Any chance to sit found him reluctant to get up too soon.

She began to tidy up, reaching for his empty beer bottle and finding the barrel-size trash can near the open garage door to toss it in. "You, me, the quarreling troupes, our work, rehearsals, the Jingle Jangle…"

"Right?" Gabe had joined her, scuttling the last of the greasy, cold lo mein and tossing it in the trash along with his dirty chopsticks. "I can't tell if it's all meant to be or we're just both equally deranged."

She chuckled heartily, the way she did when he sometimes surprised her with an errant joke or smartass reply when she least expected it. As usual, the burst of laughter sent ripples of desire through his body. "Maybe a little bit of both?" she offered as he glanced around the storage shed to see if they'd missed anything.

"You want the rest of your beer?" he asked as she slid just outside the open door.

"Keep it," she insisted. "We'll need it for rehearsal tomorrow, right?"

He beamed, the thought searing itself through his entire body. "My turn to bring dinner," he enthused, admiring the way a soft blush rose to her cheeks, reaching all the way to those sizzling green eyes. "Pizza sound good?"

Carol nodded shyly all of a sudden, tucking a stray lock of hair behind one vibrant pink ear. He slid the door down noisily, making the silence that followed all the more awkward. "What is it?" he asked as they stood face to face outside the forest green garage door.

"Nothing," she said. "I just wish I didn't have to go back to work tonight."

"Yeah?" he nudged, sensing a compliment in there somewhere.

"Sure," she said, making no move to race to her car like usual. "This has been…nice."

"I agree," he blurted too loudly. "Thanks for dinner."

"Not just the dinner," she pointed out.

Their eyes met in the shimmering darkness, making him wonder if they'd ever seen each other in the light of day. "I know that," he said bluntly. "Of course I know that."

That seemed the right answer, somehow. She smiled and inched toward their cars, the only two left in the long, narrow parking lot. The sky was dark but the night was bright, a blanket of stars shimmering overhead and the half-moon illuminating their side of Bald Mountain.

He walked her to her car, struggling to avoid the way her skirt shimmied and danced in the back.

"Crazy to think we both have to work after this," she commented as she unlocked her door but didn't open it.

Gabe nodded. He had inventory waiting on him back at the store, but also the flickering TV and Retro Reels and the hope that, on its gaily animated screen, he might find another old chestnut from their childhood for Hot Cocoa to sing. "Do you have a long shift left?"

She nodded. "My boss replaced me in Victorian Voices, so…I'm covering for him the way he used to for me."

Gabe took an involuntary step back at the news. "No shit?"

She nodded, meeting his eyes in the clear moonlight. Her lips were glossy, to match her wide, bright gaze. In her casual heels, they were nearly the same height. "None whatsoever."

"So, what, you're going to be rivals this season?"

She clucked a tongue. "I hadn't quite thought of it that way. I doubt he has, either. I think we both just like to sing, so..."

Gabe grinned. "Maybe if this goes well, you can poach him for next season."

"What, and mess up our good thing?" She pretended to be hurt, but Gabe knew better.

"We can still have our good thing," he blurted before stopping himself.

She cocked an auburn eyebrow, thinly manicured to match the rest of her modern businesswoman perfection.

"Is that right?" she all but purred.

"You know," he stammered to correct himself. "Pistachio swirl and late-night convo on the way home from work every night?"

Her stiff shoulders sagged and, as usual, Gabe realized he'd missed another opportunity to inch them closer together by somehow, stupidly, pushing them even further apart.

"Sure," she said briskly, opening her door at last and slinking in with one last glimpse of long, smooth thigh.

Jesus, but I'm stupid!

"Same time tomorrow?" she asked as she rolled her window down. He nodded, afraid that his stupid mouth might push her even further away if he dared speak.

"One last thing?" she said before backing out.

He brightened. Maybe he hadn't screwed things up after all! "Anything!"

"No onions on that pizza, okay, Big Guy?" she teased before pulling effortlessly away and leaving him, as always, with his foot in his mouth and balls as blue as the moonlit side of old Bald Mountain.

Chapter Thirty-Five

Carol

"We could try to slow the tempo even more, I suppose?"

Gabe nodded at her suggestion, no longer shy enough to turn his back when he sang his part in front of her. "Ernie Elf went back inside," he crooned confidently, the words of the cheesy nineties Christmas cartoon sliding from between those ripe, full lips. "To have a cup of tea, while Santa and the other elves they worked so busily."

Carol did another of her encouraging golf-claps. "*Much* better."

Gabe blushed sweetly above the collar of his clingy Soft Swerve T-shirt. This one was white, highlighting his naturally ruddy complexion and the way the single exposed bulb above their heads danced across the stubble of his dirty-blond hair.

"Your turn now," he encouraged with an eager nod, standing closer than he had the night before. Then, as if uncertain, he added, "Okay?"

She nodded and took over. They'd decided that, sans background music or so much as a single instrument to accompany them, their dueling voices alone would have to provide any contrast they needed to heighten or lower the emotions of each long-buried children's song.

"But Santa wouldn't have it," Carol all but whispered, slowing down the typically high-tempo cartoon carol to make it more palatable for modern, more mature audiences. "And knocked on Ernie's door…"

Gabe smiled his approval as their voices blended for the final verse, nodding toward one another as they crooned, "That Christmas nap he'd wanted? Was bound to be no more, as Ernie followed Santa to the busy workroom floor…"

Their voices faded in the open storage unit, the smell of pizza strong from the unopened box nearby but the need to rehearse even stronger as they nailed down the last of the twelve silly, lovable little carols they wanted to try out on their first gig the next day.

"Nice," Gabe insisted, big hands flopping restlessly at his side as if he either wanted to high-five her or wrap her whole body up in those long, sinewy arms.

"Right?" she squealed instead, sharing his enthusiasm, if not his reluctance. Carol hadn't come just to rehearse that night. She'd come with bigger plans, and held one hand high for him to slap. He did so, warm flesh smacking tentatively upon her own, hopefully just the prelude to so.

Much.

More.

"We good?" he asked, always so eager to please. She wondered, idly, if he'd be the same in bed, then wiped the thought away. *First things first*, she told herself. "Or do you want to do one more take?"

"I think we're good, right?" she croaked, voice taut from all the rehearsing they'd been doing. "I mean, we could go over *Buddy Bear* once more if you're still feeling a way about it?"

He smiled reassuringly. "I think we're good. My hope is that the crowd joins in anyway, so whatever kinks we still have could work themselves out that way?"

Carol nodded eagerly. "I mean, if everybody else in town knows the songs as well as we do, I would think they couldn't help but chime in and sing along."

"And if they don't?" Gabe was already halfway to the fridge, Carol admiring the sleekness of his movements.

"We'll just have to give them a little nudge," Carol finished for him, gaze flitting next to the shopping bags she'd brought instead of Chinese takeaway.

He turned with two fresh beers, twisting the caps off with those big, capable fingers. "Nervous?" she asked, taking the bottle he offered. He paused, as if caught with his hands in the cookie jar.

"About what?" he asked suspiciously, eyes widening a careful notch.

She chuckled, sinking down onto the same folding chair as the night before. "Tomorrow night, silly."

He seemed relieved. "Oh, that? Yes, obviously."

"But you've done this for years," she reminded him, enjoying his fumbling antics as he dished out slices of pizza on stiff white paper plates, big veiny hands trembling all the while.

"With people I didn't really care for," he explained, handing one over.

"And now?" she teased, flattered by the implications.

"Now I've got you to worry about."

"The hell?"

"Sorry, I mean…I just don't want to let you down."

"You won't, Gabe," she reassured him for the millionth time. "Honestly, what's the worst that can happen tomorrow?"

"Uh," he grunted, sinking onto the by-now-familiar boxes of extra floor tiles across from her. "Embarrassing ourselves silly in front of half the town. How's that for starters?"

She chuckled, unconcerned. "Well, when you put it that way…"

They nibbled their pizza slices quietly, the familiar hints of provolone and spicy sausage stinging her tongue in a most delectable way. "Is this from Broccolini's?"

Gabe brightened. "You know it?"

"We've ordered it during work a few times," she explained between cold sips of beer and gazes in Gabe's general direction. "It's right around the corner from our office building."

"Yeah?" Gabe cocked his pretty little head, the single bulb above him glinting in his curious eyes. "It's funny—you know my workplace so well and I can't even imagine yours."

"You'll have to visit sometime," she said coyly.

"When?" He snorted with the same world-weariness she felt down to her very bones. "In my sleep?"

She nodded with deep, sleep-deprived understanding. "True, maybe after the holidays?"

He finished his pizza and smiled, letting his eyes linger on hers as he nodded. "I'd like that."

She was done, too. No longer hungry, she took a sip of beer to bolster her courage and stood abruptly. "Where are you going?" he asked, as if alarmed.

"Our first gig's tomorrow night," she announced, belly taut with simmering desire as she took the few paces required to reach her ultimate destination. "We should probably pick our outfits by then, don't you think?"

"Oh shit!" Gabe stood, wiping his pizza-greasy hands off on the sides of his jeans despite the stack of napkins right next to the pizza box. "I totally forgot."

"I knew you would," she chided, sliding several bags onto a nearby pallet of powdered waffle cone mix.

"Or did I?" he joked, a bag of his own joining the fray.

"What's this?" Carol asked, surprised.

"Jalise does all our marketing," he explained. "Website updates, social media posts, that kind of thing. She also dabbles in graphic design."

"Yeah?"

Gabe nodded, rustling around in the stiff paper bag. "Yeah, she designed our store mascot, Sir Swerve."

Carol snorted at the forced formality. "Sir Swerve?"

He tapped the outside of the gift bag he'd brought along to rehearsal, fingers dancing along the cute little ice cream cone mascot with the top hat and fancy black dress shoes. "Yeah, most people just call him 'Mister Twistee' but..."

"His real name's 'Sir Swerve'?" *Of course it is,* she thought. *Why would sweet, shy, awkward, earnest Gabe call him anything else?*

Gabe blushed and held out a shirt. "Anyway, she worked up some new designs for Hot Cocoa, and I just thought—"

"Oh my God!" Carol interrupted him, unfurling the soft T-shirt Gabe had handed her. It was the color of, well…a cup of hot cocoa, a rich milky brown she knew would look dreamy on Gabe's taut, lean body. Across the front, emblazoned in cheery pink and white balloon letters like some nineteen-seventies soft rock album cover, the words "Hot Cocoa" rested above a dancing mug of, well, hot cocoa. Sentient, of course. Smiling, with cute little arms and legs, one little gloved hand holding a microphone!

"Captain Cocoa!" she squealed, admiring the clever little mascot and abruptly naming it.

Gabe snorted. "I've been calling him Mister Mug," he said charmingly. Dorkily. Predictably. "But I think I like yours better."

"Duh!" she teased, nodding toward the shirt in his hand and seizing on the opportunity she'd been waiting for all night. All day, if she was being honest with herself. Hell, ever since they'd first met, to speak the God's honest truth. "Let me see yours."

He held it up, the same retro-vibing shirt in the same milk-chocolate hue with the same cheery little dancing hot cocoa mug mascot, just slightly larger than her baby-doll tee. "Cute, huh?"

She cocked a hip and slid an over-obvious finger beneath her chin, hoping Gabe wouldn't notice the desperation of her gesture. "Not sure yet," she teased, even though it had to be the most adorable thing ever. "I'll have to see it on."

As usual, Gabe missed the hint. By a mile. "Yeah, well, you will eventually."

"No," she said more firmly, using that boss-bitch tone she knew he secretly liked so much. "*Now*."

Gabe rolled his eyes, glancing around the open storage unit. As usual, the parking lot was deserted, their cars the only two in the vast, paved lot. "What? Here?"

"Why not?" she teased, her belly gurgling with playful sin. Then, as he eyed her cautiously, she sank the hook in. "What're you, *scared* or something?"

He bristled predictably. "No, I just..." He glanced around the storage shed, piled high with extra chairs and powdered cone mix and not much else. "Where?"

"Jesus, you prude." She chuckled, the hungry sound echoing off the cinderblock walls. "I'll turn my head, if that helps?"

But Gabe was warming to the idea. Carol could tell. Smiling shyly, blushing wildly, he stammered out another lame excuse. "No, no, I'm not chicken, it's just...cold?"

Carol glanced outside. "Really? I thought it felt unseasonably warm out tonight. Otherwise, I wouldn't have suggested it, silly."

Gabe nodded, setting the shirt down next to the plain white Soft Swerve bag. "I am being silly, right?" he said, reaching for the hem of his work tee. "I mean, we're going to be joined at the hip here for the next week or so, right?"

Carol heard the words the way one might hear a mosquito buzzing nearby, indistinct but full of warning. She nodded, struggling not to lick her lips as she muttered something unintelligible like "Mmmm-hhhmmmm" as, casually, just like she'd hoped, Gabe lifted up his shirt. Time froze in the cluttered storage unit, with its stacks of boxes and great acoustics. Her eyes drank in every ridge of his defined abs and smooth, flawless young skin, made all the more distinct in the dim but dangerous glow of the single exposed bulb overhead.

A thin, almost invisible line of dirty-blond hair ran from just above the button of his faded blue jeans to his belly button before her gaze lifted to savor his thick, almost puffy pink nipples, the perfect complement to his smooth, unblemished pale skin. Too soon the shirt had lifted off altogether, Gabe's face appearing above bare shoulders that begged to be caressed by her greedy, hungry fingers.

The silence in the strangely intimate shed had grown to an almost fever pitch, so much that when he almost whispered "Take a picture," her snort of laughter seemed to burst the bubble of mounting tension for both of them.

"Sorry," she said, suddenly demure as he tugged on the new Hot Cocoa shirt which, of course, fit perfectly. "It's just…been a while."

Chapter Thirty-Six

Gabe

"What, no coed changing rooms at work?"

Carol snorted at his offhand remark, still standing mere inches away as he wriggled into his new shirt. It was comfy and cozy. Fleetingly he reminded himself to compliment Jalise on the choice of fabric, buttery soft with just enough give. But only fleetingly.

On this night, he only had eyes, ears and enough bandwidth to focus on Carol. Sweet, sexy, confusing Carol. She was warm, almost hot, the heat shimmering off her body in waves. "We're progressive, but not that progressive," she muttered in reply to a question Gabe had already forgotten he'd asked.

"I guess the kids and I don't have a choice at work," he insisted, smoothing out his new T-shirt with a vaguely trembling hand. "Coming and going at odd hours, tugging on work smocks and ball caps and shedding backpacks and it's always a hustle-bustle…"

She nodded at him then, gaze still glued to his torso as if afraid to meet his hungry eyes. "Then why were you so shy just now?" Her voice was low and tight. "When I asked you to change in front of me?"

"I guess," he began as her eyes crept up to meet his, "it's been a while for me, too. With a woman, I mean. A *real* woman. Someone…"

They were standing too close. Both of them could feel it. He'd stumbled forward while taking off his shirt, and she'd stood her ground ever since watching him change. Yet, unlike other times — make that, every other time — Gabe couldn't back away.

"Someone what?" she almost whispered, nodding as if to urge him to say the words he wouldn't let himself.

Then he did anyway. "Someone I care about."

She smiled. Her lips were always full but never fuller than on this night, damp with some kind of mysterious gloss and parted as if in invitation. "Thanks," she croaked.

"For what?"

"For saying that," Carol blurted. "I needed…needed to hear that tonight."

They stood staring at each other. Tonight she'd worn a navy dress, clingy but sedate, and higher heels so that he almost didn't have to look down to peer into her luminous, hungry green eyes. "I've wanted…"

The kiss came suddenly. Hotly. Wetly. Carol had to simply lean forward and, blam, their lips pressed against one another. He froze in reply, panicking and grunting and, God love him, pushing her away. Her eyes were wide, first with desire then, suddenly, with shock.

"Oh." It was all she said. Maybe even all she *could* say. Their eyes met for a moment, his wide as well. Then she turned, abruptly.

"Carol!" he called after her, his voice tight. Her steps were hurried as she snatched up her work valise and clattered across the drab storage shed concrete floor.

"No," she cried, turning just outside the entrance. "Please, don't..."

"Don't what?" Gabe cried, voice still cracking. "I'm sorry, I didn't mean—"

"Me either," she interrupted as he struggled to explain, their voices melding one over the other in the tidal wave of excuses that followed.

"I didn't—"

"I shouldn't have—"

"Yes, you should have—"

"No, please, just—"

Gabe was tempted to laugh, the scene was so ridiculous—him lingering just inside the storage shed as if separated by some unseen force field and Carol, radiant and flustered, standing just beyond. Behind her, Bald Mountain once again glowed majestically in the half-moonlight, stars winking high above. But all he could see was the pain, the embarrassment, the betrayal splashed across her flushed face.

"Carol, I..." He took a step forward but she stopped him with a firm hand, the handle of her valise dangling from the crook in her elbow.

"Gabe, honestly, I get it."

"You can't possibly," he insisted, following her anyway. "I don't even get it. I've wanted that so long and now?"

"Now I've ruined it." Her voice was miserable, a faint hum just above the clattering of her sensible work heels as she escaped to her fancy car.

"No, Carol, I did!"

She whipped open her door. "Just, please, it's embarrassing enough."

"Carol, I—" The slamming door cut off his words and, in moments, she'd backed out of the space and paused. His heart soared as she rolled down the driver's-side window.

"The clothes," she said, all business again.

Gabe marveled at the transformation, taking an involuntary step back. "Yes?"

"They're yours, for tomorrow." Her voice was firm, her eyes blank with an emotion he couldn't quite recognize. "What time again?" she blurted before he had time to respond.

"Seven," he replied. "I thought we'd meet at Soft Swerve a little early to rehearse and warm up since the courtyard's right there?"

Carol nodded, the window going up so fast he was just getting used to his own shocked reflection when her car leapt forward, speeding from the parking lot as quickly as her lips had found his.

He sagged against the work van, heart still racing and the warm, fragrant taste of her still lingering on his lips. "Jesus," he said aloud, struggling for words in the wake of his utter, ridiculous, sheer stupidity. "Jesus."

Chapter Thirty-Seven

Carol

"How much extra credit is it worth, exactly?"

Carol kept her voice steady, calm, as if in sharp contrast to the runny-nosed, sniffling, obviously crying caller on the other end of the line. "Like," the young woman on the other end of the Homework Helpers hotline gasped, "a lot!"

Carol stifled a knowing smile. "Okay," she crooned as she'd been trained weeks earlier in the intensive weekend course headed by the recruiting team at Homework Helpers. "Take a breath," she urged, struggling not to sound maternal. "We're going to get through this. Together."

The voice that replied was barely above a squeak. "P-p-promise?"

Carol put a hand over the mouthpiece of her high-tech headset as if it was a video call. Clenching her teeth, she counted to ten — well, she only made it as far as seven—before nodding. "Of course," she promised patiently. "Of course we are. Now, first things first, are you comfortable sharing your name?"

"Astrid," the faint whisper on the other end of the line replied.

Carol nodded. Of course she'd be named Astrid. "Okay, Astrid," she said smoothly in reply. "Well, I'm Carol and I'm a supervisor here at Homework Helpers—"

"Is it that bad?" Astrid interrupted in a woeful tone suitable for most telenovelas.

"Is what that bad, dear?"

"My case?" Astrid cried so pathetically Carol could almost picture the pile of balled-up tissues lying at her feet.

"Of course not," Carol assured her, glancing across the rows of empty cubicles to find Rome grinning at her from his corner office doorway. In his ear was a winking earbud so he could listen along and, if necessary, join in. "Why would you say that?"

"I mean, they assigned me to a *supervisor*?"

Carol stifled a sudden snort before forcing herself to remember a time when she, too, had been nineteen, overcome with emotions over something that seemed so very important at the time but now, years later, couldn't have mattered less. "No, no," she assured poor, dramatic, wispy, weepy Astrid. "It's just that, as finals wind down, we're staffing fewer Homework Helpers so I'm the lucky one manning the phones today."

"Oh." Astrid was back to being all business, her once-weepy voice now blunt and brittle. "Okay, well, about my extra credit?"

"I'm struggling to find the problem," Carol said, which was putting it mildly.

"Uh..." Astrid's weepiness took a backseat to her entitled haughtiness. "As I've explained, I can't very well stay and earn extra credit when I've got a ski trip planned with my girlies!"

Carol shot Rome a side-eye that would have melted most mortal beings. They'd tossed a coin to see which one of them would take the call, and obviously she'd lost. In more ways than one, apparently. "Unfortunately, Astrid," Carol cautioned in a steady tone, "sometimes to get the things we need, we have to sacrifice the things we *want*."

"But this is a need," Astrid insisted.

"Of course it is." Carol misunderstood. "If you need this extra credit to pass your humanities course, well, you'll just have to — "

"No!" Astrid wailed. "I *need* this ski trip! Badly!"

This time Carol made it all the way to ten. "Astrid, I need you to put on your big-girl panties and stick with me on this one. You called tonight because you wanted advice, correct?"

There was a pause on the other end of the line that sounded very much like a large land mammal jettisoning its snout. Shortly afterward, a sniveling Astrid replied meekly, "Obviously."

"Well then, my advice to you is to start doing that extra-credit project the minute you get off this call and when it's done and turned in, and only when it's done and turned in, maybe you'll still have time to plan a ski trip with your BFFs."

"But it's already planned!" Astrid's voice was suddenly back to sounding stringent, bossy and, Carol sensed, unwavering.

Carol recalled her training and engaged in what the company called a "temporary tune-out," letting Astrid vent as she struggled to find keywords in the following diatribe to assist her.

"I assume your assignment was *also* planned, am I right?" Carol interjected at last.

"Who plans an assignment during prime ski season?" Astrid whined as they began a quick back-and-forth that was far too trying, considering its brevity. But when all Carol had to offer was advice — firm but fair advice — Astrid huffed "I thought you were a supervisor," and promptly hung up!

Carol sat, stunned, listening to the drone of the dial tone in her headset. She pinched the handy little switch midway down her throat to silence it, but even then, it echoed in her ears. Much the same way Gabe's protests had the night before.

She exhaled, slid the headset free and stood, arching her back as the pressure of the day rested there, coiled and angry, like the tightly coiled ball in her stomach.

"You owe me one," she said, wagging a playful finger as Rome joined her on their well-worn path to the employee breakroom, where a lukewarm cup of shitty coffee was all but screaming her name.

"Me?" Rome was frisky, his holiday garb radiant in its vibrant hues of green and flashy red. "I've got to cover for you all night, missy!"

"Not all night," Carol reminded him gratefully. "Just until nine."

"Yeah, well, alone in this place?" Rome shivered beneath his shimmering suit jacket. "It's gonna feel like all night."

"You sure you don't mind?"

Rome loosened his green-and-red-striped tie a smidge and smiled warmly. "Not a bit." She handed him a cup of coffee before swiping her ID badge across the pay screen for a second cup. "Especially now."

Carol nodded in commiseration, even though her mind was ten thousand miles away. "Hard to believe the mall canceled your gig tonight."

Rome nodded above his bland paper cup of coffee. "Reggie was *so* pissed," he exclaimed with the same kind of schadenfreude she'd felt when hearing the news. "Naturally he tried to find a backup gig, but every other venue in town was booked, so now we're sitting idle on the first Saturday night of winter break."

Carol rolled her eyes. "You don't have to be, Rome. He could volunteer at a dozen or more worthy places who would love to hear you guys. Places you don't have to 'book' but can just show up, stroll around, sing and make people happy. Isn't that why we do this in the first place?"

"Who, Reggie?" Rome clucked his tongue and crept past her to snag a holiday snack cake — or two — from the vending machine just to her right. "Volunteer? At some lowkey apartment complex or student center? That greedy so-and-so?"

"Still, a whole Saturday night sitting on the sidelines? What a waste."

He held his ID badge high, waiting for her to make a choice. She waved a hand in denial, too nervous to eat for far too many reasons to explain. Rome shrugged and swiped it anyway, snatching another snack cake for himself. "Too bad I'm stuck here," he teased, drifting back to their favorite table in the breakroom corner. "Or I'd come see your big debut."

Carol slumped into the chair across from him, the hot coffee doing little to revive her cold feet. "If it even happens, that is."

Rome paused, a frosted gingerbread cookie halfway to his adoring lips. "What? Why?"

"Oh, Rome." Carol's voice cracked. She shook her head as it dipped nearly to the surface of the trendy hi-top table between them. "I screwed up. So bad."

"How?" Rome sounded doubtful. "How could you, of all people, screw up?"

"I kissed him," she blurted.

Rome literally sat back on his stool. "First?"

"Right?"

He struggled to backtrack. "No, I just mean, I thought you were playing hard to get."

"Yeah, well, I stupidly had him change in front of me and the minute I saw that stretchy young taffy-ass body of his, I couldn't help myself."

Rome swallowed audibly, shifting uncomfortably in his seat. "Damn, girl, you sure have a way with words."

She sighed. "Trust me, boss, words can't begin to describe the bountiful pleasures of that boy's body."

"Damn, okay!" Rome held his hands up in mock surrender. "Stop before my snack cake melts!"

"I'm just saying, I literally couldn't help myself."

Rome scoffed. "I just listened to you handle some hysterical prep school debutante with aplomb and grace, you're telling me you couldn't keep your hands off your little boy toy until after the holidays?"

"Guess not," she admitted glumly. And even now? After a sleepless night of regret and worry? The very thought of Gabe's lean, taut torso and soft, pale skin had her wriggling subconsciously in her seat. She knew, in a hot minute, she'd do it all over again.

Consequences be damned.

Unaware of the sudden rush of her unwelcome libido, Rome washed down his first snack cake with an impatient slurp of vending machine coffee. "Back up, back up," he insisted. "You kissed him, but...I'm still not getting how that ruined everything?"

"He pushed me away," Carol admitted, struggling to say the words out loud.

Rome wasn't having it. "Is that how you *remember* it?" he cautioned. "Or is that what really happened?"

"Does it matter?" Carol hemmed, still struggling to put the pieces together all these hours later.

"It does if I'm going to help you salvage this situation, yes. It matters a great deal."

"Trust me, Rome, I'm beyond help."

Rome tore at the wrapper of his second chocolate-frosted, sprinkle-covered, evergreen-shaped snack cake. "You're not beyond help, Carol, you're just...beyond stressed, that's all."

"How so?"

"You're not interpreting the signs accurately." His tone was clinical, even as his eyes bugged out comically over the XXL-sized holiday treat.

"Pretty easy to interpret being cock-blocked after our very first kiss, Rome."

He chuckled at last. "Sure, I get it, but here's my take, for what it's worth—the dude started a caroling troupe for you. *For* you. He's been giving you free ice cream for nearly two weeks. Created whole-ass imaginary extended business hours just to accommodate your wonky-ass work schedule. For who? For you. He's totally into you. Maybe he just has his reasons for spurning your advances last night, in particular."

"Like what?"

Rome shrugged, too polite to talk with his mouth full. Or, perhaps, too focused on his sugar rush to concentrate on little old her. Eventually, as Carol sipped her coffee and counted the moments until she could see Gabe again, he spoke. "Dude's got a business to run, right?" he pointed out. "All by himself, from the sounds of it."

"Yeah, but he makes it look so easy."

"I doubt it is," Rome harumphed, glancing past the trendy breakroom doorway to the hallway just beyond. "Just running this one place is stressful enough, even with a whip-smart partner like you by my side. And he's got, what did you say, three of them around town? Then go and add starting up a new caroling troupe on top of that? No wonder the poor guy was too pooped to pop!"

Carol rolled her eyes. "What are you, his hype man?"

Rome guffawed at the sudden shift in tone. "Hardly, Carol. I'm on your side, obviously. I just think...you're busy, too. New town. New job. New man?"

"We were talking about *him*, remember?"

"Maybe he's just nervous about tonight," Rome pointed out. "Dude's been a part of the second-best caroling troupe in town since forever, to hear you tell it. Suddenly he's branching out on his own. New songs, new 'fit, new partner..." He let one cocked eyebrow be his punctuation mark.

Carol sighed, sagged and relented. Slightly. "Fine, I just...I've never thrown myself at a guy before. Let me have one day to do the mental walk of shame, okay?"

Rome's sudden bark of laughter was warm. And surprisingly comforting. "A kiss is hardly throwing yourself at the guy, sheesh."

"Felt like it at the time, okay?" Carol crossed her arms over her sensible work jacket, slumping back in her chair like a petulant child.

Rome noticed. "Listen, don't take this the wrong way but...right now? You're acting a little like Astrid."

Carol leapt forward, wagging a playful finger. "You take that back!"

Rome played along, hands up in mock surrender. "What I meant was, you were clearly a far cry from where she was. Objective. Calm. Rational. Reasonable. That stupid ski trip meant everything to that girl and you tried to get her to focus on reality."

"A fat lot of good that did either of us."

"Well, right now I'm trying to show you that throwing yourself at a half-naked man half your age on the eve of your caroling debut isn't necessarily the end of the world, either."

"He's not half my age!" She pouted, very Astrid-like. "And I know you're right, it just...feels like it, that's all."

Rome was gently patting the top of her hand when his blinking earpiece went off, signaling a fresh call to the Homework Helpers hotline. "My turn," he said, standing abruptly.

"No." She sighed, sliding her own headset from around her neck and into place against one ear. "I owe you another one for that pep talk, boss."

Rome snickered, giddily hoisting his ID badge high as he slid back toward the vending machine in his camel-colored dress shoes. "Deal!" he cried as she accepted the fresh call, wishing a simple snack cake could cure all her ills the way it seemed to cure Rome's.

Chapter Thirty-Eight

Gabe

"Think she'll show?"

Jalise bided her time between stocking the new holiday waffle cone bowls behind the sales counter—now with fresh candy cane sprinkles!—and admonishing Gabe as he struggled into his new duds.

"Hell if I know," he grunted, sliding one arm into the cream-colored track jacket Carol had so thoughtfully bought for him. For them, obviously, but still. It fit perfectly—no surprise there. Carol was nothing if not a stickler for details, probably measuring his jacket size with some digital fashion app on her phone when he wasn't looking.

"Nice," Jalise murmured, admiring the chocolate-brown stripes down the sleeve. "She's got good taste. I'll give her that."

Gabe paused, hand half shoved in the crinkly brown gift bag from Slick's Sporting Goods that Carol had left behind in the storage shed the night before. "Wait, are you talking about the track jacket? Or me?"

Jalise rolled her eyes. "Gross," she said, turning so he could change into the matching track pants. These were brown, the same chocolate color as the stripes on his sleeve, and bearing cream racing stripes down each leg. "Damn," he marveled, sliding them on for another perfect fit. "She's good."

Jalise smirked, revealing she'd been gawking the whole time. "Just not good enough to kiss, huh?"

"Ja-*lise*!" Gabe spat, ducking his head out of the breakroom to make sure the dining room was still empty. "I told you that in confidence."

Jalise was wholly unrepentant. "Yeah, and…I told you not to, so there."

"Come on, man," Gabe whined, polishing off his Hot-Cocoa-inspired outfit with a pair of mismatched chocolate and cream socks before stumbling back into his sneakers. "This is bad enough."

"You just got cold feet," she assured him for the umpteenth time, her tone implying she was as tired of saying it as he was of hearing it. "I'm sure she'll understand."

"You didn't see her last night." Gabe groaned, emerging from the breakroom in his full Hot Cocoa regalia. Well, minus a few finishing touches he was hoping to spring on Carol any moment now. "She most definitely did *not* understand."

Jalise considered this with a grim nod. "Yeah, it's never much fun being shot down, but personally? It always makes me try harder the next time, if only to prove to myself that it had nothing to do with me."

Through the windows fronting Soft Swerve, Gabe saw headlights cruising into the same spot Carol used most nights. "Ugh," was his most unusual response.

Naturally, Jalise's was quite the opposite. "Sweet," she crooned, admiring Carol stepping from the driver's seat. "Break time for Mama!"

She sped from the store, making Gabe wonder if it was just to visit her favorite food truck in the galleria courtyard or to avoid the potential fireworks to come. Gabe leaned on the sales counter as casually as possible, as if to stay standing, admiring the way Carol's matching tracksuit hugged the very curves he could have had beneath his grubby little paws the night before.

Gabe swallowed one last time before Carol swung wide the ice cream parlor door. "Well," she announced diplomatically, "he's smiling. I hope that's a good sign?"

Gabe's whole body flooded with relief. "Well," he teased back, "she's speaking to me. I hope *that's* a good sign?"

She inched closer, gaze subtly — but far from racily — appraising his new outfit. "They fit," she said, ignoring his over-enthusiastic reply and getting straight down to business.

Naturally, Gabe wondered what *that* might mean.

"I love them," he sang.

She frowned. "Yeah? I wasn't sure and, well...we didn't quite have time to discuss it last night."

"About that—"

She silenced him with a very boss-bitch hand-wave. "I can't apologize any more, Gabe, except maybe to say this one last time. I'm sorry. It won't happen again."

"Like hell it won't."

Carol paused on her way to the breakroom. "Beg your pardon?"

"You heard me." Gabe was back on solid ground again, on his home turf and fighting for whatever it was they still had together—that fragile thing he'd almost torn apart the night before but that, somehow, still stubbornly held on for dear life.

"Like hell *what* won't?" She tossed the question over her shoulder, adjourning to the breakroom as if she owned the place. He followed her, he supposed, as if she did, too.

"It *will* happen again," Gabe insisted, tempted to slam the breakroom door shut and ravish her right then and there. "Over and over and over again. That is, if I have anything to do with it."

"Gabe, honestly." Carol had the same tone as Jalise, making him wonder if he was the problem after all. "It was stupid of me. I'm sorry. Again. I just—"

"It wasn't stupid," he insisted. "I just..."

"Bad timing." Carol harumphed, as if reading his mind. "I get it."

"No, you really don't," Gabe insisted desperately, as if his very life depended on it. "It's not *just* bad timing. I just...want things to be right, just right, for when...it happens again."

Carol huffed, putting her hands on her generous hips and jutting out her chin. "More 'just right' than me ogling your half-naked body and trying to jump your bones in a deserted storage space with no one around for miles?"

"No," he insisted. "Yes, I mean, maybe, I just... I panicked, that's all. I mean, how else do you react when the woman of your dreams makes the first move?"

"I dunno, Gabe," Carol huffed, sliding her valise off her arm and onto the breakroom table next to a half-empty box of stale donuts Gabe had brought in for Jalise earlier that day. "By making the *second* move?"

"I will," he said, voice cracking as if he had just reached puberty, and wasn't just acting like it. "I was just hoping to get through the holidays and then..."

Carol rolled her eyes. "Look, pal, if you can last that long, great. I shot my shot, and now I remember why I don't do that type of thing anymore."

"Anymore?"

Carol started to speak, perhaps to explain, then clearly thought better of it. She closed her eyes instead, pinched her thumb and pinky together as if she'd just arrived at a yoga retreat and literally counted to ten. Not out loud, but Gabe could read lips. Kind of.

When she opened her eyes, Carol's smile was wide but insincere, not quite reaching her cool-for-a-change green eyes. "Look, this is a good thing we're doing. You, me, here, tonight. Hot Cocoa, I mean. I'm proud of it, I'm grateful for it and believe me, Gabe? The last thing I want to do is screw it up. So, let's get past last night, go out there in our poppin' new 'fits and blow the doors off Birchwood's caroling scene, okay?"

Gabe sagged with relief. "Fine, yes, thank you!"

Carol watched him carefully, as if waiting for more. Instead of giving it to her, he handed over the contents of one last bag instead. "Listen, the suits are great, I love the fit and the vibe, I just thought..."

"So cute!" Carol finished for him, snatching one of the brown and cream striped scarves from his hand before he could finish. "I love it!"

"Yeah? I mean, I thought no matter what you'd chosen for us, it would still match, right?"

She ignored him, twirling the scarf elegantly around her throat until the ends fell majestically across her pert breasts. Gabe swallowed audibly, the sound amplified in the small breakroom. She noticed. "See something you like?" she teased, twirling the tassels at the end of one side of her scarf provocatively.

"Carol, I…"

She ruffled the stubbly hair atop his head playfully. "Just kidding, kid. Come on, we've got a gig to perform and, well…no complications tonight, right?"

He nodded eagerly. "That's all I was trying to say."

"I know, Gabe."

"I just…I want it like it was before."

"Before last night?"

He nodded. She frowned. "I can't…can't take it back, Gabe."

"I don't want you to," he insisted.

"Then why—" Carol started to ask when, suddenly, he kissed her. Hard, fast, gentle, soft, slow and just about everything in between. She made a kind of awkward, desperate, helpless sound then gently pushed him away.

"The hell?" Her tone might have been harsh but her eyes were warm, her lips bruised and parted, her hands clinging desperately to his chest even as she struggled to distance herself from the impromptu lip-lock.

"Now we're even?"

An awkward silence of approximately two point seven seconds followed before they both broke into nervous, perhaps even relieved laughter. Gradually they drifted apart, gazes dancing around the room as they patted their pockets and Gabe reached for the door. "So, ready for this?"

Carol chuckled, inching closer as they paused. "Not at all. You?"

He resisted the urge to kiss her again. Sadly, so did she. "Not even one bit," he promised conspiratorially, shoving the door wide and inching past the sales counter. "But if I'm going to do it, there's no one I'd rather do it with than you."

For once, Carol's eyes were more vulnerable than confident. "You mean that?"

"Every word," he insisted, reaching out to hold the door open for her. Across from Soft Swerve, Jalise sat on a bench, munching a corn dog and nodding as he signaled break time was nearly over.

She stood, tossing the empty corndog wrapper in a trash can by the bench. Shuffling closer, she gave them each a good once-over as Gabe and Carol tugged at their zippers and straightened their hems.

"So? Waddya think?" Gabe asked nervously, even a tad impatiently.

Jalise winked at each of them in turn. "Well, I was gonna say 'Hot Damn,' but instead I'll just say...Hot *Cocoa*!"

They shared nervous chuckles all around, perhaps each for different reasons. "Seriously, though," Jalise said, taking the door from Gabe and shooing them forward like an overbearing mother on prom night. She propped it open, leaning in the doorway as she nodded at the small crowd assembled in the courtyard, waiting for them patiently. "I've been listening to the crowd murmur and the general consensus is that folks in town are curious to see what you two are all about."

"Yeah?" Gabe asked, admiring the crowd nervously. It was bigger than he'd expected, but not quite big enough to inspire awe. At least, not yet. If things went as planned, however, Gabe hoped the crowd would grow larger with each song. Then again, if his worst nightmares came true, the Birchwood Galleria courtyard would be empty after their first song!

Jalise nodded, nudging them forward a little farther. "Now it's time to show them what you've got."

"Don't watch!" Gabe pleaded as Jalise stood by the open door, making it clear she was going to do just that. And probably much more, if he knew her as well as he thought he did.

"What? And miss your big debut? Fat chance. Now…go out there and break a leg!"

Chapter Thirty-Nine

Carol

"What time is it?"

Carol stood beside him, wriggling in anticipation as Gabe whipped the crowd into a near frenzy one last time. She wasn't the only one—around the charming courtyard of the Birchwood Galleria, anchored by a towering Christmas tree, were at least eighty people, maybe even more. The crowd replied enthusiastically.

"Carol time!" they all chanted. "Carol. Time!"

Gabe and Carol shared a knowing, almost triumphant look. They were at the end of their set, hardly believing the crowd's response. Gabe frowned dramatically, proving himself a master ringleader. "Hmmm," he dithered, really hamming it up as Carol egged him on with big, wide eyes. "I was going to say 'bedtime,' but…"

The crowd "booed," playing along as Carol turned the page in one of the twin songbooks she'd printed up at work that afternoon. "Okay, okay," Gabe teased, nudging her with his hip even as he addressed the crowd. "I suppose we have time for just. One. More. Carol!"

Gabe admired the page in front of him for a quick moment before nodding at Carol. Although she lacked the panache of her clearly more extrovert singing partner, she couldn't help but adopt the energy of the assembled crowd.

"Okay, gang," she crowed above the murmurs and mumbling of the holiday revelers gathered before them in the mall's courtyard. "This one's about a tiny little mouse who just happened to be neighbors with...Santa Claus!"

The crowd cheered, eagerly chanting the correct name of the holiday special in question. "Morgan Mouse! Morgan Mouse!"

Gabe chuckled, admiring her performance. "That's right, gang," he chimed in, like the polished host of some after-school kids' program. "And what's the favorite-est, best-est, most singable song from *Morgan Mouse and the Christmas House*?"

"House Party!" the crowd chanted, children and grownups alike already wriggling and some of them even starting to dance in place where they stood. "*Mouse* Party!"

Carol waited for the crowd's enthusiasm to dim, though not entirely, before nodding and waving her songbook dramatically. Dozens of strangers—men, women, young, old, parent, child, brother, sister, grandparent—watched expectantly. "That's right, and for our final song of the evening, we're going to sing...*House Party, Mouse Party!*"

The crowd erupted, primed after over a straight hour of pure, holiday, feel-good, cheesy eighties and nineties Christmas cartoon nostalgia. As they had from their very first song, Gabe and Carol patiently — gratefully — waited out the crowd's mass eruption. Gone were the jitters Carol had suffered as Gabe introduced them some sixty minutes earlier. Gone was that first initial crack in her voice as they'd launched into song, the crowd waiting only moments to recognize the familiar strains of *Penguin Parade* from *Penguin's Polar Christmas* before joining in.

And, to Carol's amazement, they'd never quite stopped. If Gabe and Carol had worried about performing as a duo, they needn't have. They had a whole crowd singing along with them, note for note, word for word, never once having to resort to *Jingle Bells* or *Silent Night* for filler, as they'd once feared that first tentative night of rehearsal.

Indeed, a solid hour of nonstop caroling had flown by in an instant, partially because it had been such an interactive performance. Setups for each song lasted a good long while, Carol and Gabe both egging on the crowd and, in reply, the crowd eating it up. Shouts of "Encore, Encore" had erupted immediately after their first song, then every song thereafter, until finally Gabe and Carol were giving the crowd one last bonus song, saved up just in case.

Though the crowd had never really been silent, at least not after the first few strains of *Penguin Parade*, Gabe recognized when the lull was right and quietly, but confidently, launched into the first line of *House Party, Mouse Party.* "We're having a house party," he sang richly, no longer coy or doubtful about either his voice or the crowd's response. "We're having a mouse party!"

Kids danced, lined up in front of a massive throng of equally giddy parents. "House party," they chanted as Carol joined the fray. "Mouse party!"

Then they quieted just long enough for her to continue alone. "Santa stopped in briefly, just to say hello, while Ralphie Elf showed up to share his favorite lime Jell-O!"

Carol and Gabe grooved together all the while, scarves swinging, sneakers scraping, dancing side to side and hip to hip in their matching Hot Cocoa tracksuits as if to rival the contagious energy of the several dozen kids doing impromptu interpretive dance in front of the towering Christmas tree.

When at last the song was through and Marty Mouse had cleaned up all the punch bowls and Jell-O spoons, the crowd roared its approval one last time. Gabe and Carol grinned at each other before taking a modest bow, and the minute they stood back up, *wham!* Children ran to embrace them as if they were actually Morgan Mouse. Or Marty Mule. Or Buddy Bear or any of the other dozen or so apparently beloved and no-longer-forgotten heroes from a slew of retro Christmas cartoons.

"Oh my," Carol gasped as two little girls hugged her on either side.

"Umph," Gabe grunted as a throng of ten-year-olds nearly bowled him over. "Thank you," he recovered quickly, remembering where he was. "And Merry Christmas!"

One by one the children inched closer, sometimes just to pet their dangling scarves or give a quick high-five, sometimes to bear-hug them into submission. Grateful parents, still jazzed after being thoroughly entertained, lingered just out of range, nodding or clapping or sometimes even mumbling their approval before drifting away, their happy children still dancing and shimmying by their sides while they hummed their favorite tunes until their voices drifted into the night.

The crowd thinned quickly after that, muttering and mumbling and nodding as they passed, until only Carol and Gabe remained, risking one last glance up at the towering Christmas tree before fleeing on tired feet for the relative safety of Soft Swerve.

Chapter Forty

Gabe

"Damn, kids!"

Jalise ushered them both inside, standing at the open door and glancing both ways before shutting it decisively behind them. "Great job!"

Gabe was flushed as he sank into the nearest booth seat, overwhelmed and exhausted from the push and pull of their first live performance together. "Yeah? You think?"

"Do I think?" Jalise retreated to the sales counter, snagging bottles of water for both of them. Carol managed to grab the bottles before she, too, sank into the booth across from Gabe. Jalise continued gushing, "Did you hear that crowd out there tonight? It's what they think that matters and, guys? They loved you!"

"Damn," Carol muttered to herself as the booth seat threatened to swallow her exhausted body whole. "Damn."

"Right?" Gabe almost whispered, voice raw from commanding the crowd for over an hour. He'd always been the passenger to Jasmine's expert crowd control before, but hadn't realized how much he'd learned from her. Or how hard it was!

"On the house," Jalise snickered, placing two waffle cone bowls full of chocolate chip mint and, appropriately enough, hot cocoa swirl in front of them. It was only when she passed out two pink spoons that Gabe noted the backpack slung over one shoulder.

"Leaving so soon?" he teased, although sitting with Carol, alone for a few quiet moments, was exactly what Gabe had been looking forward to the minute their debut performance had ended.

"Wasn't that the deal?" she sassed him back. "I cover for you and now...you cover for me?"

"Obviously." Gabe exhaled, nearly halfway through his water bottle already. "And thanks for the snacks!"

"Indeed," Carol chimed in, even though Jalise was halfway through the door already. "Thanks?" But her last word had fallen on deaf ears. Jalise was already hopping onto her motorcycle and blasting off for parts unknown.

"Don't take it personally," Gabe warned, waving his spoon wearily. Damn, but wasn't he pooped after that performance! "This whole caroling thing and covering for me really eats into her social life."

"Same with my boss." Carol sighed, swiping her familiar pink spoon through the soft-serve swirls and lapping at it eagerly as she savored the sweet, creamy treat. "I'm lucky enough that a Victorian Voices gig got canceled tonight or I might have had to work."

"Victorian Voices? Dropped from a gig?" Gabe could hardly believe his ears.

Carol nodded, her lips delectably pink and creamy from the holiday-inspired soft serve. "First cancellation I can remember — not that I was with them very long."

"Well, I was with their direct competition for years," Gabe recalled. "And we were both booked solid every night straight through to the Jingle Jangle."

Carol shrugged, making quick work of her frozen dairy treat. "Maybe the whole town's gotten sick of Reggie's shtick, huh?"

"It'd be too good to be true," Gabe cautioned, knowing full well Reginald Archibald the Third's stranglehold on local caroling festivities. "Probably just a scheduling conflict."

"Speaking of..." Carol was down to nibbling her waffle bowl now, little bites between sips of bottled water. "When are we up next?"

"Tomorrow if you can swing it?" Gabe offered. "I'm calling in favors with each of my store locations and so far they've all been on board. I don't want to jinx it, but...after tonight's success? I dare say other businesses will be eager to book us, too."

Carol nodded distractedly. "All good?" he asked, glad for the peaceful moment after last night's debacle and the boisterous live performance they'd both just given.

"Sure, fine, I just...is the time fixed?"

Gabe shrugged. "I mean, we didn't move much from where we started tonight but we're supposed to be strolling carolers, so a fixed time isn't necessarily a deal breaker. Why, what were you thinking?"

Carol's gaze flitted back to him, fixing him as a jolt of desire swept through his already wired body. "Nothing, I just think my boss is performing later in the evening so if we could do it sooner?"

"Not a problem," Gabe assured her. "We're just strolling at the outdoor mall where my second Soft Swerve is located. It's not as big or centrally located as this one, so chances are it will be a little less, uh…intense than tonight?"

"Intense is right," Carol gushed, pushing her empty bowl away as she wriggled to get more comfortable in the seat across from him. "I had high hopes, tentatively speaking. A few dozen people, some polite applause, folks sticking around until the last carol just to be polite. To me, that would have been a successful debut. But tonight? That crowd? Those kids? Wow, just…wow."

"Same," Gabe agreed, adding his half-eaten cone to her stack of leftovers. He somehow stood up from the booth they were sharing, not knowing where he'd found the energy, to close up shop early, locking the door, switching the "Open" sign to "Closed" and dimming the lights until, once again, they sat in neon silence, Carol's beautiful face bathed in the unnatural colors of a bygone era.

"Not up for the late-night rush tonight?" she mused, seeming to relax all the more now that the door was locked. Or maybe he was just imagining things, as usual.

"I think I've had enough rush for one night, don't you?"

"I still have to relieve my boss after this," she grumbled—a first, since Carol was always so positive about her job.

"Blech."

She nodded before she insisted, "Yeah, but it's only fair, though."

"It won't be forever," he promised, tempted to reach over and place his hands over hers.

"I'm not complaining, really," she admitted breathlessly with all the enthusiasm of a teammate after a big win. "I just... That really drained me back there, you know?"

Gabe grinned and slid his sneaker alongside hers, admiring the way she leapt at the sudden contact. "I bet," he teased. "I couldn't imagine expending all that energy at your, uh...advanced age!"

"You little shit!" She tossed a balled-up napkin at him, clearly enjoying the late-night banter after last night's miserable stage exit. "I was singing circles around you back there."

They both chuckled, Gabe admiring the way her track jacket had opened to reveal those pert, perfect breasts beneath the clingy cotton of her Hot Cocoa T-shirt.

"Probably because you skipped a bra tonight," he chided.

For once, she didn't deny it. Or, for that matter, put up much of a fight. "It's a little snug," she pointed out, her nipples replying wordlessly as they joked about her apparent lack of undergarments. "No room."

"I'd ask Jalise to make you a bigger size," he offered, voice growing low to match the tense ball of desire forming in his throat, "but where's the fun in that?"

Carol met his gaze and let it linger there, warming him from the inside out and back again. "I'll admit it *is* fun," she confessed, all joking aside, "being ogled by some gangly boy toy."

"You didn't think I was so gangly last night," he reminded her, voice thick with the implications.

She merely nodded. "Did you enjoy it?" she asked with another jut of her chin, the bold move undercut by the insecurity in her gaze. "Being ogled, I mean?"

Gabe beamed in reply, nodding. "You make me feel sexy," he confided. "Of course I dig it."

"Surely I'm not the first woman to ogle you?"

Gabe shook his head. "No, I've had my share but also? Not for a while now."

Carol frowned dubiously. "Define a while."

"Years."

She rolled her eyes. "Oh. Bull. Shit."

"I'm serious!" Gabe insisted, hardly believing that this was what they were talking about instead of, say, an appreciation of the show they'd just put on for nearly a hundred giddy audience members.

Chapter Forty-One

Carol

"You're telling me you haven't, uh, you know? In years?"

Gabe nodded, looking for all the world like some hipster record label owner in his comfy tracksuit and retro T-shirt combo, the neon lights casting intense shadows across his lean, hungry face. She made a mental note to ask Jalise to make him a trucker cap with the Hot Cocoa logo to complete the 'fit.

"That's *exactly* what I'm saying," he insisted so earnestly Carol had no reason to doubt it.

Yet, for obvious reasons, she still called BS.

As if to prove it, Carol sat back and crossed her arms over her own costumed chest. "I don't buy it."

"Why do you think I got so freaked out last night?" Gabe insisted sheepishly. "I thought I'd never get laid again."

"You weren't getting laid, Jesus," Carol lied. Out loud. And easily, to boot. "It was just a kiss."

"Shit." Gabe wasn't having it, either. "I saw you scoping me out. Those were definitely 'I'm getting laid tonight' eyes, be honest."

She snorted self-consciously, giving him little more than a quick nod to confirm his suspicions. "Yeah, well, you think I'd be that obvious if I'd been getting it on the regular myself these last few years?"

Gabe's eyes widened magnificently. "Okay, well...that's a mouthful."

"You have no idea," she muttered, hardly believing how quickly their sweet, innocent, childlike night of Christmas caroling had devolved into dirty talk so steamy it could melt soft-serve ice cream at a glance.

"Why, how long's it been for you?" Gabe's eyes were probing, but also vulnerable.

"Same as you, bud," she said without getting specific. After all, why should she take first prize in their sudden "Who's Got the Most Pathetic Sex Life" competition?

"You don't know that," he bluffed. "All I said was years. That could mean two."

"Does it?"

"No."

"So what *does* it mean, Gabe? I need a number here. Firm, hard facts before I divulge any further information."

"Two and a half," he blurted, blushing all the while. "But it feels like ten."

"What the hell is wrong with you?" she clapped back. "I mean, unless this is some parallel universe, you should be beating girls off with a stick."

Gabe seemed as nonplussed as ever. "I mean, I'm a townie. Plain and simple. Grew up here, never left. Everyone else I knew did. Off to college, or the military or to some job as far away from stuffy little Birchwood as they could get. The chicks who are still here are either too young or…"

"Too old?" she finished for him, the quick taste of acid on her tongue.

He smiled back at her like a parent dealing with a toddler's unruly tantrum. "I was going to say 'not my type,' but…"

"What a waste," she moaned, feeling it all the way to her coiled gut. *Why, oh why, are we still talking about this instead of doing something about it?*

"Why, what's your number?"

"Four years," she confessed before she could give herself a good reason to lie.

This time Gabe's shock and awe were all too real. "Damn, talk about a waste. I mean, for the love of God, why?"

"Until the call center job here in Birchwood," she explained, giving him the sanitized version, "I was always working in university settings. Older professors, middle-aged administrators who were straight-up leches or frat-boy types who weren't much better. Take your pick. Hard to find an in-between in that environment, I suppose."

"And now?"

"Now what?"

"Now, suddenly, you're willing to give it a try?"

"Only with you," she confessed, glancing out through the window at her silent car and knowing she should have left minutes ago.

He nodded. Smiled. "Same."

At last, he reached a hand over to join hers. She let him clasp the top of hers for a moment, maybe two, then stiffened and pulled away. "Hey," he protested, making her instantly regret it. "What gives?"

Carol stood, using whatever willpower she had left to extricate herself from his long, rangy, easy temptation. "Last night wasn't just because you were startled," she pressed him. "Face it, neither of us is ready to jump into this thing or we would have already, right?"

Gabe joined her on his feet, unfolding to his full height and peering down at her as they stood beside the silent booth. "Can I help it if I'm shy?"

"Don't change a thing," she said, cupping his face in one trembling hand. "Ever. But for now? At least until the Jingle Jangle is over? I think it's best if we...stay friends."

Gabe groaned, bending over at the waist. "God, I'm so stupid!"

"You're not," she insisted even as she strode for the door, not entirely opposed to giving him a taste of his own medicine after the way he'd cock-blocked her the night before.

"I am," he groaned, the sound of a frustrated teen stood up on prom night with a head full of fantasies and a pocket full of condoms. "So stupid. We could be doing this already if I wasn't such a chicken shit."

She paused at the door, by now all too familiar with locking and unlocking it all on her own. "Honestly, Gabe?" she admitted, swinging it open. "If you weren't such a chicken shit, I wouldn't have put myself out there in the first place. So keep being you, and one day will be the right day, okay?"

Gabe followed her to the door. "Or night?" he offered.

She paused halfway to her car, admiring the sight of him in the dimly lit neon of his closed ice cream parlor. So sweet and sexy and kind and gentle and patient, and joyfully, unexpectedly...weird. She'd always had a type and, though he was definitely not that, Gabe made her realize she'd been going about it all wrong this whole time.

"Or afternoon," she teased back, struggling to keep the croak out of her voice as she hurried to the car, slid inside and purposefully drove the hell away. "Or morning..." she purred to herself, blasting through a yellow light to make it back to the office on time.

Chapter Forty-Two

Gabe

"I thought we'd settled on our playlist already?"

Carol stood, casually dressed, breezy for a Thursday, hands on her hips and head cocked in that questioning way of hers.

How well I know her by now, Gabe thought. *And how little I know her at all.*

"We have, for sure, and folks are digging it, but with the Jingle Jangle this Saturday, I wanted to have at least one new number up our sleeve that absolutely no one in town has ever heard before."

Carol was nervous — he could tell. Despite all they'd achieved together since that very first performance, the closer they got to the big competition, the more uncertain she became.

"Makes sense," she said, taking another pull from the blue-and-white-striped straw dug deep inside her Burger Barn to-go cup. "Can't imagine there's a childhood song we haven't plundered yet, but if anyone could find it, it'd be you I suppose."

Gabe brightened, turning his back to her as she snatched another fry from the greasy takeout bag beside her. It had been his turn to grab the food for rehearsal and while he'd planned on something a little more appetizing, a hitch in the new software upgrade at store number three had taken longer than he'd thought. So Burger Barn it was. Thus far, Carol wasn't complaining.

Calling up the same video feed as the one that had been playing all week in his Soft Swerve stores, Gabe turned his laptop toward Carol. "Where's that been hiding?" she asked, nibbling on a brisket slider that left a slick, sexy sheen on her lips.

He glanced at the rolling desk and the basic silver laptop propped open atop it. "I use it for ordering online after I do my inventory every week," he explained. "It's easier than doing it at the store with a million interruptions."

She was sitting on the edge of the same stack of extra tile boxes he usually chose, looking breezy and radiant in a pollen-yellow sundress under an open sweater of lily white. Her hair was back, as ever, but less severely than when she wore it to work. At the moment, she was glancing out through the open storage shed door, the mid-afternoon sky radiant and sun-kissed for this time of year.

"It is peaceful here." She exhaled, as if enjoying a rare moment of solitude in her hectic day-to-day life. He kept reminding her it wouldn't always be so busy, work and caroling, rehearsing and work, lather, rinse, repeat, but at the moment he surely felt the same as she did—grateful for a break from the grind and eager to enjoy it for as long as he could.

"I could have chosen a storage space more central to all three stores," he explained as she turned her attention back his way. "But it's worth the extra drive out here for the peace and quiet. And the view."

"I bet." She sighed, more relaxed than he'd seen her in days. "Have you ever been up it?" She waved her Burger Barn soda cup at Bald Mountain, beckoning as ever through the open garage door.

Gabe shook his head. "I've been meaning to," he explained. "Same way I've been meaning to do so many things over the years."

Carol nodded, sounding a tad wistful herself. "One of the kids at work said there's a ski lodge up there."

"There are a few," he said. "Good ones, too. One even has a brewery."

"Really?"

"And bands," he added. "Big names, sometimes. And not just during winter. They have a summer festival I've been meaning to go to…"

"But never have?" she finished for him, playful as ever, her mood as breezy as the thankfully short hem of her clingy yellow sundress.

"Maybe we'll go sometime," she said cautiously. "After all this, I mean?"

"I'd like that," he said, regarding her more carefully than usual. "I feel like, ever since you got into town, you really haven't seen very much of it."

"You're right there," she huffed. "Work, Soft Swerve and home, that's been about it."

"I haven't even taken you anywhere to eat," he whined, kicking himself for the gross oversight.

She winked and wagged another fry his way. "On the contrary," she teased. "Nothing but the best when it's your turn to bring the vittles."

"I'll do better next time," he insisted. "Promise."

"What next time?" she reminded him. "We're caroling at that tree lighting ceremony at the children's hospital tomorrow and then it's the Jingle Jangle the next day."

"Shit, you're right," Gabe mused with a bittersweet tone. "Where the hell did December go?"

"Straight to my fat ass," Carol spat, seeming to surprise them both. "Thanks to you and your scrumptious pistachio swirl."

Gabe rolled his eyes. "This again?" he grumbled. "You and I have very different definitions of fat."

"Yeah, well, whatever definition you go by, if this keeps up, I'm not going to be able to fit into any of my work clothes."

"If?" Gabe wheeled the rolling laptop cart a little closer, all the better for her to see the warning gaze in his eyes. "It *better* keep up."

She nodded casually. "You know what I mean."

Gabe gave her sensual body an eager once-over. There was nothing fat about her and, even if there had been, he would have loved every sumptuous, feminine inch. He already did, as curvy and womanly as she was, a far cry from the stick-thin cheerleaders he'd thought were the height of beauty back in high school.

"Listen," he assured her, leaning closer to snatch a fry from her Burger Barn bag. "Spring in Birchwood? There's honestly nothing like it. I've got a mountain bike. I ride it to work most days once the weather gets warmer. I could help you pick one out and we could, you know…go riding together?"

Carol's eyelids fluttered almost shyly. "You'd do that?"

"Why do you sound so surprised? Sheesh."

"I'm not, I just..." Her hollow cheeks blushed. "I guess I just can't picture you anywhere other than behind the counter at Soft Swerve, let alone on a mountain bike of all things."

"You're not alone." Gabe chuckled, realizing just how sheltered, sedate and flat-out boring his life had been before Carol had stumbled into it only a few weeks earlier. "And speaking of, I've got to cover for Jalise in half an hour so we should really give this bonus song a whack, if you don't mind?"

Carol stiffened as if having just been called on in class. "Yes, sorry. But first...one more fry?" They laughed together, easy and breezy, sharing the last of her French fries before she joined him in front of the laptop.

"I know this one," she said immediately, based on only the opening credits of *Bunny's Bouncin' Christmas* still frozen on the seventeen-inch monitor when he'd hit the "pause" button earlier. "It's the one with the *Christmas Hop* song!"

"Yes!" They gave each other a little high-five before he un-paused the scene and, right on cue, the *Christmas Hop* song began.

Chapter Forty-Three

Carol

"Hop all day and hop all night..."

Gabe no longer felt shy or uncertain. Indeed, his voice rang out, smooth and assured in the flattering acoustics of his rented storage space. "Hop until the early light!"

"Hop in snow and hop on hay," Carol crooned, joining in for the second verse as Gabe swayed sexily to and fro beside her, occasionally jostling her hip with his own. "Hop until the break of day..."

The sun was warm at her back, easing in through the open storage shed door as the afternoon began in earnest. The company was casual, no longer as hesitant and nervous as they'd been together. The song was easy and breezy, childish and fun, full of giddy little rhymes and even a full-on dance routine full of hopping and hand-jiving that, to Gabe's credit, he'd agreed they could recreate when the time came on the

Jingle Jangle stage and not, thank *God*, during that day's rehearsal.

For now they just sang it, slowly, sweetly, familiarly, Hop the Bunny dancing on the small laptop screen, hopping through Santa's workshop, hopping away from a harmless polar bear, hopping all the way into Santa's big gold bag.

The scene, and the song, ended with the bittersweet chorus they sang sweetly together, their harmony never sounding stronger as they crooned, "Hop hopped until he hopped no more, asleep at Santa's feet. As Santa, tired as he was, sang a lullaby soft and sweet..."

Their voices faded out at the same time. They both were smiling, Carol figured, at their own set of childhood memories. Gabe seemed not overly fond of his growing-up years, and Carol could certainly commiserate in that regard. Still, nothing erased the blemishes of an uncertain youth like the cheery glow of a child's Christmas cartoon, and somehow Hot Cocoa had tapped into the retro-vintage-nostalgia market for what seemed like the whole town of Birchwood.

Carol had feared that maybe their first rousing success back at the Birchwood Galleria earlier that week had merely been a case of beginner's luck. But if anything, the crowds since then had only gotten bigger, more lively and interactive. Between Jalise hyping them up on social media and her cute little "Captain Cocoa" stickers popping up all over town—Carol had even seen one beaming at her from a telephone pole on the way to work earlier that week—the word was out and Hot Cocoa had become, for lack of a better term, a hit. Now all that remained was to win over the judges at the Jingle Jangle and—

"Nice, right?"

Gabe's voice, so soft and encouraging, dragged her back from her pleasant reverie. "I think so." She sighed, tidying up after their greasy but indulgent fast-food lunch. "But will the judges?"

Gabe's pinched expression belied his offhand reply. "Of course they will. How could they not?"

"Your voice says 'yes,'" she called him out. "Your face says 'hell no.'"

Gabe chuckled. "You know me so well." He bundled up his own Burger Barn bag and tossed it in the rapidly filling garbage can by the door. Despite his insistence that he had to cover for Jalise soon, he sank onto the folding chair where she usually sat.

"Be honest." Carol turned to face him, crossing her legs once she'd gotten settled. "What are our chances of winning this year?"

Gabe looked effortlessly edible in a pair of khaki cargo pants and a V-neck T-shirt boasting thick stripes of navy and light blue. They'd both been off today, a rarity for once. Or so she'd thought. But the emergency call from Jalise made it clear a business owner like Gabe, despite his casual college boy dress, was never truly "off."

He crossed his legs as well, swinging one sockless foot buried deep inside a stylish canvas loafer. "I mean, I feel like we've definitely got momentum and the popular vote," Gabe began with the wariness of a boss after calling in an employee for a "little chat."

"But…" Carol finished for him.

"But…the judges are so far up Reggie's ass it's always hard to tell."

"How can that be?" Carol mused. "Far as I can see, Birchwood's a pretty liberal, easygoing place."

"It is," Gabe insisted. "Everywhere but the stupid Jingle Jangle!"

"How? It's a Christmas carol competition."

"In name only," Gabe huffed, crossing his arms over his chest as if to prove it. "But one judge works at the Factory Warehouse with Reggie's mother and the other was in the same fraternity as Reggie's uncle, so…"

"But aren't there three?" Carol seemed to recall reading the phrase "trio of judges" on the Jingle Jangle website at some point.

"Yeah, our only hope is that this year's celebrity guest judge isn't as big a fan of Regency-era BS as the other two."

"How do they pick him? Or her?" Carol sipped her soda absently, feeling like a teen on an after-school date as she wriggled beneath her clingy sundress in the warm, afternoon light. Despite the late December date on the calendar, the day had begun unseasonably warm and had only gotten warmer throughout. Sure, it was still in the high sixties, but after a full week in the mid-fifties, she'd thought a sundress and sweater combo had been a perfect fit. From the way Gabe had been ogling her throughout the day's rehearsal, Carol's instincts must have proved correct.

"Some super-secret spy committee," Gabe scoffed. "It's all kind of rigged but I'm hoping that just showing up and rocking the crowd is enough to make Jazz's head explode."

Carol chuckled wickedly. "And Reggie's," she pointed out. "But I thought this wasn't about revenge, remember?"

"I know, I know, feel-good, kids bopping to and fro, parents reminiscing, yada-yada, but would it kill the karmic universe to let us at least get second place?"

"Why not first?" Carol scolded playfully, the long moments of admiring Gabe's sleek, young body making her belly loose and fragile once more. "That's not very 'Hot Cocoa' of you."

"Listen, no one wants to win Jingle Jangle more than I do," Gabe assured her.

"Uh, I do," Carol clapped back.

"No," he said simply. "You don't."

"What? Why not?"

"This is your *first* Jingle Jangle," he reminded her. "It'll be my, what...fifth? That's a lot of going home empty-handed over the years, so...trust me when I say I'm in it to win it."

Carol smirked, standing as the sun caressed her frustrated body. "Oh, I know the feeling lately," she purred as he followed suit. "Trust *me*."

"You know what I mean," he said, joining her on his feet as they shuffled around the storage shed straightening up.

"I know all too well." She gathered up her cute little backpack purse and slung it over one shoulder. She'd been going for young coed on the prowl, but wasn't quite sure she was pulling it off.

"Your rules, remember?" he reminded her, sliding the accordion garage door shut behind them with a practiced ease. Even so, the simple effort brought forth a welcome flex of the long, sinewy muscles hidden just beneath his shirtsleeves.

"Stupid ones," she agreed, the day off stretching out in front of her like an endless highway on a solo road trip across the country, "I'll admit."

Gabe laughed out loud, patting the side panel of his pink and blue Soft Swerve work van. "Plenty of room back here if you'd care to break it in," he teased, pretending to reach for the side door handle with a leering, if harmless, grin.

"Don't tempt me." She sighed wearily, both of them knowing she was the kind to keep rules rather than break them. Even so, she lingered near her car. She wasn't alone. Gabe lingered, too, leaning back against the side panel of his van as she reclined against her car directly opposite him.

"Thought you had to cover Jalise," she countered with a nod toward his empty driver's seat.

"I do." Gabe made no move to leave as the waning sun caressed his attractive features.

"Aren't you gonna be late?"

"Me?" he huffed, shifting from foot to foot in his very collegiate, very sexy, very distracting outfit. "She's late all the time. Constantly."

"Constantly?" Carol countered suspiciously, arching one eyebrow to plead her case. "From what I can see, she's pretty darn responsible."

Gabe sagged back even harder against his van. "Fine, yes, she's the best assistant manager ever in the whole wide world, but if she could see the way the sun is hitting your face and the way you look in that sundress right now? She wouldn't blame me for not being able to tear myself away from you for five more minutes."

Carol blinked in the soft sunlight, hoping the tears of joy could wait until just a little later. Preferably until *after* she got home. Or at least in her car alone. Her throat taut, she croaked out a tentative, "Wow, Gabe, that...that's just about the nicest thing anybody's said to me."

"Ever?" He wasn't bragging. Poor boy seemed genuinely surprised.

"Yeah, bud. Ever."

"Well, it's true."

She nodded, uncrossed her arms and propelled herself toward him. Landing with a gentle "oof" sound, she slid her arms around his neck and achingly, hungrily, pressed her lips against his. This was not the kiss from earlier that week — tentative, probing, searching. This kiss was commanding, summoning all her years of sexual prowess to unleash an embrace the poor boy might never forget. Then, just as he slid his hands to clasp her trembling waist, just as his lips parted to draw her in, just as his breath surged to form an almost unintelligible grunt, she pulled herself away, licking her own lips before sinking back into her car.

"See you tomorrow, Gabe," she murmured over the sound of blood rushing through her ears and her engine revving to back away and just as quickly speed from the parking lot before she could take him up on his offer of joining him in the back of the stupid pink and blue van!

Chapter Forty-Four

Gabe

"Thanks for coming, by the way."

Jalise got out slowly of the work van, joining him at the front. "What?" she huffed, never one to take things too seriously, least of all where Gabe was concerned. "Like I'm gonna miss this year's battle of the carolers?"

Gabe shot her an appraising glance. "You know, I honestly can't say I've ever seen you at one of these before."

"I never *cared* about one of these before," she insisted, tugging at the hem of her ugly Christmas sweater. It was a little too tight, something she was always self-conscious about. "But seeing Hot Cocoa go up against those pesky Mistle Tones? *And* the frickin' Victorian Voices? All on the same night? I had to be here for this one, boss. Had to be."

Gabe gave her an uncharacteristic, if awkward, hug around the shoulders. "I appreciate it," he mumbled before she pushed him away playfully.

"Don't waste your energy getting all mushy with me," she teased, though even Gabe could see the blush rising to her cheeks and the awkward way she still stood so close to him. "You'll need it for tonight's big showdown."

Gabe swallowed audibly, making a face. "Don't remind me."

"You love all this," she insisted, slugging him on the shoulder as they both turned toward the Birchwood Community Center where, every December twenty-fourth, the Jingle Jangle Competition was held. They'd arrived early, as was Gabe's custom, to warm up and prepare with the other carolers in the dressing rooms backstage.

But for once Gabe lingered near the parking lot, side by side with Jalise as they admired the big Christmas tree out front. "Wow," she said, tugging nervously on the hem of each sleeve of her ill-fitting sweater. She looked so different in "civilian" clothes—Gabe always forgot how young, sweet and pretty she could be. That was, when she wasn't teasing him mercilessly back at work. "I've seen it passing by, but it's way nicer up close and personal."

"And big," Gabe noted.

She gave him an odd look. "What, don't you see it every year?"

"I mean, I usually park in back," he reminded her, jerking a thumb toward the rear of the sprawling, if drab, community center. "But it's nicer this way."

Jalise stepped aside as a family of four jostled by, the little tykes giving Gabe—or, at the very least, his by-now-familiar Hot Cocoa tracksuit—lingering glances before whispering excitedly to their folks. They paused near the giant tree, turning back with embarrassed smiles. "We're rooting for you," the father said, nodding to his family before they all trundled toward the gaily decorated doorway of the sprawling community center.

"See there?" Jalise slugged him again, harder this time. "You guys are a shoe-in."

"Don't jinx it," Gabe hissed, instantly regretting it.

Jalise noticed, scolding him with two arched brows. "Damn, boss. I've never seen you this jumpy before."

"Sorry, I just… We've never really had a chance before, you know?" His voice was heavy, like the lead balloon in the pit of his stomach. "It's almost easier knowing you're going to lose every year."

Jalise nodded as another family hustled by, the kids pointing and giggling at Gabe's tracksuit this time. "Yay!" one said before his mother hushed him, making Gabe wonder if that was a good sign.

Or a bad one?

"True," Jalise conceded between the steady buildup of parking cars, slamming doors and jostling families. "But it should feel good, too. I mean, having a chance is always better than *not* having one, right?"

"I suppose." He sighed. "But *way* more nerve-wracking, that's for sure."

She chuckled, giving him a good once-over. "I can see that," she agreed before tugging him to one side just in time to avoid the flow of busy foot traffic as two, then three more families hustled past in all their green and red holiday finery. "Damn, is it always this busy?"

They glanced toward the parking lot, rapidly filling, with headlights aplenty still lined up at the front entrance, waiting to turn in. There was a sizzle of excitement in the air, and not just because it was the night before Christmas.

"Again," he reminded her, "I usually park in the back, so…"

"Okay, okay," Jalise harumphed. "You and your bad mood can just walk on back there by yourself then."

"No," Gabe whined. "You said you'd walk me in."

"Hell naw," she huffed, nodding at the tree and, beyond it, the line already growing to get in at the front door. "I'm going in with the rest of the early birds before I have to stand in the back all night."

Gabe nodded. "I can't blame you." He gave her an earnest hug this time. "I guess I'm just not very good company tonight."

She hugged him back, even patting him for good measure. "You will be," she teased, dancing out of range before he could have another panic attack. "After you kick everyone's ass in there!"

He was still chuckling as he turned and walked to the left, following the sidewalk past the towering Christmas tree to the side of the building. All the same he lingered, walking slowly as if to dispel the butterflies that had been dancing around inside his fluttering belly all day.

He scuffed the heels of his new tan sneakers, bought special to go with his trendy Hot Cocoa costume. Jalise had been right about one thing — Gabe had never before been quite this nervous about the stupid, totally harmless Jingle Jangle Competition.

Then again, he'd always been part of a bigger troupe before, just along for the ride as Jasmine called the shots, picked the songs for their competition set and fixed the special Christmas Eve mistletoe pins to their lapels. Suddenly he was part of a much smaller duo, one that called the shots equally. Then he thought of Carol — sweet, confident, capable Carol — and his mind stilled a bit.

Only a little. Or, at least, just enough to allow him to linger on the walkway to the side of the community center. From here, quiet and out of the way, he could turn to see the line of cars easing into the parking lot. Dusk had fallen over tiny little Birchwood, the evening air cooler, crisper than it had been all week. "An early Christmas present," the local radio station had called it, between playing nonstop carols.

Gabe dug his hands in his tracksuit pockets, grateful for the scarf around his neck and, of late, the Hot Cocoa trucker cap Jalise had made just for him. He knew it made him look silly. At least, from a grownup point of view. But the kids simply loved it. Loved it all — the look, the logo, the songs, the little dances he and Carol had been incorporating into each gig to join along, but especially the audience participation.

The thought warmed him much as the pockets and scarf did, inside and out. Then, as he turned toward the backstage entrance, the sound of throats clearing and scales singing from just inside brought the butterflies right back again. He froze, light spilling from under the closed backstage door — warm, but not quite warm enough to invite him in.

Indeed, in many ways, he'd never felt so out of place or unwelcome before. In all the time they'd been out singing and crooning and cavorting and dancing together as Hot Cocoa, Gabe had lost sight of the fact that he'd entered them into the Jingle Jangle in the first place. He knew it was looming, closer and closer with every performance, but suddenly it was here and he had no idea how to —

The scrape of sneakers on cold, gray cement behind him interrupted his latest panic attack. Turning, Gabe caught sight of the only living human that could make him feel somewhat less than brittle at that very moment.

Chapter Forty-Five

Carol

"Hey, stranger."

Carol held her arms out instinctively, sensing from Gabe's wounded expression and hunched-over body language that the poor guy needed a hug. Stat. He snuggled into them immediately, like a cat on a couch, long, strong arms wrapping around her so comfortably it made her wonder if she'd needed the hug even more than he had.

"Thank God you're here!" he gasped, pulling away and pinning her with those soft gray-brown eyes of his.

"Of course I am!" Carol chuckled at his histrionics. "Why wouldn't I be?"

"I dunno," he groaned. "To punish me or something."

"For what?"

"I dunno," he groaned again. "I just..."

His voice trailed off as she assured him, "I would have been here sooner but the traffic is insane out there. Is it always like this?"

Gabe shrugged. "Not sure. I usually get here earlier and come in the back way, so..."

Carol nodded, noting Gabe's obvious discomfort. "Babe," she snorted, only able to laugh because she'd found someone more nervous about the Jingle Jangle than her own damn, pitiful self. "You've *got* to relax. You've got kids in there counting on you. Parents too. We can't let them down!"

Gabe took a deep breath, then glanced back at her and smiled. "You're right." He exhaled as if shedding the weight of the world off his shoulders. "I guess I've just been inside my head all day."

"Same," she gushed, glad that Gabe at least was feeling the same way she'd been all afternoon. "I was all but worthless at work."

"You?" Gabe gasped breathily, as if they were old sorority sisters running into each other at the airport after not seeing each other for thirty years. "Jalise had to give me a 'time out' in the breakroom after I poured the wrong order one too many times."

They both shared a nervous laugh at the very thought of it. "Listen," she assured him, sliding a hand onto his shoulder and admiring the glow of winking Christmas lights around the backstage door. "It's Christmas Eve. We're together, amazingly, randomly together, but I'm also hoping...happily? Together?"

He grabbed her hand instinctively, a warm and sincere gesture. "Very. Happily," he said slowly, as if to indicate just how *very* happy the thought made him. "Together."

"Then, baby?" she said, using the term of endearment for the very first time. "That's all that matters."

"Let's hope so," a voice boomed from behind them, surprising them both in the tender moment of affection. Carol turned first, recognizing the telltale pomposity of the tone perhaps a beat faster than Gabe did. "Because happiness is the only thing you two are walking away with tonight."

Reggie's face beamed under his giant burgundy top hat, festooned with a fresh twig of holly, no doubt organically grown and sourced from some local farmer, if only in a bid to secure his vote at the Jingle Jangle Competition.

"Reggie," Gabe boomed sarcastically, turning to grip the bigger man's hand and pumping it not just richly but strenuously. "What a predictably basic dad joke from Birchwood's worst. Winner. Ever!"

Carol stifled a belly laugh as Reggie struggled to absorb the pure, unadulterated shade Gabe was effortlessly throwing his way. "Well," Reggie hemmed, somehow managing to slide his hand from Gabe's viselike grip and rubbing his thick palm noticeably as he took a step slightly backward in his ridiculously era-accurate boots, "it's not as if you two have any chance of winning tonight."

"Reggie dear," Carol oozed, inching closer to Gabe's side as she peered into the suddenly nervous eyes of her former troupe leader. "Let's just say we didn't come here to lose."

Reggie brayed laughter, but even Carol could see it was the false bravado of a silly, insecure little man unused to a little healthy competition, and grossly unsure how to handle it.

"Besides," Gabe enthused, taking Carol's hand and dragging her past their old nemesis toward a door marked "Backstage — Employees Only," "we're here to spread a little joy tonight, right? Sing some carols, have some fun, raise some money for charity. That's why *you're* here tonight, right, *Reggie*?"

"In your dreams, Pretty Boy," Reggie snapped back, flustered and flushed as Gabe held the backstage door open for Carol. "I'm here to sing carols and chew bubble gum, and I'm all out of — "

Gabe swung the door shut on the last of Reggie's ill-timed movie quote, making Carol giggle as she quickly assessed the jumble and jangle of bodies that suddenly greeted her backstage. Almost as one, the faces of her old troupe turned to assess them.

Gabe turned to her, blushing and chuckling and apologizing all at once. "Um, I may have forgotten to mention that...we all share one big dressing room?"

Behind him, smiling gaily beneath a stiff Victorian bowler, Rome inched closer, resplendent in a golden brocade vest over a spotless stiff white shirt.

"Carol!" He beamed, clapping Gabe on the shoulder. "This must be your Mystery Man."

"Rome," she cautioned, but Gabe had already turned, hand extended.

Then he paused playfully. "Not sure I should shake the hand of a competitor just before the big show," Gabe bluffed, taking Rome's anyway. "But I've heard so much about you, I feel like I already know you."

"Same here," Rome announced before lowering his voice and drawing them in conspiratorially. "And listen, no hard feelings about tonight, okay?"

"Why?" Carol teased, enjoying the surprised expression on her boss's face as she engaged in a little harmless trash talk for good measure. "Are you giving up already?"

Rome snorted, releasing Gabe's hand and inching even closer. "I'm just saying, I heard Reggie blathering out there and just want you to know…"

"We know," Carol said, patting Rome on the shoulder. "We already know. I just hope you're having fun."

Rome nodded. "Are you?" Gabe asked. "Because we are. And if you're not, well…you can always join us for a singalong when we're out there."

Rome glanced from one to the other uncertainly. "Can we… Is that…allowed?"

Gabe shrugged. "Not sure," he said, gaze meeting Carol's as he winked playfully. "But in less than an hour, it's all gonna be decided one way or another, so why not have some fun while we're out there, right?"

Carol saw the glimmer in Rome's eye and winked in reply. "I know how badly you want that trophy for your office, Rome, but…if we're all just having fun out there tonight, then we're all winners, right?"

Rome glanced toward the backstage door where a blushing Reggie was stumbling his way inside, dressed to the nines and already grumbling to his cohorts to "Gather round, ye lads and lasses." The very sound of his mockney accent made Carol blanch.

She wasn't alone. She recognized the hangdog expression as it spread across her young employer's face, so very much at odds with his jovial, cheery holiday-edition Regency garb.

"Later," Rome whispered, as if passing them both a note about the big party later in class. "Before I can even think about having any fun, you know I gotta do the whole Victorian Voices thing, right?"

As if to prove it, he popped the stiff collar beneath his broad, sporty chin and tipped his heavy top hat before slinking away to join the rest of the troupe. Behind him, Bertha gave Carol an apologetic smile, no doubt waiting for one in reply.

Carol glanced at Gabe, so youthful and generous in his forgiving state, so fresh-faced and eager to put the past behind him. Behind *them*. Relenting despite herself, Carol gave her old troupe mate what she wanted and flashed Bertha a cheery, perhaps even forgiving smile.

What harm could come in making peace now?

After all, it was Christmas Eve.

Chapter Forty-Six

Gabe

"How are you, Gabe?"

Gabe turned from meeting Carol's boss to find Jasmine peering back at him, resplendent in a supremely special edition, vintage Regency costume, emerald-green skirt blossoming everywhere from beneath a tight burgundy vest jacket. Her bonnet was a briskly bleached white featuring a fresh mistletoe sprig, the kind Gabe used to wear on his lapel for the big competition.

"Hi, Jazz," he said casually, as if she hadn't fired him in the pettiest, most belittling way possible. "You look great tonight!"

Jazz seemed taken aback by the positive greeting, but what did Gabe have to lose by being gracious now? After all, with Carol by his side, who needed any of these cut-rate wannabe British shmucks in the first place? Of course, frigid and bossy as she was, Jasmine couldn't return the favor but said, instead, with that pause of the entitled elite just beforehand, "You both look...interesting."

Gabe was about to reply, though he wasn't quite sure how, when Carol breezed in and popped the collar of her sexy track jacket, striking a pose that would make any man drool. "Good to hear," she murmured as she passed them both without a backward glance, Gabe noting the extra bounce in her step and shimmy in her hips on the way by. "That's what we were after, right, *Gabe*?"

He winked at Jazz and began following Carol to a far corner of the room. Not far enough, of course, but at least far enough away to not be tripping over the fake friends of his past. Before he could get there, of course, Ray snagged his sleeve with a playful tug.

"Gabe," his old Mistle Tones pal said gaily, as if he too hadn't thrown him under a bus in the not-so-distant past. "Looking great, pal."

Gabe gave Ray a quick once-over, admiring his own version of the special super-duper deluxe edition of his Regency-era caroling garb. "You too, bud," he said evenly, fixing Ray with a firm but clear gaze. "Best of luck out there tonight, okay?"

He turned then, ignoring Ray's stammering comeback to smile at Carol and join her in the corner of the backstage dressing room, where they were both keenly aware that all eyes in the room were upon them.

"What should we do now?" Carol mouthed, her voice barely above a whisper as all of her previous bravado seemed to evaporate once they were all alone.

Gabe glanced back over his shoulder, offering the startled onlookers a confident smile before turning back to her. "Well," he said, rolling his head around his shoulders as if stretching before a track meet, "tonight we unleash *The Christmas Hop* on an unsuspecting public, so if neither of us wants to tear an ACL the minute we start hopping, we should probably...stretch a little, right?"

Carol grinned and promptly touched her toes.

"Damn," Gabe marveled, struggling to do the same.

"Yoga," she explained, as if they were indeed alone and not surrounded by the passive-aggressive glances of the town's most exclusive caroling troupes, all gathered in one claustrophobic space. "You should try it sometime."

Gabe was grunting as it was, struggling to touch his fingertips to his brand-spanking-new sneakers. Or at least the laces. Or, perhaps...his socks? He risked a glance over at Carol to grin. "I suppose, after tonight, we'll have a lot more time on our hands."

"Whatever will we do with it?" she purred, not straining in the least as Gabe's every tendon quaked and threatened to pop before they even hit the stage.

"Take up yoga, I guess," Gabe chuffed before standing back up and dragging one arm over his shoulder, then the next.

"Get a bike." Carol sighed, following suit.

"Eat something other than soft serve." Gabe chuckled, extending an arm across his chest as they continued to fantasize about their off-season exploits.

"And Burger Barn," she teased, risking a glance across the crowded dressing room as the back door opened once more. "It's getting crowded in here," she observed.

Gabe recognized the six older women in the shimmering silver ball gowns they wore to the Jingle Jangle every year. "The Silver Belles," he explained as the ladies proceeded, chins held high, past the other troupes already gathered backstage. Behind them, four younger but still mature gentlemen in matching candy-cane-striped sweater vests and straw hats strolled in, waving the wicker canes that were part of their shtick.

"The Merry Gents," Gabe explained as they followed the Silver Belles toward the center of the long, narrow backstage dressing area.

Although they weren't necessarily the friendly types, both troupes glanced over at Gabe and Carol and smiled. One of the Silver Belles even gave a little wave. "Probably an audience member's grandmother," Carol remarked as, suddenly, Trevor Hartford, a local car dealership owner and a familiar face from local television thanks to his nightly TV commercials, appeared through a curtain to beam at them.

"Merry Gents," he crooned in that melodic voice, nodding at the four McMullen brothers as they stood, shoulder to shoulder and toe to toe, before him. "You're up first. And the rest of you?" Trevor glanced from left to right, scanning the room with a practiced smile and slicked-back hair. "Break a leg!"

There were nervous murmurs, polite twitters and soft replies as, one by one, the Merry Gents strode away from the rest of the troupes and through the velvet curtains to follow Trevor onto the stage. Gabe and Carol glanced at one another before instinctively gripping one another's hands.

"Holy shit," Gabe chuckled, stomach empty after having been too nervous to eat all day. "Here we actually go."

"Almost," Trevor noted as he nodded Gabe's way. "As with every year, those wanting to watch from the wings know where to go. Otherwise, wait until called to go onstage and, as always, best of luck to all the carolers. In my eyes, you're all winners!"

There was a robust round of applause, mostly from last year's winners — and the year before that, and the year before that — the members of Victorian Voices. Shortly after the curtain closed, the Merry Gents took the stage and the crowd inside the auditorium applauded loudly. Without preamble, the four brothers who made up the troupe broke into a lively, if predictable, version of *Here Comes Santa Claus*, much to the standing-room-only crowd's delight.

"Dang," Carol had to almost shout over the sound of the thundering applause that continued, unabated, through the opening strains of the beloved Christmas carol before finally settling down. "They're really into this."

Carol and Gabe gave each other worried glances before he winked and said, "Listen, as long as they don't do *The Christmas Hop*, we've still got a fighting chance!"

Chapter Forty-Seven

Carol

"Hop! Hop! Hop!"

Gabe's voice was merry as he curled his hands in front of his chest, miming a bunny hopping as, new sneakers squeaking on the varnished stage floor beneath him, he began to hop up and down beside her.

"Clop! Clop! Clop!"

In front of them, having rushed the community center stage like a crowd of hormonal teenagers at their very first Beatles concert, was what felt like every child in all of Birchwood, and perhaps even several neighboring counties from the looks of it, who followed suit—dozens of fresh-faced children decked out for the season hopping and bopping and shaking their heads to their little hearts' content.

They weren't alone. Standing, or even sitting, their parents and grandparents joined in, hands poised like little bunnies in front of them as they clopped and hopped where they sat or stood. Or shimmied or shook.

"The Christmas Hop," Carol sang, bolstered by the crowd's energy and, of course, her partner's apparently boundless enthusiasm. "The Christmas Hop. Let's all do the Christmas Hop."

Carol was hopping too now, swept up by the moment, the majesty, the energy, the very holiday spirit in the standing-room-only community center that night.

"Hopping here and hopping there," Gabe sang, hopping gaily beside her as the little kiddies in their Santa hats and striped pajama bottoms and blinking red reindeer nose necklaces mimicked their festive dance moves in the frenetic front row. "Snowflakes dancing in mid-air!"

Voices began to join them as the tune picked up momentum, the childhood memories flooding back to the grownups while the little kiddies sang along as if they'd just watched the cartoon on their tablets that very morning.

"Santa kicked off both his boots, and Mrs. Santa, too," Gabe sang, louder than usual to be heard over the rapturous audience. "Elves began to hop around, and even reindeer, too!"

"Polar bears had joined the fun," Carol sang out, loud and clear. "To dance and boogie, too. While snowmen rose from frozen ground, to do a jig or two!"

Carol was shimmying from side to side, imitating a dancing snowman—*please God, let no one be filming this!*—when she spotted several of the other carolers watching from the wings backstage. Well, more than watching—they were singing along!

Other troupes, their competition, were singing along!

"The Christmas Hop," Carol belted, nudging Gabe's side to get him to glance her way. "The Christmas Hop. Let's all do the Christmas Hop."

When he did, she nodded toward the vibrating stage curtains, currently lined with half the competition! Gabe took a pause from singing — good timing since the crowd was cheering so wildly anyway — to whisper in her ear, "Go get 'em, Carol!"

And, God love her, Carol did just that, playfully hopping toward the curtain as Gabe kept the crowd singing along in turn. "Hop! Hop! Hop!"

Carol saw one of the Silver Belles clapping and shimmying, not sure if it was the same one who had waved at them earlier backstage, but no longer caring. She held out a hand and, after a short pause, the older woman grabbed it eagerly, joining her onstage as the crowd roared their approval at the sudden display of good sportsmanship.

"Clop! Clop! Clop!" they all sang together, generations merging as the rest of the octogenarian Silver Belles flooded on stage one by one, neither too old — nor too shy — to set the floorboards quaking with their flapper-era-inspired dance moves as the crowd erupted, even the last few holdouts launching from their seats to shimmy from where they stood in the auditorium. "Let's all do the Christmas Hop!"

What the Silver Belles began, the other troupes finished. One by one they appeared on stage, doing their own version of *The Christmas Hop*, some hopping higher, some in better shoes, some baritone, some bass, but all smiling to beat the band as they wriggled and shimmied their way onstage. "Let's all do the Christmas Hop!"

There was no need for sheet music. No need for songbooks. No need for key whistles or rehearsal or elephant-tipped canes waving higher or lower to guide them here or there. Every child and inner child in the room knew the song by heart, and sang it straight from there as well. "Cookies flopping off the plate, milk jugs held up high, the North Pole hopping off the charts, with reindeer on standby!"

Carol felt a presence beside her and beamed to find Rome hopping along at last, stiff top hat jostled slightly to the left and his gaudy vest unbuttoned halfway as the two coworkers found their rhythm and hopped in time to the infectious beat. "Hop! Hop! Hop!"

The stage wobbled and buckled and creaked and sang out, as if wanting to get in on the act as well. For once, perhaps even the first time in history, *all* the caroling troupes in Birchwood were on the same stage, at the same time, not just singing the same carol but hopping around while doing so!

Carol took the opportunity of others joining their duo to admire the solidarity, watching Reggie's flushed face as he pretended to be a grown-ass rabbit alongside the rest of her former troupe. Not surprisingly, he caught her looking, returning her look of shock and awe with, well, what could only be considered an embarrassed smile and a vaguely humble shrug before joining Gabe in another chorus of, "Hop! Hop! Hop! Clop! Clop! Clop! Let's all do the Christmas Hop!"

Even Gabe had made peace with his old troupe, dancing alongside them — or were they dancing alongside *him*? — as they feigned sentient bunny-ship for one night only. Even Jazz, looking far less frosty than the reputation that preceded her, wore a smile not even an actress could feign, eyes lit up like the giant Christmas tree out front.

And at the judges' table? A most unlikely sight indeed — they were standing and hopping and singing alongside, too! Rules, decorum and score pads be damned.

As the song wound down, the crowd cheered and the kids booed — they wanted more, more, more — and eventually the judges sat back down to tally their votes at last. Turned out Hot Cocoa, being the newest caroling duo on the scene, was also the last to go onstage, so now that they'd sung the last carol of the evening, the judging would officially begin.

Gabe and Carol took their bows, the other carolers spread out behind them and, at last, the kids returned to their seats, squirming as the noise inside the auditorium dulled to a controlled, almost distant roar. Trevor, the VIP MC, bounded out, pretending to be a bunny as well, much to the crowd's delight.

"Truly great performances here tonight," he crowed, nodding for Gabe and Carol to join the other troupes behind him. "So much fun and such great music. And isn't that what it's all about, folks?"

Trevor waited out the dutiful, almost predictable applause that followed his sappy sentiment before continuing with even greater aplomb, "We hope you've enjoyed this year's Jingle Jangle and, in just a few moments, we'll have those votes tallied for you and, well…hold up…" Trevor glanced toward the judges' table where two men and a woman, each retirement age and dressed to the nines in holiday garb, nodded that they were ready to make the big announcement.

"Let me just 'hop' on over and see who this year's winner is," Trevor proclaimed in his effortlessly smooth announcer's voice, the crowd cheering as he hopped — or at least attempted to — across the stage to the judges' table. Eventually he gave up, the distance too far to keep the charade up too long, especially not in his fancy dress shoes.

Gabe slid his hand, warm and trembling, into her own and she gripped it for dear life, drawing him close as if to shield herself from the inevitable disappointment to come. She glanced down the row of carolers that lined the stage beside them, most still breathless from the Jingle Jangle's rousing finale, to find them commiserating as well, murmuring and crossing their fingers and huddling together in advance of the night's big announcement.

Trevor's voice boomed. He was holding a giant Christmas card covered in bright red glitter, just passed to him from the judges' table. "Here it is, folks," he said in that voice so recognizable from the hundred or more car commercials Carol had endured since moving to town. "The moment we've all been waiting for. The entire caroling season boiled down to this...very...night. But first, please join me in thanking all of these marvelous carolers for putting on a show, not just tonight but all season long..."

Trevor, ever the dutiful host, waited for the applause that followed to die out before he continued. For her part, Carol cursed the vainglorious blowhard for dragging things out so long. Sure, yes, everyone had done a great job all season long, yada-yada. Great, super, fine, but who had done the *best* job? She was breathless with anticipation, no doubt squeezing Gabe's hand to within an inch of actual bone breakage.

Then, before she could snap each finger out of sheer frustration, Trevor yanked open the glittery Christmas card and beamed, breaking into that award-winning smile before announcing, "And now, without further delay, the surprise winner of this year's Jingle Jangle Competition, taking home the trophy for the very first time, is…"

Chapter Forty-Eight

Gabe

"Let me in before I catch a charge out here!"

Gabe snorted, whisking his front door open as Carol rushed past, a literal breath of fresh air after he'd spent the last hour and a half pacing the length of his loft apartment waiting for her.

"On what grounds?" he teased, sounding every bit the nineteen-seventies TV detective.

Carol stood demurely in a puffy pink bathrobe and matching slippers, looking for all the world like she'd recently stepped out of the shower and not just driven halfway across town.

"Indecent exposure," she murmured, glancing past him to the stairwell just beyond. "For starters!"

Gabe poked his head out into the hallway, spacious and beamed with rich, glossy blond wood to match the rest of the ski lodge aesthetic of the brand-spanking-new Century Arms apartments.

"It's one in the morning," he pointed out, though it might as well have been noon judging by how wired he felt. "Who could have possibly seen you?"

"Some old woman and her dog, apparently," Carol said, inching backward into the foyer as if attempting to blend into the very wall itself.

Gabe shut the door behind her, chuckling as he leaned his back against it. "Mrs. Breckenridge," he explained gleefully, struggling to imagine the late-night exchange between both women. "Don't worry, she can hardly see."

"Yeah, well, she sure was trying her best to keep me from getting in downstairs."

Gabe could only imagine his older neighbor trying to protect him from some crazed, half-naked intruder. "What'd you tell her?" As the always-pleasant shock of seeing Carol again began to wear off, he focused in on what she was wearing.

Or, for that matter, *wasn't* wearing.

"That I'd forgotten my key, obviously." Carol brushed a stray lock of auburn hair behind one pale, freckled ear, favoring him with that wicked smile of hers. "And that you were waiting for me to open your present."

Gabe chuckled. "I'm sure I'll hear about that at the next condo board meeting." Then he glanced more closely at the robe. It wasn't just pink—it was pearly pink, covered in little white and red candy canes. "Are your bags downstairs?"

She shot him a look like he had three heads. "What bags?"

Gabe felt positively overdressed as he inched away from the front door. "Is that all you brought?"

Carol rolled her eyes, digging deep into one of the pockets in the front of her fuzzy pink robe. "Obviously not," she explained, dragging out the torn piece of Jingle Jangle program he'd written his address down on after the competition. "How do you think I found this place?"

He laughed, breezing past her as his mock-Regency boots echoed on the hardwood floors. "You must need a drink after all that excitement," he teased, admiring the way her long, bare legs poked from out of the bottom of her scandalously short bathrobe.

"Indeed!"

He'd expected her to follow him into the kitchen, with its open floor plan and inviting smattering of flickering jar candles. Instead she lingered by the Christmas tree. "Were you going for something minimalist here?" she mused, as if to herself.

He chuckled, the bottle of bubbly in one hand and two champagne flutes dangling upside down from the other. "I put the tree up the weekend you first walked into Soft Swerve," he explained, joining her by the towering spruce and examining it the way she might, with its three quiet strings of white lights and less than a dozen ornaments scattered up and down its seven-foot length. "But never found the time to finish it after that."

She turned toward him, several inches shorter without the aid of her usual work heels. Her quiet gaze was magnetic above her softly curling smile. "I like it," she said, voice just above a whisper now that they stood so close. "It suits you."

"Yeah?" He made no move to open the champagne. "Speaking of, I thought you asked me to dress like this because…you would too?"

She snorted, inching away lest his hungry gaze short-circuit some master plan gurgling up there in her always working noggin. "I never said *that*," she said, taking the two quick steps down into the sunken living room before dropping into one of the two leather wing chairs facing the tree. "I just said I wanted to see you in all that Regency splendor one last time."

He followed her, pausing at the coffee table in front of her to wriggle the cork free and fill the glasses. She watched him carefully, smiling as he handed over one of the flutes and sank into the chair beside her with his own.

"Toast?" he asked, nervous for reasons he couldn't quite articulate, let alone comprehend.

She nodded, just as reserved, little ponytail bobbing in the back as he noted how the act of sitting had tugged the sides of her robe apart to reveal more of her awe-inspiring cleavage, hinting at the soft expanse of her pale belly.

"Here's to making sweet music together," she cooed, as if inspired.

He nodded eagerly, clinking her glass with his own before taking a smooth, silky sip of the champagne he'd bought on the way home from the community center earlier that night.

"I like that," he said, wriggling to get comfortable in his stiff breeches. "Did you just think of it?"

"God no," she admitted, crossing her legs to reveal a glimpse of creamy white thigh just beneath the robe's fuzzy pink hem. "I've been dreaming of, and planning for, this very moment all day."

"Really?"

"What, you haven't?"

He rolled his eyes, ruffling the frilly cravat at the base of his throat as the veins alongside each temple throbbed beneath his cloying top hat. "You think I'd get back into this stupid thing if I *hadn't*?"

She took another sip of champagne, big green eyes glued to him the whole while. "Don't worry," she promised after swallowing. "You won't be in it long."

His chuckle was dry and soft, barely loud enough to cover the sound of traditional Christmas carols drifting from an unseen speaker high atop the ladder shelf beside her.

"Well then…" he babbled incoherently. "I suppose it's all worth it then."

Despite her erotic promise, she sank deeper into the comfy leather chair, twice her size and seeming to gobble her up with every coy little wriggle. He smiled, nodding her way.

"You're the first person to ever sit in that chair," he realized out loud.

"Really?" She glanced past him to the rest of the store-bought furnishings, trendy and comfy and stylish but, as yet, unseen by human eye. Other than his own, that is.

"First human to be in my new place, actually."

She cocked a ginger eyebrow, eyes settling on his after quickly appraising the stylish, spacious loft. "It does have that 'new place' feel about it," she noted. "When did you move in?"

"Toward the end of summer," he admitted, embarrassed about the unopened moving boxes he'd scuttled away in the guest room while getting ready for his first official visitor. "I just, with the new store taking up most of my time, and then you showing up, well…"

"I'm flattered to at least be *one* of your diversions," she purred before taking another luxurious sip of champagne.

He followed suit, topping off their glasses from the bottle on the table between them. "I'd consider you my *main* diversion," he corrected her. "If we're being completely honest."

"Are we?" she teased, wriggling her fuzzy slipper playfully as she re-crossed her long, slender legs.

"I can't think of a better time to be," he pointed out, waving his glass around the subtly decorated living room. "Just after midnight on Christmas? Isn't this supposed to be a magical time?"

Carol smiled. "You've certainly set the scene for magic."

He followed her eyes around the spacious loft once more, seeing the vaulted ceilings and bamboo-covered walls and black and white art prints as if for the first time. "Honestly? It's the first time I've just sat and enjoyed the holiday all season."

She set down her champagne flute and hugged her belly as if savoring a fine meal. "Same here," she sighed, voice all soft and fuzzy like her tiny little robe. "It's been so busy and exciting and, well…fast."

"It *has* been fast," he agreed. "Feels like I need an extra month to sit back and enjoy it all."

She stood at last, rising from the wing chair like sex on legs as the fuzzy pink robe hugged the ripe and ready curves of her sultry body. "I can't give you a whole month," she confessed, reaching for his hand to pull him up from his own chair. "But I can make tonight and tomorrow feel like one."

He stood, towering above her as she lightly teased the brocade material of his fancy riding jacket with her fingers. "No helpline on Christmas?" he asked as she undid one of the seven brass buttons that reined in his quietly panting chest.

"Or the day after," she murmured, shaking her head so that the ponytail rasped across the shoulders of her soft, clingy robe.

"Wish I could say the same." He sighed, voice hitching as the jacket front finally gave way with a rustling whisper. "But the day after Christmas starts one of the busiest weeks of the year."

"Shame," she purred, helping him shrug free of the jacket altogether. "I had *such* plans for you."

He laughed nervously as she repeated the process on his dandy vest, each layer of clothing slipping away beneath her expert touch. "Well, I mean, I'll have time for a quick break here and there I suppose."

She arched her feet, inching up on her tippy toes to whisper in his left ear. "Trust me, baby, you won't want to rush a minute of what I've got planned for you."

He nodded, short-circuits in his brain overriding at the sudden influx of pleasure impulses. "Well then" — he grunted as they slid off his vest together — "guess we'll just have to make the most of tonight then."

"And today," she teased, reaching for each wrist to undo his puffy white shirtsleeves. "Don't forget today."

He smiled down at her. "Funny, Carol. I have a feeling today's gonna be pretty unforgettable."

She blushed quickly, making Gabe wonder what her whole body might look like, bare and sweaty and blossoming in reply to his tender touch. Then he scrubbed the thought away, too eager to enjoy every moment in its place rather than rush a single one.

"It already is," she said. "I mean, tonight? My God, I've never seen anything like that before!"

He chuckled as she set each brass cufflink down next to the long-forgotten champagne flutes. "Hard to believe that was all just a few hours ago."

She shook her head. "You're not disappointed?" she asked, reaching to tug the cravat loose from around his rapidly swallowing throat. "Losing out to a rival troupe like that?"

Gabe shook his head. "I thought I would be," he insisted. The emerald cravat joined the pile of clothes on the chair where she'd sat. "When Trevor announced the winner? I thought for sure it would be us, you know? I mean, how couldn't it be?"

"At least it wasn't Victorian Voices this year," she said, tackling the first of twelve ivory buttons down the front of his elegant dress shirt.

"There's that," he said. "I mean, the look on those ladies' faces as the Silver Belles walked up to take first prize? I think they were more shocked than the rest of us."

"Not more shocked than Reggie," she insisted, halfway down his shirt front and clearly in no hurry to finish the deed.

"Or Jasmine," he noted proudly. "Although, I have to say, a part of me feels bad for them."

"Really?" Carol paused at a fresh button to peer curiously up at him. "Really?"

"Yeah, I mean, you and I? I feel like all we needed tonight was to see those families, clapping and hopping and having a great time together. To hear the laughter and the singing and all that hopping. But to the other troupes? The Jingle Jangle is really important."

"But not to you?"

"Sure, but there's no doubt in my mind that Hot Cocoa was the clear winner."

Carol glanced toward the ladder shelf behind him, nodding at the gleaming trophy freshly installed on the third shelf down. "Honorable Mention," she murmured, reaching the last button before tugging the shirt free from where it had been hastily tucked inside his breeches. "Not bad for our first outing, huh?"

He patiently slid each arm through its sleeve, until he stood, bare-chested before her. "Had to be your doing." He grunted as the last sleeve slid free of his arm.

"Why do you say that?" she asked, kneeling at his feet.

"Five years in a row of doing this and that's my very first trophy," he pointed out.

"Just wait until next year," she purred, unzipping the first of his stylish blond boots.

"Can't wait," he said, distracted, feeling bad for the way she'd gone to her knees so quickly. "Here, I can do that."

She glanced up, eyes wide and nostrils flared. "Honestly, Gabe? I'm enjoying this. Immensely."

He arched one eyebrow in reply. "Really?"

She nodded, returning to her work. "Kind of like giving a gift to myself," she said, helping him out of one shoe before turning to the other.

"Well then," he chuckled as they slid off the other shoe together. "Knock yourself out."

"Trust me, slugger," she crooned, sliding off each silk stocking as if peeling a banana. "I won't rest until we *both* feel knocked out."

Once his feet were bare, toes curling against the hardwood floor in anticipation of whatever his own saucy little minx had in store for him, he reached out to help her up. They stood, face to face, the only light in the room coming from the sparsely lit, half-decorated spruce glowing quietly in the corner. The dim lighting highlighted Carol's sensual curves, scarcely hidden beneath her sorry excuse for a robe.

As always, he'd gone commando, so the only thing standing between him and his birthday suit were the blond woolen breeches still left to unbutton. Carol reached for his waistband, the mere touch of her fingertips sending jolts of anticipation through his already trembling body.

"I've waited for this so long," she confessed, "I'm afraid to actually get started."

"We've got all night," he promised, even as his pants tightened from the strain of his excitement.

"And day." She tapped his flat belly absently, as if it was perfectly natural to stand this way together in the middle of the night. "Don't forget day."

"We can just sit here for a while, if you like?"

She winked saucily. "I didn't come here to sit," she blurted before reconsidering. "Well, maybe some of the time, I mean…"

They both giggled nervously, like two teens at a house party about to hook up in some random parents' bedroom while the rest of their senior class did keg stands downstairs. He nodded down at her loosely clinging robe. "I think the problem is we're a little one-sided at the moment."

"How do you figure?" she asked, one button on the front panel of his breeches down and five more to go before they got to full frontal and whatever lay beyond that.

Gabe grinned. "I mean, you're standing there in that little robe, making me wonder what's underneath."

She nodded, snapping one last button free before taking a single step backward. "Oh, I see," she teased, gripping the sash of her robe with both hands as she started to tug it loose. "You want a little eye candy too, is that it?"

"I mean, it's only fair," he argued. "Seeing as I went to all the trouble of setting the mood."

"Ah yes," she exclaimed, admiring the tree before turning back to admire him once more. "You must be exhausted from stringing all those lights."

All the same, she tugged a little more strongly on the sash. He watched her breathlessly, especially when she paused. "Then again, maybe you'd like to unwrap your present...yourself?"

His swallow could be heard for miles. Or at the very least two floors down to Mrs. Breckenridge's apartment. "Oh. My." He somehow stumbled forward, bare-chested, bare-footed, pants barely hanging from his narrow hips as he reached with trembling hands to take over the job of tugging free her saucy little robe. "When you put it that way..."

He took his time, fantasies blending with reality as the sash fell free. Stubbornly, the sides of her little pink robe clung to those elusive breasts, the ones he'd fantasized about all this time and had still yet to see with his own, hungry eyes. Then, just as he reached to tug the robe free, he glanced down the expanse of her soft, pale belly to spy the pair of baby doll panties beneath.

He squinted, just to make sure his eyes weren't fooling him, before glancing back up at her grinning face. "Are those..."

"Hot Cocoa panties?" she teased, dancing just out of view to wriggle her hips for a better view, the shimmering pink robe somehow clinging to each perky breast in the process. "Damn straight they are."

"But how? When?"

She shrugged, the chocolate brown bikini panties clinging to the ripe curves of her hips with soft pink strings, leaving little to the imagination beneath the dancing Captain Cocoa mascot resting atop her thick, ginger bush.

"Grabbed the logo from our website," she explained, still just out of range as he struggled to memorize her pubic thatch by the light of the winking Christmas tree. "Uploaded it to an intimate lingerie site and, one very expensive rush delivery later, it got here just in time for, well…"

"Time for me to take them off," he moaned, voice taut with exquisite anticipation.

"Only when you're good and ready," she said. He crossed the distance between them in two quick paces, but not before stumbling free of his Victorian pants along the way. Her gasp was audible, Gabe not sure whether from seeing him naked at last or from the way he slid the robe open to reveal the bare expanse of her perfect, pert, exquisite breasts.

"Ready or not," he murmured before kissing her breathless, his stiff top hat tumbling to the floor after he clumsily brushed against her blushing forehead. "I think we've both waited long enough for this."

Chapter Forty-Nine

Carol

"Shit! I was trying to be quiet..."

Carol stood, clad only in Gabe's cast-off flouncy dress shirt, midway to the kitchen. "By knocking over the coffee table?" Gabe snorted, sprawled atop a tasseled throw rug beneath the tree.

"It's still standing," Carol promised. "Sort of."

He sat up, bare to the world and glistening with sweat. Reaching out a hand to steady herself, or perhaps prevent herself from jumping his bones yet again, Carol struggled to contain herself.

"Probably my fault," he said before yawning, stretching those long, veiny arms above his head to reveal the bushy sprays of sexy hair beneath each arm. "I bought everything DIY and wasn't exactly the most patient about assembling stuff."

Carol ignored him, striding awkwardly for the kitchen, knowing it wasn't the shoddy assembly job that had managed to jostle the stylish end table but her jelly-like legs, wobbly and practically useless after the waves of pleasure he'd urged from her, time and time again over the last few hours of nonstop, well...catching up.

"Good luck in there by the way," Gabe warned her, struggling to cover his obvious charms with the micro-robe she'd worn to his apartment.

"Don't you ever shop?" she grumbled good-naturedly, settling on a fresh bottle of bubbly and the last wedge of non-moldy cheese from his crisper drawer.

"What, in my spare time?" He chuckled, sweaty shoulders gleaming in the light of the still winking Christmas tree.

"True." She sighed, slinking back to him after making sure his borrowed shirt had swung open in the front. Carol couldn't help but be flattered by the way Gabe still ogled her, hungrily, tenderly, despite having had her in a dozen different ways since that first, maddening kiss of the night. "If it wasn't for takeout, I'd probably have starved to death by now."

"I dunno," he teased, patting the space next to him protectively. As if she might sit anywhere else! "Not sure how many nutrients there are in soft serve, but..."

"Oh, Gabe." She grunted, struggling to wriggle the cork from the fresh bottle of bubbly. "You think I came there for the ice cream?"

"What?" he asked around a healthy nibble of hard Cheddar, looking ridiculous with the wedge of cheese hoisted in his bare hand like some overgrown mouse from one of his beloved nineties Christmas cartoons. "You said you were starving that first night you stumbled in, and I was the only place open on the way home."

"Silly man," she purred, trading the bubbly for the cheese after taking a healthy swallow. "I was stopped at the light on Forest Street, glanced over and saw you in the window. It was a long light, and I got a good look, enough to know I wanted to see more, so I hung a U-turn at the next street and circled around to come back in."

Gabe pretended to be shocked, sipping straight from the bottle before handing it back as they gobbled and sipped a late-night snack.

Or is it morning? Carol wondered, the sky still dark outside his floor-to-ceiling windows as Christmas crept across Birchwood like a slow, quiet thief in the night.

"What?" she sassed, the bottle already half-empty as they struggled to slake their insatiable thirst after three straight hours of getting to know each other on the floor beneath the tree. "Like you're so innocent?"

"Obviously." His lips were bruised from all the kissing, moist from the champagne and chock full of little white lies.

"I know you close at eight," she bluffed, snuggling up against him as Gabe reached out to draw her even closer.

"Bullshit," he assured her, warm breath preceding a tender kiss against her tousled hair. "I had Jalise work her magic and mock up special holiday hours, just in case you got suspicious."

"You forgot to change the website, Einstein," she pointed out as, once again, they drifted down atop the carpet beneath the tree. Gabe sprawled on his back, the pink robe slipping away to reveal the defined abs hidden beneath, to say nothing of the delightfully furry bush of dirty-blond hair just below.

"Let's face it." He turned to face her as the robe slid away altogether. "You're just too smart for me."

She sighed, gently tracing the line of his jaw as she lay beneath him, the shirt wide open and doing little to hide the way her tender nipples responded to the very sight of him.

"If I was so smart," she mused, head resting atop a faux-fur throw pillow that had somehow toppled from the couch in the midst of their handsy explorations, "would I be considering quitting my job so I could lie here with you for the rest of the year?"

"Would that be so bad?" he crooned before bending low to silence her with another of his persistent kisses.

"With the spring semester looming and all those parents calling the hotline to help their kids register for classes?" she asked, scooting out of range before he could silence her with another scorching glance of those pink, puffy lips.

"Don't remind me." He propped himself up on one elbow as his free hand trailed the expanse of flesh between her already stiffening breasts. "A quarter of my staff will be heading back to school the first week of January, meaning I'll have to work double-time until I can hire their replacements."

Carol sighed, the thoughts of the real world an unwelcome intrusion upon their holiday love nest. "I guess I'll have to live on memories then." She groaned, arching her back so that her borrowed shirt drifted open all the more.

"Guess we should make some more then, huh?" he murmured, bending close to kiss her back down into the pillow before bounding up like some spring toy to dance just out of range.

"The hell?" she gasped, still breathless from his latest kiss.

"Sorry," he lied, reaching for a single Christmas sock hanging from a shelf near the tree. "But I figured we should exchange presents at some point today, right?"

She sat up, hair tousled, breasts piqued, belly quivering, bush sticky and thighs sore, a mess from head to toe but clearly no less attractive to her sweet and persistent beau. "But I didn't bring you anything!"

"Sure you did," he teased, bare to the world, flouncing to and fro as if they were changing in the locker room after some big game as he reached down to retrieve something from the nearest leather chair. Dangling from his finger, he waved her rush-order pair of scandalous lacy Hot Cocoa panties in her face. "Remember these babies?"

"They weren't your *real* present," she insisted, snatching them away lest the world see such evidence of her unbridled, foolish lust.

"Neither is this," he said, sinking down next to her and handing over the sock.

She regarded the man's sock, made to look like a reindeer. "Is this…supposed to be a stocking?"

Gabe chuckled. "I wasn't expecting company or it would have been a real stocking. Jalise buys me Christmas socks every year. This was the closest thing I had."

Inside was a rolled-up piece of paper. "For me?"

Gabe nodded, watching as she slid it free of the sock and unfurled it. It was a flyer, silver foil around the edges and fancy cursive script announcing some ritzy event called the Bald Mountain Ski Lodge's Annual

Year-End Ball. She scanned the itinerary, from hot toddies to hot hors d'oeuvres, from a candlelight ski run to live entertainment featuring the hottest strolling carol duo in Birchwood...

"Hot Cocoa?" she gasped, reading the whole flyer three more times to be sure it said what she *hoped* it did. "Is this...fake? Like your fictional holiday hours?"

He shook his head, sitting cross-legged across from her as if he didn't realize just how distracting his long, tender body — and its anatomically accurate accessories — could be to a girl in such a vulnerable state.

"Ever since you asked me about Bald Mountain, I thought, why wait? I got in touch with the entertainment division and it just so happened the string quartet they'd hired for this year's event had backed out, so I sent them some of the videos of our performances Jalise had uploaded to the website and, well...they hired us."

"For New Year's Eve?"

He nodded cautiously. "Is that okay? Can you get off?"

"I mean..."

"For a few days, that is?" he insisted, voice low and gently demanding. "I figured, since we were there, why not make the best of it? I rented a chalet for a couple of nights and..."

She remained silent, gripping the flyer in trembling hands as he reached out with one of his own to squeeze her shoulder. "I can reschedule," he insisted, "if it's a problem? I was just so excited I guess I got carried away..."

"I just..." Carol's voice was raw, her eyes moist as she glanced up into the face of her sweet young lover. "It's not that, Gabe."

He cocked his head, dirty-blond stubble aglow beneath the winking Christmas lights. "Then what, babe? What is it?"

"I guess I'm just waiting for the other shoe to drop," she admitted.

He frowned, shaking his head. "Why ever would it?"

"It just always does," she insisted, thinking of the failed relationships in her past. "Always. Every time."

"Not this time," he promised, gripping both shoulders now so that his dress shirt slipped away and down each of her suddenly trembling arms. "New year, Carol. New...us. We can do this, you and I. Work. Caroling. Each other. It's not that hard if we just...try."

"That's just it," she said, the flyer falling away as Carol reached out to cling to Gabe's impossibly narrow waist. "I don't have to try with you. That's what scares me so much."

He chuckled hoarsely, drawing her close until, at last, she slid her thighs atop his, opening herself to him yet again. "Why would that scare you?"

"Not sure," she confessed, clinging to him as if for dear life. "It's just never been like this before."

"For me either, Carol," he insisted. "For me either, but that's a good thing, right? That we've finally found a...good thing?"

She nodded, struggling to regain control. "It's not you I'm worried about, Gabe."

"Then who?" He was tugging her closer still, those big, strong arms making light work of dragging their bodies together once more. Her heart pounded, and her lips parted as he kissed her silent, again and again.

"I'm afraid of myself," she gasped, collapsing against his chest. "And how I always screw things up."

"You?" His self-deprecating laughter dashed across her damp cheeks and ruffled her tousled hair. "Until this place, I was living in the same crappy apartment I'd rented after high school. Until you, I hadn't felt my heart race in years. Until you, the only thing that even kept me going was leaping from one new Soft Swerve to another. I was so lonely I didn't even realize it until you walked in that night, dressed to the nines, asking for a pistachio and peanut butter waffle cone. Now I'm spending Christmas in the arms of someone I truly care about, and she's just agreed to share the new year with me, too. I'm the one who should be pinching myself, Carol. Not you."

Her heart swooned as the lights from the tree reflected in his own wide, damp eyes. "Oh, I dunno," she found the strength to purr, sliding her hands southward to tweak his flawless flanks. "You kind of like it when I do the pinching."

Their nervous laughter burst forth, raw and hungry, like the naked flesh that writhed together there on his living room floor. Their words fell away, their concerns, their doubts, their fears, or at least Carol's did as she rocked against her tender lover once more, inspiring him to new heights as they slid down and against and into one another there in the winking light of the half-naked Christmas tree.

She'd come empty-handed, wanting little more than to fulfill the fantasies that had kept her up every night since they'd first met. Instead she'd been given the most precious gift of all—the chance to start over. To trust herself to find love in the most unexpected of places, with the most unexpected of men, at the absolute worst time and still, nothing had ever felt more right in her whole, entire life.

Merry Christmas indeed.

Epilogue

Gabe

"Should auld acquaintance be forgot…"

Carol's voice was crisp and clear, a thing of beauty in the middle of the vast ski lodge, bouncing off wooden beams and dancing off rough-hewn walls and the massive windows overlooking glistening snow as far as the eye could see.

Above her towered an awe-inspiring Christmas tree, the decorations all taken down but the white lights strung round and round, reflected in the beaded cocktail dress she'd chosen for the occasion.

Gabe joined her, stiff but regal in his ill-fitting rental tux. "And never brought to mind…"

One by one, the assembled crowd of similarly dressed partygoers crooned in time, eyes moist beneath crooked party hats as they raised their half-empty champagne flutes and sang out in unison, "For auld lang syne, my dear, for auld lang syne…"

The voices swelled, the room filling with the bittersweet emotion of another year gone by and a new one on the cusp of beginning as, in perfect harmony, Gabe and Carol led the crowd through the final verse. "We'll take a cup of kindness yet, for auld lang syne..."

The pause that followed filled the entire room, Gabe and Carol glancing at each other nervously until the crowd broke into applause, cheers and more. They gasped with relief, taking mock bows and jostling each other's hips as they slid from the impromptu stage in front of the tree to make way for the night's epic grand finale — a towering, seven-tiered cake festooned with sparklers, glitter and more.

Gabe was grateful for the quick brush-off, more eager to spend time with Carol than a flock of new admirers drunk on bubbly and emotion as they circled round the towering cake instead of embracing Hot Cocoa as most crowds might after the evening of nonstop entertainment they'd just provided.

"I'll give the lodge this much," Carol murmured, snatching two champagne flutes from a passing server as if they were guests and not just the hired help. "They sure know how to throw a party."

He couldn't argue with that logic. Glancing around the room at the cake sparkling, the tree shimmering, the snow falling outside the massive windows, Gabe felt like he was trapped in the most realistic of snow globes.

"I've never been much for New Year's before," he confessed, sidling up next to Carol in a little nook overlooking a gurgling indoor stream. "But they're making it pretty hard to resist its charms this year."

"You know," Carol glanced past him to the bubbling brook at their feet. "Since our Christmas is so busy, maybe we'll have to treat New Year's as our holiday."

"I'm down," he gushed before Carol could come to her senses and retract her offer. "And speaking of busy, I'm already getting little nudges from the other troupes about next Christmas."

"You too?" Carol blurted before savoring a fresh sip of bubbly. "I thought it was just me."

"First my old pal Ray reached out," Gabe confessed, recalling the flurry of texts his old caroling buddy had sent him shortly after Christmas. "Then Jasmine, of all people."

Carol's wide eyes revealed her surprise. "What do they want, do you think?"

"More of what happened onstage during the Jingle Jangle, I suppose," Gabe explained with a shrug. "I figured I'd answer them once we get back to town."

"Same," Carol sighed, looking doubly glamorous in her shimmering silver cocktail dress.

"Why, who hit you up?" Gabe pressed.

"Reggie, for one."

"No shit?"

She shook her head. "Said he enjoyed our 'collaboration' and wouldn't be opposed to 'more of the same' in 'the near future.'"

Gabe chuckled. "Can't say as I blame him."

"No," Carol agreed, turning to face him as she leaned against the log-cabin-inspired railing that ran throughout the length of the ski lodge. "Plus Rome is all up my ass about joining us, too."

Gabe chuckled. "I bet." He sighed, feeling triumphant in ways he'd never imagined before.

"Would you be...open to that?" she asked cautiously.

Gabe was surprised she had to ask. "Of course I would."

"Really?"

"Are you so surprised?"

"No, I mean…yes."

"What? Why?"

"I thought you wanted me all to yourself." She pretended to pout, and not very well at that. Gabe couldn't blame her. Hard to wear a frown on a night like this one.

"Of course I do," Gabe insisted, inching even closer as the party behind them revved into high gear, forgetting entirely about the caroling duo that had entertained them for the last two hours with slow-tempo versions of *Silent Night* and *What Are You Doing New Year's Eve*? "But I was thinking, we rushed it so much this year, we hardly had time to enjoy it."

"I agree with that much," she said. "And besides, traditionally, folks start decorating and playing carols over Thanksgiving weekend, so…"

"So maybe if we were to start caroling before December even began—"

"I mean, most folks wouldn't be into it yet—"

"But some would—"

"And for those folks, we could perform as a duet or—"

"A trio," Gabe hastened to add, enjoying the way their voices so often danced over one another's to finish the same sentence. "If only Rome were available for that performance, say."

Carol nodded eagerly. "Or a quartet, if Rome and Ray both had the same night off."

"I mean, a quintet wouldn't be out of the question," Gabe offered as they both nodded at the unlimited possibilities. "That is, if Jazz was really serious about joining forces at some point."

"Would mean a lot more rehearsing," Carol pointed out.

"Starting around Halloween, I would think," Gabe reasoned. "With that many big personalities, you know?"

"And schedules," Carol pointed out, biting her lower lip gently the way she often did when absorbed in thought.

"Gonna make the Jingle Jangle harder to judge," he offered.

Carol nodded, their eyes meeting in the warm glow of the distant tree. "Maybe they need a little shakeup after this Christmas," she huffed.

Gabe chuckled. "I thought you were okay with Honorable Mention."

"I was at first," she admitted, mirroring Gabe's own thoughts. "Until I had time to think about it a little more and... Honorable Mention, my ass!"

They shared a hearty chuckle, the raucous sound lost in the growing hum of the mounting new year. Behind them, jostling and cavorting, well-heeled travelers in tuxes and gowns vied for selfie position in front of the tree as a giant digital clock just above it began to count down to the new year in real time.

"Only a few minutes left now," Gabe pointed out.

"Gosh," she gushed dramatically, setting her glass down on a nearby railing and plucking one finger beneath her chin. "If only I had somebody to kiss."

Gabe blushed and mumbled and pulled her close, a quick glimpse down the front of her dress revealing that she'd gone without a bra. Again. He marveled at how much he wanted her still. Despite all they'd shared that first Christmas together, and the next day, and the next, his hunger for her had only grown exponentially as the new year drew close.

"You know," she purred, hot breath in his ear as his hands clasped around the small of her back, "our chalet is only a few steps away."

"And ours for the whole weekend," Gabe reminded her. "No need to rush, right?"

"Speak for yourself." She grunted, reaching even lower to squeeze one ripe, firm cheek. "You sure you don't want to start right away?" she asked in that come-hither voice that never failed to rack his entire body with thick, urgent desire.

"Seems like we already have," he croaked, drawing her against his thickening manhood.

"Naughty boy." She sighed, collapsing against him as they both turned to watch the countdown together. "One minute left."

"I've never been to one of these before," he admitted.

"A countdown?" Carol glanced away before smiling. "Me either, come to think of it."

"Another first?" Gabe offered as a kind of shimmer passed through the crowd.

"Not sure how many more firsts I can handle, Big Guy," Carol teased.

"Not sure we have a choice, with the way things are going."

Carol toyed with one of his lapels, smoothing it out with one hand while the other rested against his quivering belly. "Gonna be quite a year," she offered, gazing up at him.

"Promise?" he teased.

"You first," she murmured as, behind them, the crowd began to count down as one. "Ten, nine, eight..."

"I have a feeling that together," Gabe offered, struggling to be heard over the bellowing crowd, "we can do anything."

"I'm game if you are." She sighed, wilting against his urgent young body.

"Seven, six, five..."

"You should know I am by now," he insisted, pushing her gently away. "You should know, by now, I'm *all* in."

"Four, three, two..."

"Are *you*?" he pressed.

Carol nodded as, behind them, the crowd erupted, cheering and kissing and toasting and reveling as a fresh round of drinks assured the party would go on well past midnight.

But here, in their private little corner, the artificial brook babbling beside them, Gabe and Carol shared more than just urgent glances. "Of course I am," she insisted. "I just..."

"Stop that," he hissed. "Whatever differences we have, age, income, schedules or otherwise, stop right here, right now. I...I love you, Carol. Can't you see?"

Carol took a quick stagger-step back before tugging on his lapels to make him follow. "Gabe, I... Have you...ever said that before?"

"Hell no!" he all but shouted as the crowd continued to cheer and hoot and holler in the background, none the wiser to the earth-shattering pronouncements being flung about only a few steps away from them.

"Me either," she confessed, the hint of a smile curling up her lips.

"Yeah, well," he grunted playfully. "You *still* haven't."

"I think I said it about a dozen times last night," she reminded him.

"Doesn't count when we're"—he glanced around the crowd, as if someone might actually be listening to two random strangers on the periphery—"doing stuff, you know?"

"Who made you boss of what does or doesn't count during S-E-X?"

"I did," he bragged, puffing out his chest playfully.

Her laughter was raw and honest, showing Gabe a different side of the self-proclaimed "boss bitch" who'd taken over his very existence that first night in the ice cream parlor. "Well then, if it only counts with our clothes on, then yes... I love you *too*, Gabe."

He beamed, dragging her in for a breathless kiss to rival every new year to ever come before it, and several more still to come. When at last they parted, dragging each other from the alcove and out through the side door, out into the bracing snow for the short walk—make that sprint—to chalet number three just down the lane, words were no longer necessary. Gabe had known the minute he'd locked eyes on Carol that he'd make her love him, whatever it took.

Funny thing was, it only took being himself.

Sign up for our newsletter and find out about all our romance book releases, eBook sales and promotions, sneak peeks and FREE romance books!

Want to see more from this author? Here's a taster for you to enjoy!

Modern Herstory: Beat It
Alex Winters

Excerpt

Cleo

"Completely?"

I glance across the cluttered desk at Austen Sturges. I should have known I was in trouble the minute they'd assigned me a new editor named Austen Flippin' Sturges. In his late forties, with salt-and-pepper hair, pastel-yellow sweater vest over a button-down dress shirt and paisley tie, the man puts the stuff right into "stuffy." Austen arches a bushy grey eyebrow over his thick, round, tortoiseshell glasses.

"Did I stutter?" His voice is cool and calm and *definitely* collected. Much more so than mine, anyway.

"Mr. Sturges, if you could just—"

His withering glance softens a smidge. "Please, Cleo, call me Austen."

"Fine, yes, I just…" I let out a sigh, cutting myself off in mid-stream. And why not? I've got nowhere else to go. Five minutes into meeting my new editor and he's just set off a nuclear bomb imploding what I intended to be my next bestseller.

He softens still. "Listen, I know it's not what you came all the way into the office to hear today, but I'm afraid I can't see any other way to make this manuscript even…" Austen struggles to find a punchline, rattling his manicured fingernails across the title page of the 389-page manuscript in question. "Salvageable."

"Salvageable?" I hear the harshness in my voice but can't help it. Nor can I help all but bolting out of my chair in protest. "My manuscripts have been called a lot of things in the past, Austen. 'Charming.' 'Dreamy.' The phrase 'Yummy' has been used more than once, I believe. But this one is barely salvageable?"

"If you want to continue the First-Timers Club series here at Backstage Books, Cleo, then yes. A complete overhaul from start to finish. I'm afraid I can't see any other way to, well...salvage it."

Austen gives me an almost apologetic shrug, as if to soften the blow. It doesn't. Not even a little.

"Can't we just...take out the parts that aren't very eighties?"

I'm aware that I'm whining now—pouting, even, slumping back in my chair and crossing my arms over my chest and doing everything but stomping my feet up and down like a toddler having a tantrum—but again...nuclear bomb blast. Shrapnel piercing my poor little writer's heart. No control whatsoever over my fight or flight response to this devastating news.

Complete and utter career meltdown here, people!

"Aren't *very* eighties?" Austen tosses his first sneer back across the desk. I've been waiting for it ever since I walked in and he didn't stand up to greet me. "Forgive me for saying so, Cleo, but this manuscript as delivered?" He shakes his head with vigorous aplomb, as if saying "no" to a very bad idea. "Not even eighties adjacent."

The fancy, city-bred snippiness to his voice leaves no doubt as to what Austen would sound like bitching to his age-appropriate brunch mates on a late Sunday morning, three mimosas deep and complaining about his poached eggs being "not even runny adjacent."

This rye bread? Not even toast adjacent.

This mimosa? Uhm, I'm sorry, not even prosecco adjacent.

Adjacent. Who even *says* shit like that? Then again, he's kind of got a point. I sigh and lean forward, placing my hands against his desk as if to keep myself from bolting out of my chair and, in five short flights, sprinting from the entire Backstage Books corporate headquarters itself. "Listen, I may not have been as rigid in my research on this one, I get that."

"If we're being honest, Cleo?" Austen's chiseled face is somber, but also somewhat understanding. You might even say... understanding adjacent. "It shows."

"Right, yes, I get that now, but...why scrap the whole book just because of a few technology slips, am I right?"

"A few technology slips?" Austen looks offended, glancing down at the manuscript beneath his tapping fingertips. He rifles through it, yanking free a few pages from the middle. "Let's just read a random passage chosen without preamble, shall we?"

I frown, stomach blanching at the very words. "Must we?"

"If I'm to get my point across, yes. We must."

I beg him with panicking eyes and clenched fists. "It's just that...I dread hearing my stuff read aloud."

"Be that is it may — and I'll keep it brief — but allow me to prove my point?"

I glance out through the window at downtown Atlanta, toward the coliseum where I'm due to see none other than the hottest band in the country, Torn Blankets, visible outside Austen's office window, just a few short city blocks away. So close and yet, at the moment? A world away. He's fumbling through the pages. I'm staring at the coliseum, as if I can will myself there to avoid the sound of him reading my words out loud.

"Aha." He's found a passage he likes. Or dislikes. Or likes to dislike. Either way, I dig my fingers into the armrests of my leather wing chair, dreading the next three point five minutes. Clearing his throat, Austen reads in a clinical tone, as if unaware of my poor little writer's heart breaking with every wrong-headed syllable.

"Her playlist oozed from some unseen speaker, Madonna wailing in time to Emily's pounding heartbeat. Brody's eyes shone brighter than the pale moonlight filtering in through the open window at his back, taking the phone off the hook so they wouldn't be disturbed.

"The thought of the captain of the pickleball team wanting her, and only her, undivided attention made her weak in the knees. Emily reached for the tennis sweater wrapped around his broad shoulders, struggling to untie it. Brody stopped her, big hands engulfing her own as the glow from his digital watch showed the time – six minutes before midnight.

"'Holy shit!' she gasped. 'You have to take me home. I'll be late for my curfew!'"

I wince. Not because I hear a ton of errors but once I've hit "The End" on my final, off-to-the-printer, no-more-chances-for-take-backs   or   last-minute-edits manuscript, I tend not to read my books ever again, let alone out loud. This is the exact reason why.

Utter cringe factor.

I stare back. Austen holds the pages out in accusation.

"Okay, and?" I press, all but waving my hands in the universal symbol for "hurry the fuck up and put this meeting out of its misery already!"

Austen sighs and sets the pages back in the manuscript where they belong. "So, there *were* digital watches in the eighties, as a five-second Google search might indicate, but what the internet won't tell you is that more often than not a trendy frat chode like Brody would be wearing a Swatch of some variety."

I nod, not seeing the problem. "Okay, so…'edit and replace' much?"

Austen clenches and unclenches his jaw a total of three times before continuing. "Fine, yes, if it was *just* the watch. Every time you mention it, which is…a lot. I mean, we sure get hit over the head with this poor guy's love for all things digital watches. It's—and forgive me if I'm wrong here—it's *almost* like you were trying to hit your minimum word count and figured describing this digital watch again—and again and again—might somehow burn through another hundred or two words?"

I blush and avoid his eyes. *I so totally was!*

He nods as if I've already acknowledged as much. "But wait…there's more. Taking the phone off the hook? Yes. Gold-star effort there. Clever little detail there, actually. However, the minute you do that in real life, the busy signal starts bleeping and doesn't stop until you hang up the phone again, so they wouldn't do that to 'achieve undivided attention.' Also? Pickleball is a relatively new trend and sure wasn't popular enough, or endorsed enough, to build a whole high school team around back then, so…"

I nod, face flushed. Big head deflated. Book tour canceled. Career ruined. I may even have to go off-grid for a few years just to recover from this epic fail. "Just so you know," I bluff, avoiding his eyes with such vigor I'm afraid they'll pop right out of my skull and roll across my poor, ill-conceived manuscript pages. "I *did* research the eighties for this. Like. A lot."

But I didn't. Not "a lot," anyway, and if we're being honest here? Barely even a little. I did a few image searches, bookmarked some song lists, movie titles, trends but…romance is romance. A good book should transcend all that fussy research, right?

Austen nods, inching back in his chair as if to make me feel less threatened. "I can see that, Cleo. And don't get me wrong—the book itself is great. It's just…you can see how much work this would be to edit just in one sample paragraph. On *one* sample page, pulled at random. Now magnify that by almost four hundred pages? It's not fair to let this one get a pass when all your others have been so camera-ready."

I sigh and wince in advance before offering the vaguest excuse possible. "I suppose I thought the story itself was camera-ready."

He nods as if desperate for something positive to latch on to just so I won't walk straight into traffic after leaving the building. "Look, it's not the writing, okay? Let's get that out of the way first thing. Fact is, we *love* your books, Cleo. Obviously…"

Austen swipes a hand at the bestselling book covers lining his walls, blown up to poster-sized and framed like fine-art prints. There are twelve of them hanging around the office and, not to brag or anything, but three of them are mine. Make that the first three installments of the First-Timers Club series. "You've been integral to Backstage's success and we're eternally grateful."

I wink and slither a little to the end of my chair. It's late afternoon, the concert starts in three hours and I want to pregame at this trendy new downtown club I saw on Slicktok so I've worn my brand-new champagne-colored, off-the-shoulder, glitter bedecked jumpsuit to our meeting. It's skimpy, but not too revealing. Stylish, but not slutty. Slutty *adjacent*, I might say. Still, my flesh feels ready to burst out in this position. "So can't I get a pass on this one, Austen?"

He frowns and wrinkles his nose and sits back in his chair all the further. "I'm afraid not," he says with dismissive finality.

I straighten up. "Oh, okay then."

He picks up my manuscript and sets it aside, as if indicating that's where my career is heading if I don't shape the hell up. "I do appreciate you coming in today, Cleo. We could have just as easily done this on a Zoom call."

"Happy to," I insist, struggling to keep the illusion that I drove all the way to Atlanta just to hear how shitty, gross, dumb, shoddy, slapdash and downright unrealistic my latest manuscript is. He doesn't need to know about the concert. "I just wish, well, things had wound up different, that's all."

"Different efforts produce different results," Austen insists, sitting back in his desk chair as I stand, sweeping the cute little beaded handbag I'd bought for the concert over one bare shoulder. It's shaped like a goldfish, with alternating orange and yellow beads, in honor of *Fish Food*, my favorite song by the band.

He nods at it. "Cute purse," he says.

"You like it?" I hoist it up for his benefit, batting my lashes and striking a pose like I'm about to take my first selfie of the night in front of the coliseum.

"It'll be perfect for the concert tonight."

I take an involuntary step backward, almost stumbling over the chair where I'd heard the verdict about my "unsalvageable" manuscript. "W-w-what concert?" I stammer like some bumbling side character in my own life.

"Torn Blankets," he observes, waving a fancy pen at my purse. "Your ticket is sticking out."

I glance down and, sure enough, there it sits, poking out of the thin space between the goldfish-shaped clasps at the top. "Dammit!"

"It's fine, Cleo. You deserve a little fun. But tomorrow? Once you've washed all that glitter off your face and put your feet on ice after a night in those heels? Straight to work, okay? We'll need that manuscript by early September at the latest if it's going to be in shape for holiday sales."

I give a half-hearted salute. "Aye-aye, Captain," I tease, hoping to salvage what's left of this very bad, miserable, horrible, borderline apocalyptic editorial meeting.

He offers me a placid smile, the same kind I'd give some breathless reviewer who obviously hadn't read my book but still wants an "exclusive" interview anyway. "Before you leave?"

I'm halfway through the door already, teetering on my brand-new high-heeled sneakers — also champagne-colored, also blinged out and also totally fab, if I do say so myself. I nod at the door, his brass nameplate so fresh I can still smell the glue they used to hang it there. "But I thought you already gave me my marching orders, right?"

Austen offers a rare, handsome, smile followed by a borderline comforting nod. "No, I meant...before you leave the *building*, Trixie would like a word."

"A word?" I croak, almost dissolving right there in my four-hundred-dollar jumpsuit. "With Trixie?"

"You're not in trouble," he insists, not very reassuringly. "Honest."

I roll my eyes. "Then I must not be, Austen, since the one thing you are is absolutely, utterly, brutally honest..."

About the Author

Alex Winters is an Amazon bestselling romance author with a passion for holiday music, junk food, cheesy 80s horror movies and Epcot. His series feature a variety of romantic pairings (M/F, M/M, F/F AND MMF) and include Campus Crush, Slightly Sinful, Good, High-Stakes Heroines, and more. His stories tend to be sizzling and sweet, with a whole lot of laughs — and spice — along the way!

Alex loves to hear from readers. You can find his contact information, website details and author profile page at https://www.firstforromance.com

ENTWINED PUBLISHING